C

Viking Treasure

Book 13 in the
Dragon Heart Series
By
Griff Hosker

Viking Treasure

Published by Sword Books Ltd 2016
Copyright © Griff Hosker First Edition

A CIP catalogue record for this title is available from the British Library.
Cover by Design for Writers

Prologue

When we had defeated King Coenwulf and King Egbert in sight of Old Olaf it had been a mixed victory. We had gained great quantities of ransom for the crowns I sold back to King Egbert and we had gained peace from both the men of Wessex and the men of Mercia yet we had lost many fine warriors. There were empty hearths in my land and that saddened me. My only consolation was that my young son, Gruffyd, and my grandson, Ragnar, had both shown that they were Vikings. They had both faced the enemy and not flinched.

As I rode my horse, Storm Rider, along the shores of the water at Cyninges-tūn I wondered if we could continue to hold on to this precious jewel that was known as the Land of the Wolf. The Danes of Eoforwic, now called Jorvik, both hated and feared us. It was still Northumbria but King Eanred had a tenuous hold on the land. They were waxing in power as that of the Saxons waned. There would come a time when their hatred would overcome their fear of me or perhaps a young warrior would decide to take on the old man that was Jarl Dragonheart. That day would come and I was not becoming younger. Wessex had sworn to keep the peace but King Egbert hated my family so much that I knew the oath would mean nothing to them. We were barbarians and their priests would condone such an act.

Sometimes the Weird Sisters acted in conjunction with the spirits which protected my land. I often wondered if they all sat together watching. Did the Gods in Asgard move us around as pieces of carved bone on a board? Perhaps I amused them. Did they set me challenges wondering if I would overcome them?

That morning, as I rode in the chilly early morning air I was alone. The fog on the water lay like a thick blanket so that I could not see the far shore. What I could see was Olaf's craggy top. That morning his face seemed even more pronounced. I could see his empty mouth and it seemed to be smiling. That had been a rare occurrence when Olaf the Toothless was alive. A shaft of sunlight suddenly glinted on his face and it seemed to me that his eye winked. Then more sunlight flooded from the east and Olaf's features disappeared. I could just see the mountain rising above the fog.

I kicked Storm Rider on and headed towards the lower slopes of our holy mountain. Olaf wished me to visit. I do not know how the thought came to me but it became clear as day and I decided to visit the lofty crag. By the time I had reached the Blue Water, where I would leave my horse, the fog had disappeared and the valley was bathed in sunlight. I saw the tiny dots that were my people as they began their daily work. On the hillsides, warriors and their sons tended sheep and cattle. Smoke rose from their farms as their wives and daughters cooked food. Bjorn Bagsecgson's smiths' hammers rang out like bells as they worked their metal. Life was going on.

I ascended to the top and sat on a flat rock, taking in all that I could see. It was such a clear day that I saw Man and Hibernia. Looking north I saw the Wolf Mountain and beyond it, the wall the Romans had built. Finally, my eye was drawn to the east. The Danes lived there but, strangely, I seemed to look beyond the sea which bounded this island the Romans called Britannia. I saw the land of Ragnar and Prince Butar; the land of the Norse. I saw the home in which I had grown and become a warrior. It seemed to me that I was taken there and saw myself and the old, crippled man. I closed my eyes and felt a sudden shiver. The old women said that was someone walking over your grave while others said it meant your death was imminent. I did not know what it meant but I knew it meant something. I stood. I surveyed the Land of the Wolf and I felt proud. If those who determined such things, the Weird Sisters, the Gods, the Spirits, had decided that my life had run its course and my thread was ended then I could be proud. I had ringed my land with strongly fortified halls ruled by Hersir and Jarls who were superior to any foe who came. My people were rich and enjoyed a life free from the fear of famine. The land was fertile and we prospered. We had not had a wolf winter for some years. Perhaps my time was coming to an end. I was now the same age that Prince Butar had been when he had been slain on Man. But if it was coming to a close I would not go quietly to the otherworld. I would do as I had always done; the best I could for my people.

I nodded and said, loudly, "If it is *wyrd* that I join you, Olaf and Ragnar, then so be it. But do not expect me to rush to see you. I still have much to do. I am still Dragonheart; I am still Lord of the Land of the Wolf!"

Chapter 1

The recent wars and battles meant that my warriors had no reason to seek glory in raiding. We had gained much booty from the Saxons and Danes. They had been both well-armed and laden with riches. My warriors tended their fields and their animals; they watched their children play. They hunted in the forests which covered the land of the Wolf. Those who had no farms or were single ventured across my land hunting and exploring the high places. Snorri and Beorn the Scout spent many days away from the stad. Beorn had almost lost a leg in the recent war and the two of them tramped for miles strengthening his leg.

I practised swordplay with my young son, Gruffyd. He was growing rapidly. I did not bother overmuch with my new daughter, Erika. She clung to her mother or, if they visited, Kara and Ylva. The two nuns who lived with us, Macha and Deidra, made a great deal of fuss of her. I just smiled at her when she recited something she had been taught. A short time of smiling back made my face ache and I would play with my son instead. Brigid did not seem to mind. She and my daughter, Kara, shared daughters and they were happy enough. Kara's husband, Aiden, worked on potions and ointments to heal wounds and voraciously devoured any parchments and books that he could. He gathered knowledge like a squirrel gathers nuts. Fatherhood had made him more inward-looking. He rarely travelled abroad with me now. That was wyrd. I did not mind. I had my Ulfheonar.

As summer waned into harvest our lives were settled. Our new warriors practised at arms and were eager to learn how to go A-Viking and our people prospered. The Weird Sisters inevitably became bored and they spun their threads. Snorri and Beorn returned from one of their forays. They had been away for some time and, when they arrived back without game I wondered why. The sentry on the watchtower saw them approaching along the side of the Water. He shouted to me. Wolf Killer, my son, was with them.

I went to the Waterside, with Gruffyd to watch them approach. A passing fishing boat pulled over to fetch them. All knew of the prowess of Snorri and Beorn. Who knew what news they brought?

Gruffyd saw the three riders and said, "Mother said that Snorri is going to take a wife, father. Will he?"

Women liked to gossip and to matchmake. "Eystein the Rock left a widow. Snorri is just helping her at their farm as is Asbjorn the Strong. It is kindness only. In this clan, we look after all; especially the maimed, the widows and their children."

"Like Karl One Hand!" I nodded. "People say that only the Dragonheart would have offered a place for a one armed warrior." He said it with the innocence of a child.

"Karl swore an oath to me and he kept it. Every jarl who has oathsworn has a responsibility to those who give their lives for him. Remember that, my son. An oath is a sacred thing. Besides is Karl, not a good warrior yet?" Karl practised with my son when I was busy.

"He is. Even with one hand, he is faster than I am."

"There you are then. It is not kindness. It is common sense."

I was distracted by the boat which was carried by the wind to grate upon the shingle and sand beach of the Water. Snorri, not my son, was the first to land. He clasped my arm, "I bring news, Jarl, of danger. When I told Wolf Killer he thought to come too."

I gave a coin to the fisherman, Sven Audunsson, "Come we will go to my hall and talk." I saw that he had brought his youngest son, Garth. He had been named after me. He was a quiet and thoughtful child. As we walked to my hall his hand found mine. I smiled down at him. I did not see enough of him. I would wait to speak until we reached my hall for I disliked talking about danger and trouble in the open. There were many ears and some were given to gossip. They could take a half snatched conversation and make it into an apocalypse. I preferred the people calm and content than agitated."You are growing young Garth. Soon you will have your first seax!"

His face lit into a smile, "Will you have your smith, Bjorn Bagsecgson, make one for me, grandfather? Then it would be a mighty weapon."

"Of course."

We entered my hall. Uhtric, my servant, fetched us beer. Brigid was with Kara and Aiden at their hall. The four of us sat around my table and Gruffyd squatted nearby hoping I would not send him away.

Snorri began without preamble. "We went to Hwitebi."

"Hwitebi? That is as far east as a man can go. What were you hunting?"

He looked embarrassed and Beorn the Scout said, "He went find some jet. He had a mind to carve something for Eystein's widow!"

Snorri waved a hand in an irritated manner, "It matters not why we went there it is the news we discovered that is important." I saw Wolf Killer smile. Snorri was no longer a young man and he was awkward about such things. "We came across a Frisian up on the high moors close to Hwitebi. It was in a valley filled with the yellow flowers. He had been

4

attacked and left for dead. When he saw the wolf cloak he grabbed hold of me."

Beorn said, "The man was dying, Jarl. Dying men do not lie."

I nodded.

Snorri continued, "He begged to hold my sword so that he could go to Valhalla. He believed in the old ways. He said he would pay for the loan with knowledge. The son of Rurik of Dorestad, Ragnar Ruriksson, is gathering warriors. He wishes to avenge himself on you. He is being supported by Grimoald, the Mayor of Neustria. He is still angry with us for our raids. Then the man died. We buried him and returned thence."

I nodded. The three of them looked at me expectantly and Gruffyd was barely breathing he was so engrossed. I ran through what they had said in my mind. "Who killed the warrior?"

They both shrugged and Snorri said, "He did not say. I think he wanted to give the information to us."

Wolf Killer said, "I see the Weird Sisters' hands in this." He grasped his wolf amulet for protection. "Have we not enough enemies? Rurik was a nithing! He deserved to die."

I smiled, "A Viking who has no enemies is not a Viking!" I turned to Gruffyd, "Go and find Aiden. Say I have need of him." He looked disappointed, "Do not fear, you will miss nothing. Take Garth with you. He looks bored."

He raced out. I could imagine him dragging poor Aiden bodily back to my hall.

I lifted my sword out of its scabbard and laid it upon the table. "When the Gods touched this they bestowed honour and rewards. It has helped us to destroy our enemies but there is a price to pay. The Gods want it used against our enemies. We have defeated the men of Wessex, Mercia, Dyflin, Corn Walum and Eoforwic. The Welsh have been cowed and the men of Man fear us. Did you think the Gods would want us to sit in our halls growing fat and listening to Haaken One Eye's tales of our deeds?" They all smiled ruefully and shook their heads. "Then we do what we always do we consult with Aiden and Kara. I will send Raibeart ap Pasgen to spy and we will prepare for war."

Wolf Killer raised his horn of ale, "I hope my little half brother can fill your boots, father, for I fear I will not."

"A man never knows what he can do until he has no choice. Until Prince Butar was slain I did not think I would be able to lead our people and yet here I am almost twenty years later and I am still alive." I raised my own horn and drank deeply, "I am grateful for each day on this earth." Wolf Killer gave me a quizzical look.

Aiden was dragged unceremoniously into the hall. My galdramenn was laughing. "This must be important! They risked the wrath of their sister to fetch me."

I pointed to the side of my chair, "Now sit there and be quiet!" I turned to Aiden and told him our news.

He seemed as calm as I was. He nodded, "I am guessing, Jarl Dragonheart, that you are not immediately worried about this."

"Not worried; concerned, interested...."

"If Rurik's son is raising men to fight us he has two choices, as did his father. He can land in the east and cross the land of the Danes or he can board ships and sail around the coast of Wessex and Wales."

"Those were my thoughts too. But he could come through the land of Eanred, Northumbria."

"True and that is his most dangerous course of action for the Danes are unpredictable and the coast unpredictable especially for the next months. The seas can be as stormy as in winter. The Saxon king might well wish to help an army of Frisians and Franks. If they could hurt us then he might have the kingdom he inherited." Aiden nodded and drank his ale. "The more I consider it the more I think it likely that will happen. This Ragnar Ruriksson may well come through that land."

"Have you dreamed?"

"No Wolf Killer for this is the first I have heard. Your sister and I will dream but the Frisians are far away. Our power comes from this land and our people." He drank some of the beer which Uhtric had poured. "This Ragnar Ruriksson must be your age, Wolf Killer. I remember him from Dorestad. He was a pale sulky youth. There must be someone behind him who uses his name."

I nodded, "The Neustrians. They did not like our raids. The Danes," I spread my arms, "they are ever looking for a chance to expand into our lands."

"So, father, what do we do?"

"I will visit with King Eanred at Bebbanburgh. I will go as a neighbour." Enigmatically I left it at that.

Wolf Killer said, "And?"

"And I will speak with him. I will warn him of the dangers of poking the wolf. I have no doubt that he will fear my visit and mistrust my words but I will take Aiden and Ketil Windarsson with me. Perhaps I will take him a gift."

"A gift? Why?"

"Because the Saxons of the east have not bothered us for many years and I would keep it that way. It will not cost us much and if we are to face a force funded from Neustria then we will need every warrior we can get. And I will send Raibeart to Dorestad. He has sharp ears and a quick mind. We will see what he can discover. Besides we have many goods which can be sold."

I could see that Wolf Killer was still worried. He downed his ale and poured himself some more, "But if you and Aiden are successful and persuade the King not to ally himself with our enemies then it is likely they will come from Eoforwic and many Danes will join them. I am directly in their path."

I sighed. We had this debate too often. I decided to give him my thoughts, "You chose to live there, my son because you wished to be away from me and Kara." I saw him colour and begin to bluster. "It is the truth and all in this room, save Gruffyd know it." I pointed a finger at him. "And little ones should keep their counsel!" I nodded and he did too. "You are more than welcome to return here and live. There is more than enough room for you and your people to make their home where it is safe. Ketil has the same problem as you do and he complains not. You want your freedom then you have to pay the price."

He downed more ale, "It just seems wrong that my people might pay the price for something they did not do."

"Not do? As I recall Rurik came here to attack me. He brought Danes who would have ravaged your land too had we not fought together. We are one clan, my son. Or at least I thought we were."

There was an awkward silence. Gruffyd had made himself as small as he could. Aiden was closer to Wolf Killer than anyone. It was he who broke the silence. "You may be right, Wolf Killer, Ragnar Ruriksson may well come from Eoforwic and if he does then you would be correct in assuming that many Danes would flock to his banner. We are a rich prize and many would like to take this land. If that is true then they will have to come through your land."

"Your words are cold comfort, Aiden."

"Would you rather I did not speak the truth? Until we know more then we prepare for every possibility. Your father goes to Bebbanburgh. We can tell Coen ap Pasgen of the dangers and he can prepare his defences. You must do the same. If they leave Frisia now they might be at your home after the harvest. If that is true then you use the land. There are many bogs and wetlands close to you. Make them more so. Use your river to flood them. When winter comes they will be impassable. Make your ditches deep and your walls higher. Lay in food and water. Once your father knows where Ragnar Ruriksson is we can meet him and defeat him."

My son stared at the floor. "There is no honour in sitting behind a wall." He sounded petulant and I rose angrily. Erika would have calmed me. Brigid would have restrained me. As it was there was no one. "You do not want an answer! You just wish to complain! Aiden has given you ideas and yet you reject them. You would argue that black was white! Go back to your wife and decide what it is you really wish. I will visit with you before I go to Bebbanburgh!"

He was angry and he rose and faced me. Had his hand gone to his sword then there would have been bloodshed. He thought better of it. Even my son feared the sword that was touched by the gods. He stormed out. Beorn and Snorri stared at the puddles left by my son's spilt beer.

Aiden shook his head, "Lord, you have become ill-tempered of late. The old Dragonheart would have bitten back on his tongue and been more patient."

I sat down and shook my head, "Of late I am not sure how much time I actually have left." I pointed east. "I cannot see him ever being ready to rule this land. Can you?" Aiden did not answer. "Can any of you?" The silence was almost unbearable. I wanted one of them to give me a reason to hope. "I am weary and I grow old." I saw Gruffyd's terrified face. "Take no notice of me, my son, I am just out of sorts."

He nodded. "I will fight alongside you, father."

"I know. Now go and fetch your mother. I am hungry after all that shouting."

After he had gone I said to my two scouts, "I forgot to thank you two for bringing us the news. I would say it was fortunate but I sense webs being spun." They nodded. "So Snorri, did you find any yet to carve something for your woman?"

Beorn laughed and Snorri said, indignantly, "She is not my woman!"

"I think it is good that you two make a couple. Eystein would approve and it is time you fathered a child."

Aiden said, "Do you need jet?"

"I have a mind to carve an amulet for her. Do you have some?"

"I do and had you asked I would have given it to you. It would have saved a journey."

I felt the same shiver I had on the mountain top. "But you were meant to go to Hwitebi and you were meant to help the Frisian get to Valhalla. It is *wyrd*."

They all nodded and touched their amulets.

"I would like you two to summon the Ulfheonar. I will hold a feast for them tomorrow night. We will leave for Bebbanburgh the next day. We will visit Elfridaby and Windar's Mere before we see Ketil."

"You just take your oathsworn?"

"I may take some of Ketil's men but any more would seem like an invasion. We go in peace but we demonstrate our power."

I left them and headed for my smith. Bjorn was hammering a piece of twisted metal. It would become a sword eventually. "Have you a sword which would be fit for a king?"

He laughed, "All of my swords are fit for a king. Which king?"

"King Eanred."

He nodded, "Then it would have to be a fine sword. The Saxons are almost as good as me when it comes to making fine swords." He went to a rolled-up sheepskin. Unfolding it he took out a sword which was slightly shorter than Ragnar's Spirit. It had just one jewel in it. It was one of the red stones we had found in a church. "I have been working on this one. It has been quiet lately and I enjoy the craft of making something beautiful and yet deadly. I just need to etch the blade. I was going to make a dragon."

"Then do so. It is worthy of a king and the gift may buy us an ally."

"Do we need one?"

I laughed, "You may be right, Perhaps it is better to say we need no more enemies right now." I looked at the other workshops they were all busy manufacturing the weapons and tools we sold. "Have you heard from Bagsecg?" His son had left home and now plied his trade elsewhere. Thoughts of sons were in my mind.

He shook his head, "No." His face darkened. "When Anya, his wife, first came I liked her. She was lively and I thought she would bring my shy son out of himself. She is too ambitious and she likes gold too much. He would have stayed here were it not for her." He shook his head, "I do not see the children and I grow old."

"You have other sons."

"But only one is called Bagsecg. I named him for my father. My other sons are all fine smiths but Bagsecg, he understood metal the way my father did and I do. He was the best smith I sired."

"Then this is right. He can ply his trade and not compete with you. See this as a good thing."

"I wish I could." He shook his head as though to rid the picture of his son far away, "When do you need the sword?"

"Two days?"

"It will be done." He looked across the Water. "I saw Wolf Killer leaving in a hurry. It seems we both have problems with our sons."

"It starts the day they are born and ends the day that we die."

The words rang through my hall as my oathsworn sang the latest saga composed by Haaken One Eye. It told of the death of Eystein the Rock. Although Haaken had, as usual, changed some events to make a better story, it was still largely true and it was a fitting way to begin the feast.

Through the stormy Saxon Seas
The Ulfheonar they sailed
Fresh from killing faithless Danes
Their glory was assured
Heart of Dragon
Gift of a king
Two fine drekar
Flying o'er foreign seas
Then Saxons came out of the night
An ambush by their Isle of Wight
Vikings fight they do not run
The Jarl turned away from the rising sun
Heart of Dragon
Gift of a king
Two fine drekar
Flying o'er foreign seas
The galdramenn burned Dragon Fire
And the seas they burned bright red
Aboard 'The Gift' Asbjorn the Strong
And the rock Eystein
Rallied their men to board their foes
And face them beard to beard
Heart of Dragon
Gift of a king
Two fine drekar
Flying o'er foreign seas
Against great odds and back to back
The heroes fought as one
Their swords were red with Saxon blood
And the decks with bodies slain
Surrounded on all sides was he
But Eystein faltered not
He slew first one and then another
But the last one did for him
Even though he fought as a walking dead
He killed right to the end
Heart of Dragon
Gift of a king

Two fine drekar
Flying o'er foreign seas

When the song was over Uhtric ordered the slaves and servants in with the food and the beet. I had also broached a jar of wine for I knew that some of my warriors preferred it. There were just eleven Ulfheonar left and one of those, Karl One Leg, never ventured forth with us but we still counted him as one of us. He guarded my home while I travelled, trained new warriors and watched for new Ulfheonar. There had been precious few of late. That is not to say we did not have fine warriors who were the equal of any we met. It was more that they did not have the complete set of skills needed by the finest and stealthiest of warriors.

Few now lived in Cyninges-tūn and the meal was a noisy affair as they spoke to each other of their farms, their families and, inevitably, dead Ulfheonar. I daresay that Asbjorn who now had his own crew was doing the same.

When the food had all been finished save for a few morsels which my men picked at as they drank I rose and I spoke.

"Snorri and Beorn have brought us news that the son of Rurik of Dorestad is gathering warriors to raid us and avenge his father's death. Today I sent Raibeart ap Pasgen to sail to Dorestad and find as much as he can about the force he might bring. Our raids in Neustria have brought us the enmity of the leader there and the Mayor of Neustria is financing the raid. They will be hiring mercenaries."

Olaf Leather Neck snorted, "And they will flee at the first sign of opposition!"

"Perhaps, but when Rurik came last time we had to spend many months scouring the land for the last vestiges of those who remained. There were many farmsteads destroyed by hired swords. You may not fear them Olaf Leather Neck but you are a well-armed warrior and not a farmer and his wife fighting the flies of Grize's Dale."

Olaf nodded, "And that is why you are Jarl and I am just a hewer of Danish necks. Sorry, Jarl Dragonheart."

I waved his apology away. "Aiden and I agree that there are three courses of action our enemy can take. Two of them; an attack by sea and from Eoforwic would take time to organize but Northumbria is weak from war and this Frisian may take the third and seek to ally himself with Eanred."

Erik Eriksson slapped the table, "Excellent! We go to war with the Saxons! More riches for us!"

Others slapped him on the back and cheered, "No, we go to talk with Eanred."

Snorri and Beorn were silent. They knew my reasons. Haaken One Eye looked curious for he knew me well but the others began a clamour. Olaf banged the table, "Talk? We slay Saxons!"

Shaking my head I said, "We do not wish any of the Saxon lands and they have learned to fear us. I intend to persuade King Eanred to be our ally and to protect our border."

Rollo Thin Skin asked, "Why would he do that?"

"Because he fears King Egbert from Wessex. Egbert wishes to be High King of the land of the Angles. It was always the Kings of the north who were the old High Kings. Wessex will go to war with Northumbria when Mercia is cowed. It suits us to ally with them for we know they are not strong enough to fight us."

"We defeated Mercia and Wessex! No Saxon is strong enough!"

"Rolf Horse Killer, you are young. You are a fine warrior but you are still young. We are few and the Saxons are like fleas on a dog. They will return one day and in even greater numbers for we shamed Egbert in front of his army. Our ransom humiliated him. He will be brooding and plotting in his burgh. Better he attacks King Eanred and we help Northumbria than he attacks us and we fight alone."

Everyone fell silent. Haaken One Eye, who was seated next to me, said, quietly, "Have you dreamed Jarl? You seem not yourself."

"We are older, Haaken, that is all. I have not dreamed but I climbed the Old Man and I felt him pat my back." Their hands went to their amulets. They believed that warriors such as we felt our fallen comrades close by when we were close to death.

"What do Kara and Aiden say?"

"They have not yet dreamed. They are now dreaming."

I paused to fill my horn. My words had sobered them and made them reflect. Despite their words, they were all thoughtful warriors. It was what made them Ulfheonar. They realised now the wisdom of my words. Rolf Horse Killer and Rollo Thin Hair apart they were all older warriors; most with families and farms. That changed a man.

"So we ride tomorrow. Take a spare horse each and ride in your best armour. Leif, we will ride beneath my banner. I want to impress the Saxons. We visit with Wolf Killer before riding to Ketil. I will take some of his men. He is the nearest neighbour of the Saxons. It is right that we do so."

Now that they understood the mood changed and they became enthusiastic. It was a chance for them to show off with their best armour. They would wear their warrior bands and display their golden wolves around their necks. It would show any that we met who we were. The drinking went on for some time. Only those who lived within a mile or so of my hall attempted to go home. Uhtric put the rest to bed.

I had not drunk as much as my men and I rose before dawn and left Brigid sleeping. I slipped along to the hall of my daughter and Aiden. Macha and Deidra admitted me. If they wondered why I was visiting so early they knew me well enough to hold their tongues.

"My lady and her husband have just risen. They have gone to make water."

"Then I will wait in the hall. Fetch me some of your fine cheese and small beer."

The two former nuns of the White Christ made excellent cheese. They still worshipped the peacemaker god but they fitted into our world well. It was hard to imagine Cyninges-tūn without them. It was Macha who returned with warm bread, runny goat's cheese, honey and a horn of ale. Deidra followed a short while later.

"My lady will be with you when she has dressed."

There was a hint of criticism in her voice and I smiled, "This is fine cheese!"

She scurried out uncertain how to reply. I think she still feared me a little. I knew now that I looked frightening. My white-bearded face bore scars from battles and the lines upon it were like one of Aiden's charts. They reflected the life I had led. It had rarely seen peace.

"You are early, father."

I nodded, "Aye Kara for we leave as soon as we are able and I would know as much as I can before I speak with Eanred."

I wiped my mouth with the back of my hand and looked up. Kara looked drawn. She always did after dreaming. I knew not what the potion was they took but it seemed to age her each time she and Aiden dreamed. It was one of the reasons I rarely asked them to dream. She sat down and poured herself some beer from the jug.

"It was a strange dream. We saw the raven flying."

The raven? The bird of death?"

Smiling she said, "And also the sign of Jarl Gunnar Thorfinnson. We think it was both. We did not see enemies close to hand but we dreamed of a wall, far away and there was a gate. Warriors spilt out from it. There were Franks and Frisians, Saxons and Danes. They will be coming here."

"But not yet?"

Ignoring my question she continued, "We spoke with the spirits. They spoke not of danger but of treasure."

That made me sit up. It was not the reply I expected. "Treasure?"

13

"I saw mother counting coins from one chest into another and she smiled. And..." she hesitated, "there was a figure behind her but he was hidden. It was a spirit but one without features. They are not dead yet."

Once again I felt the icy fingers of Olaf the Toothless on my neck. "Someone dies?"

She drank some more of the beer as though to compose herself. "Someone dies. More than that it is someone that I know. Mother hid their spirit and I saw your mother too. She smiled at me."

"What do you deduce from all this, daughter? Am I to die?"

For the first time in many years, she looked uncertain. "I know not if you will die but it is possible. I do know that the danger to your home will not be until the winter has passed. The warriors who spilt out of the gate passed the yellow flowers of Eostre. You have until then."

I was relieved. "And has Aiden told you of my plans?"

"He has. They are good. I did not dream this but I believe it is *wyrd*. The way of the sword is not always the best."

I rose and kissed my daughter on her forehead. "Thank you, my daughter. I know how much this has taken from you. Ask your husband to meet me at Ketil's stad. I will not be there before tomorrow evening."

She nodded, "Be patient with my brother, father. He is not as you and I. There is anger inside him and that is my fault. Each morning I curse the day that Angharad came here."

"We cannot change the past."

"I know but it is just as sure that it changes our future. The ripples from that stone have not yet reached the shore. Who knows what dangers they will bring."

Chapter 2

Despite Brigid's objections, I took Gruffyd with me. I had promised him that the next time I rode beneath my banner he could accompany me. Kara had not dreamed danger to us and I felt it was safe. In fact, the dream seemed all good. The flying raven meant Jarl Gunnar Thorfinnson prospered and Erika counting out treasure was also good. It meant we prospered. My wife wept as we left but, when I returned, she would be calm. We rode down the eastern shore of the Water with the noon sun lighting Old Olaf. My men nodded when they saw him smile. It was a good omen. Leif the Banner rode next to my son. He would be his bodyguard. I rode with Haaken. We had much to say. He was my oldest and closest friend. As you grew older such friends became even more important.

"It is Wolf Killer who worries you, Jarl, and not this Ragnar Ruriksson is it not?"

"You know me well. Enemies I can deal with. With warriors like these and those we left at home I can face any foe but family? It is always difficult. They are of your blood but you cannot change their nature. Wolf Killer has ever been thus. He is headstrong and wishes things his own way."

"Perhaps he got that from Erika. You have always been one to compromise and see another's viewpoint." He laughed, "Save in battle where I would not be your foe."

"Perhaps the ride home and Elfrida's counsel will calm him. She is gentler than Brigid."

"I would not let your wife hear that lord! Her Welsh blood will rise to the fore!"

We headed up over the ridge towards the valley of Windar's Mere. I noticed that more land had been cleared and there were more farms. We were slowly taming the land. My people were prospering. Perhaps that was why Old Olaf was smiling.

Haaken asked, "What if our passage north is barred? Will we fight?"

"I would travel in peace but I asked for us all to bring two horses and our weapons and arms in case someone objects to our presence. I think Eanred's thegns will have trouble enough in the south of his land. He has all but lost Eoforwic."

"True, it is now normally called its Danish name, Jorvik."

"Aye, the Danes have insinuated themselves into that land. Within a few years, I can see it being a Danish kingdom and then Wolf Killer will really need to watch out." I looked towards the north. We had reached the high point on the ridge and I could see the Wolf Mountain to the north. "We will take the quiet road through the forests of the north. They will be fly filled at this time of year but I would avoid the Saxons until we reach the stronghold."

"Last time we were there we crept like ghosts did we not?"

"We may still not have the luxury of visiting its interior but so long as I speak with Eanred I will be happy. If he refuses my offer then we will know where we stand and we can make our plans."

It took a couple of hours to reach my son's hall. I saw men toiling in his ditches. He had heeded my words. I smiled to myself. I would not mention it. He might take it as crowing on my part.

Ragnar, my grandson, threw himself on the back of a horse as soon as we were spied and galloped towards us. Haaken laughed, "Just as reckless as his father."

"And he has grown too. Since he carried the banner to fool the Saxons he has grown a hand span."

He reined up next to me. "Gruffyd shouted to his cousin, "I am going with the Ulfheonar! We ride to Bebbanburgh!"

"Grandfather! Can I come with you? Can I?" I must have looked confused for he pointed at my son and said, "Gruffyd is going with you to meet the King of the Saxons! I am older and I have carried your banner. Can I come too?"

I saw another confrontation with my son and I said nothing. I think Ragnar took my silence as assent for he began chattering like a magpie to Gruffyd. Haaken just said, "It is at times like these I am pleased I have only girls!"

When we passed through the gates I dismounted and turned to Snorri. "Have the horses fed and watered. We leave for Ketil when I have spoken with my son."

"Aye lord." He added quietly, "Remember Aiden's words, lord. Patience."

I nodded and put on a smile to greet my son and his wife.

Elfrida threw her arms around me. She was the best wife my son could have chosen. I wondered what his nature would have been had he not met her. "Do you stay overnight?" She asked me.

"No, I ride when I have spoken with Wolf Killer. We travel to the land of Northumbria."

She nodded, "He told me he left angry. He means no disrespect, father. He is just..." She searched for words that would not hurt either of us.

"Wolf Killer. I know. But what of the time when he rules this land. What of his haste then? He cannot storm off when he is lord of the Land of the Wolf."

"He has mellowed, lord." She was clutching at straws for he had become calmer since we had rescued Elfrida from Caer Gybi but not by much.

"You are far too good for him. Let us go and beard the bear in his den then!" She took my arm as we headed indoors.

He sat at his table with a stern expression on his face. I sighed. This would not be easy. I forced the smile and extended my hand, "Son."

Ragnar and Gruffyd were behind me and he was forced to rise and clasp my arm, "Father."

"I called in as I said I would. I saw your men improving the defences. That is good."

He nodded, "I have my farmers digging channels and building dams so that we can flood the land around if anyone comes this way."

Haaken said, "With the Danes so close that is a wise move. The Frisians may or may not come but one day the Danes will decide to take this valley."

When Wolf Killer nodded I thanked the Allfather that I had brought Haaken. He had said what I could not.

"Is this enough men to take with you?"

"I will take Ketil and some of his oathsworn but it should be enough."

"I wish to go with Grandfather, father." Ragnar was not afraid of facing his father.

"But..."

It was Elfrida who came to her son's defence. "Gruffyd is going. If the Dragonheart thinks it is safe for his son then Ragnar will be safe. He is becoming a man and a warrior, husband. Soon you will have his byrnie made and he will ride to war. I lost him long ago. Your time will come. You will lose him. It happens to all fathers." She held her hand out and grasped mine. Wolf Killer looked from me to his wife and nodded. He knew when he was beaten.

Ragnar threw his arms around her and said, "Thank you, mother. I will be safe. I ride with Dragonheart and the Allfather watches him. You have often told me that, father."

"Aye. Well, you will need your leather and your helmet. Get a spare horse."

Elfrida pecked me on the cheek, "I will get him a cloak and blanket. You will watch him will you not?"

"He rides with the Ulfheonar. If anything happens to him it will be because I and all my oathsworn are dead."

Young Garth came over to me. "One day, Grandfather, I will ride with you."

"I know and that will be a great day for me with my two grandsons and two sons at my side." I reached under my cloak and took out a small piece of sheepskin. I unrolled it. "Here, I promised you a seax and here it is. Bjorn Bagsecgson made it just as you asked and in the handle is carved a wolf cub. That is for you."

The joy on his face made me smile long after we had left the hall and headed north. The road we took was much more pleasant than the road through Grize's Dale. We headed towards the pass of Shap. I hoped we would reach Ketil by dark. This was a desolate place. The valley ran north to south and it could be a cold and cheerless place in winter. The nearest settlement of any size was Penrhudd. Arne Arneson was Hersir there and he had a wall around his hall. In the past, we had been attacked too many times by the men of Northumbria. This and Ketil's Stad were two barriers on the old Roman Road to the Land of the Wolf.

He rode out to greet us when we approached our westernmost outpost, "Do you visit with me, lord?"

"No, Arne, Ketil's Stad. Tell me, have the Saxons been a nuisance of late?"

"No lord. Not since the last time you trounced them. The bones of their wounded still mark the road east. The Hibernians and the northern barbarians are more of a problem. The Jarl rides north every month or so to take a few heads and mark the border afresh. It is only the young hotheads who risk the wrath of the Jarl."

"Good. Keep a close watch and if you hear or see anything unusual then send a messenger to Cyninges-tūn."

"Aye lord."

"Have you seen my Galdramenn?"

"Aiden? Not yet, lord."

"He should be passing along the road soon. Have your men watch for him. He might be a wizard but he rides alone."

As we approached, at dusk, the lonely old Roman fort which stood astride the road from Northumbria I regretted not warning Ketil. He was no longer the single young adventurer, keen to escape his father's life of plenty. He had married and had children. I had behaved much as my son might have; recklessly. He was, however, a good host. His men had seen our approach from his walls and he was ready to greet us. His wife was Saxon; she had been captured as a slave. Like many female slaves, she became a wife and seemed, as far as I could see, to be happy.

"Welcome, Jarl Dragonheart. My wife, Seara, will see to your men. Come to my hall and we will feast you."

I could hear the unspoken questions in his words but he knew me well enough to wait.

"Thank you and I apologise for the inconvenience."

Seara gave a small bow, "How can we be inconvenienced, lord. We would have nothing without you."

As we were led away I turned to Ragnar and Gruffyd. "Tonight you keep silent. Listen and watch. This is training for when we meet King Eanred." They both nodded seriously.

Ketil and I sat before his roaring fire and the two boys squatted out of sight but not hearing. I told Ketil, briefly and succinctly what I intended.

"And how can I help?"

"If you could supply some scouts who know the land then that would help us. I do not wish to start a war."

"It would be better if I came with some of my warriors."

I nodded, "But I would not wish to take you from your children and your family; not to mention your people."

"I think you are right to bring so few warriors. A show of force would be wrong. I would bring two scouts and six oathsworn. That would be enough."

I nodded. "And what think you of the idea? Am I a foolish old man who is becoming a dotard?"

"No lord. If anything it is the opposite. I think it is astute. We need not the land to the east of us so why not make an ally of the Saxons? It would make my land safer. We could keep more animals on the fells. I am more worried about this Ragnar Ruriksson. Perhaps your son is right. He may use the southern passes or even the sea."

"That he may and having the Saxons as allies makes our task easier for then our enemy has but two choices."

He laughed and turned to the two boys. "When you grow if you are half the leader that is Dragonheart then men will follow you to the ends of the earth."

I asked that Seara join us while we ate. That was unusual. Normally the men ate separately but I wish to use her knowledge. It had been many years since I had lived amongst Saxons. She had only been married to Ketil for four years.

"Tell me how the Saxons view us."

She looked nervously at her husband. He smiled, "Speak. Nothing that you say will cause the Dragonheart offence. He was born a Saxon."

"Truly?"

I nodded, "I was but six or seven when I was taken as a slave."

"And yet you are now Jarl." She shook her head. "They fear you. They fear all Vikings for you do not respect the church. But you hold a special terror for them. Despite White Christ, they see you as the one who changes to a wolf and appears out of the dark. Their children are brought up fearing you."

"You follow the White Christ?" Her hand went involuntarily to the cross she bore around her neck. "Fear not my wife is a Christian."

"You kill priests and take the holy books. They say you burn them."

I laughed, "They are too valuable to burn. We sell them. And the king, King Eanred; what do they feel about him?"

"Some say he is not strong enough. There are those who would try to take his crown from him. It is why he stays in Bebbanburgh. He is safe there no matter how many try to take his throne."

"And has he children?"

"Prince Aethelred. He is a fine young man and very popular. There are many ladies who would have him as their husband. He leads the king's army."

Just then a weary Aiden strode into the hall.

Ketil stood, "You had better get food for the Jarl's galdramenn." Seara made the sign of the cross and hurried out. Ketil laughed, "She has many superstitions and rituals of her own but she is afraid of witches and wizards."

Aiden sat. He looked weary. "It has been many years since I have ridden so far on the back of a horse!"

"How long will it take us to reach Din Guardi from here, Ketil?"

"If we ride hard then we can do it in one day. It is a hundred miles and from here is a straight line."

"Where will be the danger?"

"There are two such places. One, when we cross the wall. At Hagustaldes ham there is an ambitious young thegn, Coenred of Hagustaldes ham. He sends his men sheep raiding. It is rumoured that he wishes to be King."

"And the other?"

"There is a hall at Alnwick. The Aln is not a deep river and we can ford it if the bridge is guarded but Hagustaldes ham is the place I worry about for we cannot avoid it and we may find trouble."

"Then it is good that we know where it is for we can be prepared."

As we had scouts we used Ketil's oathsworn to lead the horses. Leif the Banner now had two boys to watch although they felt they were guarding my standard. As soon as we left Ketil's home we were in the land of our enemy. His scouts rode ahead and returned as we headed north and east. They kept changing horses. There had been a bridge at Haydon but it had washed away in a storm and so we would have to cross the Tinea at Hagustaldes ham. We broke our journey four miles short of it. We ate and changed horses. We kept our helmets on our saddles and our shields behind our backs. We were there peacefully but we kept a hand on our swords.

We had not gone far when Oswald, Ketil's scout, galloped in. "There are Saxons ahead, lord. A horseman and thirty warriors."

Ketil deferred to me. I asked, "How many are mailed?"

"The rider and four others."

"Fetch the other scout back and stay with the spare horses." Turning to my Ulfheonar I said, "We come for peace but be prepared for war."

They chanted, "Aye Jarl!"

"Ragnar and Gruffyd stay by the banner! No matter what you see. That is an order! Aiden, stay by the banner too."

"I will."

Haaken joined Ketil and me. "What does this Coenred of Hagustaldes ham look like?"

"He is the size of Asbjorn the Rock. He has mail which has a coating to make it look like gold. It is not. His shield has a boar upon it with a bloody mouth. A human tongue hangs from it." I cocked my head to one side. He nodded, "A real one!"

Haaken asked, "Does it not rot?"

"He takes a fresh one each month I am told." Haaken looked in disbelief. "It was my wife Seara who told me. When cases are tried by the thegn his punishment for serious crimes is always the loss of a tongue." He shook his head. "And they call us barbaric!"

"And he is a rival for the throne?"

"He is ambitious and would have more power. He and Aethelred, the King's son, were friends. They had a falling out. He is an untrustworthy warrior from what my wife told me."

"She seems to know much about him."

"She is his cousin. She lived in a settlement close by. The Gesith owed allegiance to Coenred. He was punished for losing the village. He had his tongue cut out and then he was executed." He paused. "He was Seara's father."

"Then he may take exception to your presence."

"He may."

"Thank you. We will now ride on and meet this Coenred." I turned to Ketil. "Do not rise to his jibes and his insults."

"No, Jarl."

I had met Vikings as barbaric as Coenred but never a Saxon. Even old Aella had not been such a savage. I wondered how I should speak to him. I wanted no confrontation but we had to get to Eanred.

The town was to the south of the Roman Road and Coenred had his men waiting for us. They were in a shield wall with him astride his horse before them. I saw what Ketil meant about his armour. It was intended to impress. I saw the tongue. It looked ridiculous and yet grotesque. From his hip hung a Saxon sword. We rode forward. Saxons had no archers. Apart from their leader they were on foot. The danger they presented was as a barrier. When we were thirty paces from them I stopped and held my hands before me to show them I came in peace.

He rode forward five paces and drew his sword to show that he meant war. "A Viking who comes in peace? I do not trust such an action. From your cloaks, you are the men from the Land of the Wolf and as Ketil the Coward hides behind you I am guessing you are the one they call Dragonheart."

I glanced at Ketil who kept his face impassive. I nodded, "I am Jarl Dragonheart of Cyninges-tūn. From the tongue on your shield, I believe you are Coenred of Hagustaldes ham."

"I am. Now go back to your land before we slay you!"

I had his measure now. He wanted to impress his men by making me flee and yet he did not trust them to defeat us.

"I come in peace. I am on a peace mission. We are travelling to Bebbanburgh to speak with your king."

"And I will not let you pass! What say you?"

We had been speaking in Saxon and I knew his men were hanging onto every word. They would be taking in my warrior bands and my armour. They would see the jewelled sword hanging from my belt and knew it was a sword of legend. They would glimpse the golden dragon around my neck. They knew who I was. Whatever I said next would determine whether this ended peacefully or not.

"I have no quarrel with you and I do not want to kill you. Let us pass and I am sure your king will reward you."

"Reward me! Crumbs from his table?" He pointed his sword at Ketil. "You, hiding there behind this old man, come and fight me! I owe you a death! You destroyed my village and stole my cousin!"

I held my hand out to silence Ketil. "This is discourteous even for a young man like you. Ketil Windarsson is oathsworn to me. He cannot fight you without I give him permission and I do not. So let us pass." I waved a hand at those behind me. "These are Ulfheonar. There are no finer warriors in this whole land. We are all mailed and your men are not.

If you try to stop us we will slaughter you and I do not wish to do that. Let us pass peacefully."

I kept my voice calm and reasonable. I saw his men looking at each other. They did not want to die. His four oathsworn looked ready for a fight but not the rest. The Saxon thegn looked around to gauge support. He did not like what he saw.

He kicked his horse on. "Then I will fight you in his stead!" He roared it loudly so that all would hear the challenge.

"I do not wish to fight you."

"You are afraid?"

"I did not say that."

"Then fight."

I pointed to his men. "You will bear witness that I refused to fight. I want no bloodshed." I saw one or two of his men nod. "I say again, Coenred of Hagustaldes ham, let us pass peacefully."

He dismounted. "The only way is through me. Do we all fight or just you and me?"

I dismounted. "I would not have any man's blood on my hands but if this must be, then so be it. I will fight you alone." It was unspoken but we both knew that this would be to the death. I wondered if this was the first time he had done so. I had fought like this more times than I cared to recall.

I handed my reins to Haaken. He said quietly. "He will be quick, lord."

"You will be teaching my horse how to run next, Haaken." I smiled. "I know that he will be fast and I know that he will be strong. I have to trust in my sword and the Allfather."

I swung my shield around to my front. He glanced at one of his oathsworn and I knew what was coming. He would rush me before I reached the middle. I pulled my shield around tighter as I stepped towards him. He ran at me roaring a war cry and swinging his sword. He aimed it at my head. I planted my left leg on the ground and angled the shield up to cover the lower part of my face. I needed to see him. It was a mighty blow. It shivered my shield and slid up to my helmet. My thongs held it in place and the adornments Bjorn had applied prevented damage. He roared in joy and turned to face his men and their cheers. It was another trick for he hoped to entice me to attack his back while it was turned.

He suddenly spun and sliced his sword towards my shield side again. He was quick. He was like lightning. I had a sword struck by Thor's lightning and my left hand came down as I stepped forward. The sword crashed onto my shield. It was not as powerful a blow as I was closer to him. My forward movement meant he overbalanced slightly. His helmet only had a nasal and I saw the look of disbelief on his face. He had expected it to be over.

"Old man, can you no longer fight? Give me this so-called magical sword and I might let you live as a dog in my kennels!"

I said nothing but stretched my left arm out and then pulled it tight again. I knew that silence from behind my face mask would be unnerving. I had yet to use my sword which I held slightly behind my body. Once again he used brute force and speed to try to overwhelm me. He came at me swinging quickly with looping cuts. I used my shield to fend them off and my feet to keep me out of trouble. After a flurry of eight such blows, he stood, panting and sweating.

This time I spoke again and I spoke loudly enough for his men to hear. "I ask you again. End this and let us go to visit your King. This cannot end well for you."

Through gasping breath, he said, "How have you lived so long when you cannot fight? Your shield can only take so many blows!"

He was tiring and I watched as he took a deep breath to launch yet another attack. As he pulled his sword back I knew that he would strike over his head. He was a big man and he would be able to create much power when he did so. I did the unexpected. I stepped forward and punched him in the face with my shield. My left arm ached but I had a boss on my shield. The boss caught him squarely in the nose, bending his nasal. Blood and cartilage sprayed from the wound. The edge of the sword caught the rim of my shield and it stuck there. As he faltered I swung my sword from behind me and it bit into his knee. I pulled and twisted it out. This time it was not a war cry which came from his lips but a cry of pain. He did not step back but lurched back the blood pouring from the wound.

His face was a mask of blood and fury, "You trickster! Now I will end this!"

He tried to charge me again but I must have done more damage to his knee than he knew. His left leg gave way. I swung my sword in a scything sweep. His hand tried to bring his shield up but his bent nasal obscured his vision to the left and he was tired. Ragnar's spirit hacked into his neck. I had brought my sword from a long way back and I could not stop its power. It bit through the flesh and the bone. The head, helmet still attached, rolled from the body. A heartbeat later the corpse fell to the ground.

24

The Saxons were stunned. My men were too well trained to cheer. I heard swords being drawn from scabbards. Sheathing my own I took my helmet off. "Enough blood has been shed. If you draw your weapons we will slaughter you." I looked at his four oathsworn. "Your lord is dead and you will gain nothing by trying to gain revenge." Without looking behind me I said, "Snorri!"

An arrow suddenly sprouted from between the legs of the nearest mailed man. It was embedded along half its length. The man nodded and sheathed his sword. He went to take the reins of Coenred's horse.

"Leave the horse. Take your lives and leave." Scowling, the four did so. I pointed to the nearest four men. "Pick up your master's body and head. Put them on his horse. Does he have a family?"

One man ventured, "Aye lord, a wife and a bairn."

"Then take him home so that he can be buried." I pointed to the next four. "You four come with us. We go to your king but I would have you four testify to the events which took place here." Without waiting to see if they complied I shouted, "Ketil Windarsson, fetch four horses for these men." Turning back I said, "The rest of you go home. I meant what I said. We come in peace. You may well remember this day when you are greybeards bouncing grandchildren on your knee. This could be the day when the war ended and is certainly the day your lives were spared by the Dragonheart."

I mounted Storm Rider and Haaken said, wryly, "Were you trying to blunt his sword? Or waiting for him to tire himself out? It is an interesting technique, Jarl."

"I defeated him did I not? Besides he relied on my shield being as badly made as his. He should have invested his coin in a better shield rather than making his iron armour look golden."

"Aye, his byrnie was too short."

We all wore our byrnies so that they covered our knees. We had learned that the extra weight was worth it.

Ragnar said, "Were you not afraid, Grandfather, when he launched himself at you? His hands were so quick."

"And that is why you practise against two men and learn to use your shield. You have two weapons when you fight. Use them both."

He nodded, "Does this mean that the King will be angry when we meet him?"

"I hope not but I could not avoid it could I? It was the work of the Weird Sisters. Our threads were twisted. We will see what they next intend."

Gruffyd said quietly, "I prayed to the Allfather that you would be safe. He answered my prayers."

25

When we came to the Aln the Saxons there had heard our approach and they fled to their hall in the loop of the river. We did not bother them for I was keen to reach Bebbanburgh before dark. The fight had delayed us and we rode hard for the last fifteen or so miles. We made good time on the Roman Road but the last few were over a rough road covered with windblown sand.

The castle was well built and well sited. It lay at the end of a promontory which was surrounded on three sides by sea, sand dunes and boggy ground. There was but one approach and that was directly towards the castle across a neck of land. As we crested the rise I saw the mighty fortress rising ahead of me. It looked like the boss on a mighty shield. Even as we watched the last of the Saxons were hurrying along the road desperate to be within the walls of the stronghold of Northumbria. The walls were lined and King Eanred was ready for war.

Chapter 3

I turned to my men, "Take off your helmets and put your shields behind your backs. You four Saxons, ride next to me." I said quietly to Haaken, "Take my kin to the rear."

"Grandfather!"

Haaken snarled, "You heard him. If you wish to serve the Dragonheart you obey orders without questions. You get to groom all the horses tonight Ragnar Arturusson!"

We halted below the walls and waited. The entrance wound along the side of the salty swamp which would fill with the sea at high tide. The banners of Northumbria hung from the walls. Suddenly something was hurled from the walls. I dodged my head out of the way at the last moment as the lead ball thudded into the ground behind me.

"Leif, come with me."

I rode forward with my standard-bearer and we stopped in the slippery dank water close by the causeway ramp. "King Eanred I come in peace. I come to talk and not to fight." There was silence. "If I had come for war I would have brought a mighty host and you know that."

His head appeared over the wooden walls. A younger version was next to him. He shouted, "If you come in peace then why do you have four Saxon prisoners with you?"

"They are not prisoners; they are witnesses." I turned and shouted, "You four Saxons come here." When they were next to me I said, " Coenred of Hagustaldes ham would not let me pass beyond his hall. He demanded combat to the death. I brought these men so that they could bear witness of what occurred. You can take them within your castle if you wish and question them."

The heads disappeared. I turned to the Saxons. "You may dismount. I trust you to speak the truth." They nodded.

The heads reappeared. King Eanred shouted, "They may enter. You, Dragonheart, retire to yonder headland and camp. We will speak with these men first. Do not try any tricks, you will be watched!"

I nodded and led my men north. It was ironic. We had camped there when we had crept into the castle to slay our enemies. Now we would camp there and perhaps be admitted to the castle through the front gate. On the other hand, it could be where we had Dragonheart's last stand!

We made a picket line and Snorri and Beorn led Ketil's men to make a rough barricade from gorse and bramble bushes. It would not stop a determined foe but it would slow them down. I did not believe that they would attack us. We were too intriguing a prospect. Haaken grumbled. "They will probably let us freeze out here tonight and then slaughter us in the morning."

Olaf Leather Neck said derisively, "You are getting too soft, Haaken One Eye. It is one night and when we return home think of the song you can create."

He nodded, "Aye, I suppose so."

Young Ragnar asked, "We just wait?"

"We wait. My life is not filled with sword fights and battles. Oft times it is dull. Now is such a time. You two may well lead men in the future. This is part of being a leader."

We finished off our rations and drank the last of our ale. If the mission proved fruitless and we were sent on our way empty handed then we would take from the Saxons and they would pay for their king's lack of manners. Snorri and Ketil made sure that we kept a good watch overnight. I slept little. I stared at the darkened shadow of the castle. I had slain Magnus the Forsworn there. One of my ancestors had slain a false king. Was my destiny tied up in the rocky fortress?

Aiden joined me. "You cannot sleep either galdramenn?"

He pulled his cloak a little tighter around his shoulders. "This castle is special. Myrddyn is reputed to have flown in here with one of your ancestors."

I cocked a cynical eye, "And you believe that?"

He laughed, "No. You and I know of enough tricks to have an idea of how it was done. No, my point is the legend that is created from such events. When we speak with King Eanred tomorrow he will be in awe of you. He will fear you. No matter how much he blusters remember that."

"He will admit us?"

"He has to. If not he will lose even more face than he has already. You have slain one of his mighty warriors and travelled deep within his kingdom. He has to speak with you. I have not dreamed but I can make a story from the pieces I see before me. When he asked us to camp here I knew that you had won."

"You could have told me and I might have enjoyed a night's sleep."

"No, you would not for you feel Olaf's hand on your shoulder."

I whipped my head around, "You read my thoughts?"

"I know you have spent many mornings with Old Olaf much as you did on Man when you tramped to Snaefell when everyone else slept.. Your son's behaviour worries you for you see the end of your thread."

"Am I to die? Have you dreamed it?"

"No we have not dreamed it and I do not think we will. The Weird Sisters have been too kind to us and told us more than they should have. You are favoured by the Allfather but there are many gods in Asgard and some are jealous of you. Loki, for one, would resent someone who was not Norse born having the glory you have."

That thought depressed me. I had thought I would know of my own death for it would be dreamed and I would be prepared. Now I knew that it could come at any time and it was a sobering thought.

Dawn was worth the wait. The sun spread out like golden butter melting upon a deep blue sea. It lit up the seal islands which littered the coast. Aiden and I watched as the white light rose slowly in the sky. He turned to me and said, "This is a good omen, Jarl. I have never seen Ran have the sea so calm. This will be a good day."

It was mid-morning when Rollo Thin Skin shouted, "Riders leaving the castle."

Haaken shouted back, "Do they come for war?"

Ulf walked into the camp and laughed, "There are but twenty of them. If they come for war we gain twenty horses and some fine mail." Shaking his head he said, "They do not wear helmets and their shields are on their saddles."

I nodded, "Then they either come to invite us within or to tell us to go home. Either way, we should mount and be ready."

As the Saxons rode in they were greeted by a terrifying sight; fully armoured and armed Vikings. I knew how intimidating we were and this was our peaceful pose. The Saxons were led by the young warrior who had been at the walls the previous day. I hid my smile as I saw the fear on the faces of the men who followed him. Even our horses looked intimidating compared with theirs. The young man, however, seemed quite calm, almost pleased to see us. The warrior had golden hair tied in two pigtails. His armour was well made but only came to his waist. It seemed to be the way the men of Northumbria liked it.

"I am Prince Aethelred. My father King Eanred invites you to visit with him."

"In his castle?"

The Prince looked embarrassed, "No, Viking, he has had a shelter erected twixt the castle and here. It is close to the village of Bebbanburgh." Apologetically he added, "There is food and ale but I think he fears admitting warriors with such a fierce reputation.."

I smiled. I was here to make peace not to visit a castle. "That is satisfactory. Lead on Prince Aethelred."

"I will ride with you if that is agreeable."

"Very well."

29

Haaken dropped back to ride with Aiden. As we rode the prince asked, "Why did you not wish to fight Coenred?"

"You spoke with the men?" He nodded. "They told you what happened?"

"Aye. They said you gave him many chances to leave the fight with honour and he refused. He was once my friend and I knew him. He would never have backed down. Yet they said you slew him with ease and could have done so far quicker than you did. Why?"

"I told your father. I come for peace."

We descended towards the houses of the village. "I find that hard to believe. You are a fierce foe and we have many empty hearths because of you and your men."

I stopped Storm Rider and looked at him. "Have my men ever invaded your land to conquer it?"

"You came into my father's home!"

"And killed renegade Vikings. The only Saxons I slew were the ones who tried to kill me." I kicked my horse on. "We have killed many of your father's men but they came to do us harm. I defended my borders. You do not poke a tethered wolf. I live in the Land of the Wolf. We wear the skin of the wolf and we are dangerous as the wolf. We choose whom we hunt and we hunt not outside our territory. If you fear us then that is not our fault. We have never tried to take your father's lands."

He laughed, "You are not what I expected, Jarl Dragonheart. We grow up with stories of how you will come in the night and eat us if we misbehave."

I heard his words but I was busy studying the men we would meet. I saw the King ahead with his oathsworn before him. There were six priests behind him. I think that one was a bishop but I am not well up on the different types of priest. As we slowed I said, quietly, "I was born to a Saxon father on the river they call the Dunum. I was born in Northumbria. Think about that."

I dismounted and handed my reins to Finni the Dreamer. Turning to Leif I said, "Stay here with my banner and the two boys." I saw the disappointment on their faces but they heeded the words of Haaken. "Aiden, fetch the sword. Haaken, come with us."

King Eanred frowned as we approached and two of his oathsworn stepped forward. One of them was a huge warrior with a split nose and a scar which ran down his forearm. He wore many battle bands and he held a double-handed axe. He said, "I am Osric and the King's champion. Approach no closer."

I smiled, "I am here to make peace and not to fight."

Prince Aethelred said, "I have spoken with the Viking, father, and I believe he comes in peace."

"I will believe that when the sun rises at midnight!" He waved a finger at me, "I warn you Viking I have sent riders seeking your warband and I have called up the fyrd. The army you try to sneak through our lands will be destroyed!"

Aiden said, "Your men would be better working in the fields. It will be a hard winter and our army consists of the men you see here before you.."

King Eldred recoiled as he recognised the wizard; his priests made the sign of the cross and began to chant. "It is a wizard! Do you seek to enchant me?"

Aiden frowned, "If you do not believe in magic then how can it hurt you? Surely your god and your army of priests will protect you."

"Sorcerer! I will not speak in the presence of this man! Get him gone."

Osric put his hand on Aiden's chest. I removed it firmly saying, "Do not lay on hands on my friend or peace or no peace I will give you another scar that will not heal in this world." I spoke quietly but he saw that I meant my words. He stepped back. "Aiden you had best go. It seems they fear that which they neither understand nor believe." He handed the sheepskin covered sword to Haaken and nodded.

Aiden had a wicked sense of humour and as he turned he flapped his hands at the priests and mumbled gibberish. They fell to their knees. Haaken could barely control his laughter. Even Aethelred had a smile.

"This is not the beginning I wished, King Eanred. Let me start again. As I said to your son I have never invaded your land and the only Northumbrians I have killed came to harm me." I saw him start to speak and I forestalled him, "When I entered your castle it was to kill a renegade, Magnus the Forsworn and I apologise for that breach but he had to die. Now I come with an offer of peace. I am ready to swear an oath and as you have your priests here assembled we could make it binding."

"I do not fear you or your barbarians!"

I did not mention Coenred and his tongues but I could see that Aiden was right. He did fear me. "That is good but would you want a peace which would stop your men dying and your cattle being raided? We would. For that is our aim to live in peace with our neighbours and you are our nearest neighbours. Those who were here before the Saxons are our allies. Coen Ap Pasgen is descended from the kings who ruled here in the times of the Romans. They are our allies and they prosper. Why cannot you?"

"We do not raid." He said it almost petulantly. It seemed wrong for a king to speak thus.

I shook my head, "King Eanred your thegns do try to take slaves and cattle. Coenred of Hagustaldes ham did. Ask his men. They told you the truth of the fight. They will tell you the truth of that also."

He turned and beckoned over a priest who was slightly better dressed than the others. His fingers were heavily ringed. After he had spoken he said, "How do I know that you will keep your word? What assurances do I have?"

My eyes bored into his. "You have the word of Jarl Dragonheart of Cyninges-tūn. I have never broken an oath in my life. Even my enemies admit that, if I give my word, then it is so. I swear that if you agree to this treaty then we will not raid your land or take your people. More if the Danes or the Hibernians cross your border to raid and try to cross our land we will capture them and deliver them to you for punishment. And if you wish I will swear on this sword. You have heard of it I know. You may not believe the story but to us, it is the truth."

Prince Aethelred could keep silent no longer, "Take the offer, father!"

"Silence or leave us. This is the work of men and not striplings." He stood and approached me. There was still fear in his eyes but also curiosity, "It is a reasonable offer but I am suspicious of your motives. Why?"

"I will be honest. I have many enemies. King Egbert is an enemy of mine and although I have defeated him I have no doubt that he will come again to attack me. The Hibernians always raid for slaves. The Danes at Eoforwic trouble not only you but for me also. I need my northern and eastern border secure so that I can face my enemies and defeat them when they come. I have no desire to rule this land. I am happy with the Land of the Wolf."

"Which was once Northumbria."

"And which was lost in years gone by. And before that belonged to King Coel and before that..." I waved a hand as though rolling back the years. "You must look to the future, King Eanred. The time of the Dane is coming. If you waste your anger on me they will take the whole of your land, not just Eoforwic."

He returned to his seat and pondered. "This should be written down."

"Why? If a man's word cannot be trusted why should a piece of parchment? I am willing to swear and shake your hand."

"And what would you have of me?"

"I would have you swear on your Holy Book that you will neither raid nor attack my lands and you will not aid my enemies." As he considered it I said, "And as a token of my esteem I give you this gift. Haaken, give it to Prince Aethelred."

Haaken unrolled the sheepskin and handed the gleaming sword to the prince. A shaft of sunlight sparkled off it. The oathsworn were impressed as was Prince Aethelred. Once more King Eanred consulted with his priests. It seemed to me that they had more power than the King. Haaken must have thought the same. He said, out of the corner of his mouth, "Do you think he asks them when he should make water too?"

Eventually one of the priests hurried back into the castle and the King stepped forward. "I agree, Jarl Dragonheart, but I have to tell you that I am still suspicious of you. A wolf does not become a sheep overnight."

I nodded and said, "And yet we have sheepdogs at home which are descended from wolves and now protect their sheep. Does not your God tell you that men are not always what they appear on the surface? I have heard that your God's lieutenant turned against him and became the one you call the devil."

I almost undid the good work I had done for the priests recoiled when I named the Devil. We waited in silence for the Holy Book. When it arrived the King said to me, "Swear."

I took out my sword and held it in my hands. "I swear by Ragnar's Spirit that we will no longer make war on the men of Northumbria. From this day forth they are as our friends and allies."

I think the Saxons were stunned. My word was legendary and I had sworn.

The King gave his oath on the bible and the priests poured some water on his hands. I walked over and clasped his arm. I saw his priests grin. They had poured what they termed Holy Water on the King's hands and they expected it to affect me. How little they knew. I think they expected me to shrivel before their eyes. They could not keep the disappointment from them.

I stepped back, not knowing what to do. Prince Aethelred said, "We will now seal this with a feast. We have a great bounty from the sea. Let your men come forward and eat with us."

Slaves brought out tables and benches. One was laid for the King and one for me and my men. "Haaken fetch the men."

I suspect that Prince Aethelred had been responsible for the food for it was excellent and there was plenty of it. Having had dried rations for the previous day my men appreciated it. The Prince came and sat opposite me. Ragnar and Gruffyd were on either side of me and he nodded to them. "Are these your sons, Jarl?"

"This is my son and this is my grandson."

He smiled at them, "And will you two be warriors like the Dragonheart?"

Ragnar said, "We already are. We fought King Egbert! I am not afraid to fight!"

The Prince nodded, "I see even young Vikings have spirit."

"I am sorry to say, Prince Aethelred, that your White Christ stops you and your men becoming great warriors. Warriors do not forgive and forget."

"I see now; that is why you came here to kill the renegade." He leaned forward. "The killing of Coenred of Hagustaldes ham was a clever move, Jarl. He had threatened to take my father's throne."

"I told you, Prince. I tried to avoid killing him. I did not kill him to ingratiate myself to your father."

He frowned. "But you had to kill him. He was like a mad dog."

I smiled, "Ah, you mean it was meant to happen?" He nodded. "It was *wyrd*!"

"You are interesting Viking. A man who can quote the Bible and argue like a Greek. You are not what I expected."

"And that is the difference between us for I never expect anything. I use my eyes and ears to judge. All men are equal in my eyes. A man only betrays me once. Magnus the forsworn thought he had found somewhere to hide in the most heavily defended castle in the land. He was wrong. I hope your father keeps his word. I shall but if he does not then the wrath of God will seem as nothing compared with a Viking's wrath."

I kept my voice calm but I saw him recoil in fear. "And I believe you."

We left at noon when my men were full and the skies were clear. The Prince and his men escorted us as far as the Aln. He pointed to the loop in the river. "I will build a burgh here."

"A good choice. You need but a ditch across the front and it will be almost as strong as Bebbanburgh."

"Could you take Bebbanburgh, Jarl?"

"A man can take any castle. He would lose many men but it could be done. A leader has to weigh those questions up. Is it worth the effort? Besides, while men are in their castle their land can be ravaged."

"Is that why you do not build burghs?"

"We have no need. We follow the old ways and the land protects us. We live in harmony with the earth and the spirits." I smiled, "Your people did once."

"Would I be welcome if I came to visit you at Cyninges-tūn?"

"Your father would approve?"

"I am my own man and I make my own decisions."

"Then you may visit and welcome."
We bade him farewell and we headed west into the afternoon sun.

Chapter 4

"Jarl, it is Raibeart ap Pasgen. He has returned from Frisia." The message from the guard on the tower by our gate was a relief.

We had been back for half a month and the preparations were going well for whatever attack Ragnar Ruriksson had in mind. Bjorn Bagsecgson and his sons had produced arrowheads, spearheads and swords. The ditches had been deepened and the land around the walls cleared back even further than the fifty paces we already had cleared.

Those of my Ulfheonar who lived nearby made their way to my hall as did Aiden and Kara. This was of vital importance to us all. Gruffyd also sat in with me. He had been both quiet and reflective since we had returned from Bebbanburgh. He had been close enough to hear all of our discussions. His Saxon was the equal of any. Perhaps he had his skill in languages from me; I know not. He watched me more. I had also noticed him emulating my walk and my stance. It was like having a half-sized shadow following me around.

Brigid had Uhtric bring in ale, bread and some fresh and very runny goats' cheese. The fact that she stayed showed her concern too.

Raibeart looked grubby and weary as he entered my hall. "I came as fast as I could, Jarl Dragonheart."

Brigid said, "Have some ale and sit. A few more moments will not hurt your news." She glared at me and I gave her an innocent look. I had not pestered him.

He began after downing a whole horn of ale. "It is good to drink decent beer once more. It is true, Jarl. Neustria has made both funds and ships available to Ragnar son of Rurik. He is gathering men up and down the coast. He was not in Dorestad when we were there; he had travelled to Neustria."

Haaken interjected, "Franks too? They have horses."

Raibeart nodded. "I stayed to find as much information as I could." He grinned. "We brought back much profit. We can sell as many sealskin boots as the women can produce."

I shook my head irritably, "You are a spy and not a merchant, Raibeart."

"Sorry, Jarl. The good news is that he will not be ready to sail until after Samhain. The men were still gathering at Boulogne. They have a count there now and he is also aiding the Frisian leader. When we passed the port there were just three ships there. From the numbers of men we heard of they will need four times that number. Their ships are smaller than ours."

"Then we have time to prepare."

Aiden nodded, "And one route is now eliminated. He will not risk the wild seas of the west after Samhain. Frisian ships are not dragon ships. He will come across the Saxon Sea. I would bet he would come through Eoforwic. There he could pick up more men and Danes with local knowledge."

I agreed. "You have done well Raibeart."

"Thank you, Jarl. And we met Jarl Gunnar Thorfinnson. He was seeking crew in Dorestad. He had to flee when they tried to take extra taxes from him."

"He went back to Ljoðhús?"

"No Jarl. He and his men have captured an island off the coast of the Bretons. He has a stronghold of his own now. He does not have as far to sail to raid."

Aiden nodded, "That was Hrolf's dream."

Raibeart said, "Aye, he was with him. Einar sold him some boots. He has grown and is a handy warrior by all accounts. His crew think highly of him."

Aiden looked at me and smiled, "*Wyrd*."

Wyrd indeed. The Weird Sisters still entangled our threads. As much as I had liked the young slave as soon as the witch had given her prediction I knew that he was meant for other things. I had no doubt that our threads were still bound together but he would never be one of my people.

"It is good that Jarl Gunnar has his own land and if it can be defended then so much the better."

Olaf Leather Neck brought us back to the moment, "I am pleased for the Jarl too but what do we do about this Frisian? Are we to sit on our arses and wait for him to come or should we seek him out and kill him ourselves?"

The question was asked of me but most eyes were on Aiden. "Aiden has told us that he is guessing that he will come from Eoforwic. That means he has to come in that short time between Samhain and Yule or wait until the winter snows have gone. The high passes are too difficult in winter."

Karl One Leg was more thoughtful since he had been forced to stay in Cyninges-tūn where his injured leg would not impede him. He could think things through and see what other warriors could not. "A hired warband is hard to keep together, Jarl. They want food and women. A leader has many different clans to control. This Ragnar must be young and inexperienced. Even if they have a Frankish Count with him he will have to attack sooner rather than later. I do not like to argue with a galdramenn but I think they will be here by Samhain."

Karl's words brought silence. It meant that the ships could be on their way and might be able to take the longer sea passage. His words had been an unpleasant truth. We had to plan for two possible avenues of attack.

This time all eyes were on me. I was Jarl and I made the decisions. "Snorri, ride to Sigtrygg. Tell him I need him to watch the waters off the Lune and to be ready to come to our aid. You know him well and you can tell him all. Hide nothing. Speak of our visit with the Saxons."

"Aye Jarl."

"Haaken we will need Asbjorn and his men. They are the closest to Úlfarrston. I want them ready to go to Coen's aid. Raibeart you need to warn your brother. I fear that you and your people may have to bear the brunt of a seaborne attack if Karl is correct." Karl shifted uncomfortably in his seat.

"I shall take *'Red Snake'* to sea. If I sail to Man and then Dyflin I can spot such a large number of sails."

Although Raibeart was not Norse borne he had the heart of a Viking and a mind as sharp as any. "That is good. Before you leave I would have words with you for I will send a message to Jarl Gunnstein Berserk Killer."

I drank some more ale and silence filled the room until Haaken said, "And Wolf Killer? What of him Jarl?"

"I will visit with him but I will travel to Windar's Mere first. That is the richest of our stad. They have had an easy time of late. Ketil watches their northern borders. They will have to provide men to go to Wolf Killer's aid. I will visit with Wolf Killer myself. Beorn and Haaken I would have you come with me. As for the rest; let us prepare for war. This Ragnar Ruriksson will find out the true meaning of Samhain. He and his men will soon join the army of the dead!"

After they had gone I was left with Aiden and Raibeart. "Perhaps Karl is right and I am wrong Jarl. My sight seems to focus too much on Cyninges-tūn. I find it harder, these days, to see beyond the borders."

"That is the effect of your daughter, Ylva. I was the same when Wolf Killer was firstborn. She will be a powerful witch when she grows. She draws much power from you and from Kara."

Aiden smiled, "You are becoming the wizard now, Jarl."

I turned to Raibeart, "When you are in Dyflin I would have you buy two Saami bows for my son and grandson. I fear they will be with the clan when we go to war. A bow might keep them out of danger. I would have them learn to fight before they die." Raibeart nodded, "And ask Jarl Gunnstein Berserk Killer to keep watch for our foes. I cannot think that they would be foolish enough to even think about seeking his help but the young are sometimes foolish."

Raibeart shook his head, "Do not underestimate this warrior. He is of an age with Wolf Killer and men say he has been a warlord. He is both cruel and cunning. He is being backed by Neustria because they see someone who can take the Land of the Wolf from you. I believe both Karl and Aiden are correct. It will be hard to keep a hired warband together but this Ragnar seems the man who could do that. They talk of him being greater than his father. He has men who follow him like your Ulfheonar. They are intensely loyal to him. That tells you something."

"And we both know how dangerous Rurik was, Jarl Dragonheart."

"Then it is a test for me." I looked at Aiden. He knew my thoughts, "Can I hold on to this land and pass it down to my blood or will this be the end of Cyninges-tūn and our way of life?"

"I have not dreamed the end, Jarl. To answer honestly, I do not know."

When they had left me Gruffyd crawled out from under the table. I had forgotten that he had not left. "So the little mouse was listening."

"You sounded as though our world was coming to an end father. Is it?"

"All things end, my son. We pass through this land and we make a mark but in time the marks disappear and it was as though we never existed."

"That is sad."

"No, my son, you, Wolf Killer and Ragnar will carry on and, perhaps, your threads will take you to somewhere different. Jarl Gunnar Thorfinnson now has a home many leagues to the south where they know not snow. My thread began not far from Bebbanburgh. We do not know where the journey will take us. Life is an adventure. Take it as such." I ruffled his hair and looked into his eyes. "Now do not tell your mother my words. Women worry."

His back stiffened. "I will be as your oathsworn, lord."

Ketil was Jarl of Windar's Mere. He had taken over from his father but he knew that his duty lay to protect the north. I had liked his father but Windar had been no warrior. His son was. His second son, Harland, was more like his father. He stayed in the stad by the mere and ran it for his brother who lived on the border. In that, he did a fair job. It was prosperous. That prosperity came from my protection and, as I headed there with Beorn and Haaken, I intended to collect payment for that prosperity.

At the bridge of Skelwith, I said to Beorn. "Ride to Ketil and tell him what we intend. If we light the beacons then he should bring all the men he can muster."

Haaken said, "You are testing this new treaty then Jarl?"

"The best time to test it is when we are on a war footing. Besides I believe that Prince Aethelred is on our side."

Beorn rode off and the two of us rode down to the fine halls that made up this rich little stad. We passed the old Roman fort. Its stone walls had been repaired but none stood guard. That would have to change. My visits were rare enough for me to cause a stir as we rode through the streets. Here they made no swords but their craftsmen made delicate bone combs and needles. They spun wool and made fine clothes. Stone was so plentiful, as it was in Cyninges-tūn, that they had masons who turned the stone into building materials. It was a stad where men did not carry swords for they had no need to. The exception was Arne Thorirson. Harland Windarsson might organise the stad but it was Arne, one of Ketil's most trusted men, who defended it.

It was he who strode towards me. "Jarl, this is an honour."

I had fought with Arne. His arms had not only battle rings but the scars of a warrior. "I come with dire tidings. We have had word that a war band of Frisians, Franks and Danes may be heading to lay waste to our land and to slay me."

Harland arrived as I finished the sentence and he looked alarmed, "Kill you Jarl? Who would be so foolish?"

If Arne looked a warrior then Harland looked like a priest of the White Christ but Ketil trusted him. I would not like to stand in a shield wall with him but he made sure there was enough food for the people of Windar's Mere.

"There are many. Now your people will be safe here, for a time at least but Wolf Killer may well need help. We know not if they come by sea or land. If they come by land then Wolf Killer will have to endure their attack." I pointed to the beacon. "The beacon is unmanned. From now on someone is there each moment of the day and night." Arne flashed an angry look at Harland who looked abashed. "Arne I want your men ready to ride at a moment's notice. You have horses and ponies aplenty. Use them. Harland, you will mount a permanent guard on the fort. That is your refuge when Arne takes the bondi to help Wolf Killer."

It was only then that the seriousness of the threat sank in. "But what if they came here?"

"Then those who remain would have to defend the walls of the fort. You have been spared the privations of raids and wars. Be thankful. Arne here knows the dangers of enemies."

Harland was silent. Arne held his arm out for me to grasp. "I will make sure that Wolf Killer is not left alone and I promise you that we will keep watch on the beacons."

I nodded as I mounted Storm Rider, "And I will speak with the others who have beacons close by. We have grown lax and lazy. The Norns do not like complacency. Be vigilant and, Harland, if you do not wish to lose this fine life then strap on a sword and don a helmet. There will be no spectators if Ragnar Ruriksson descends upon you."

The beacons followed the track from the mere to Elfridaby. They were maintained by the farmers who lived close by them. It took some time for us to speak with them all but once we had done so then they understood the importance of their role. It was dusk when we rode through the gates of Elfridaby. I was pleased with the improvements my son had made. I was weary and Elfrida saw that.

"Let your father sit and take refreshment before you badger him with questions. He will tell you his news soon enough." She pointed to Ragnar. "Our son put your mind at rest when he returned from Bebbanburgh."

Elfrida was like a mouse but when she roared she was like a she-wolf. Wolf Killer looked abashed.

"Thank you, Elfrida, but a horn of ale will suffice for a while and then I will give my news."

Ragnar sat next to my chair between Haaken and me. I saw the frown flit across my son's face. Was he jealous?

Haaken saw the look. "We have spoken with those who guard the beacons. They will be vigilant. If our enemies come then your beacon will bring the men of Windar's mere. They have many horses and ponies. They can be here before you know it."

Wolf Killer nodded gratefully, "Then they will be coming this way?" Elfrida flashed an angry look at her husband. "I ask Haaken, not my father!"

"And is not Haaken of an age with your father? Neither is getting any younger!"

I think Haaken took offence at that last comment but he did indeed have streaks of white hair as I did. He smiled, "Do not worry, Elfrida, we have life left in us yet. Aye, Wolf Killer, they come and they may come sooner than we thought. Raibeart is patrolling the seaways. He told us that there could be ten or twelve boatloads of Frisians, Franks and Danes heading this way."

"If they come by land then they will have to pass here first."

I nodded, "They will and therein lies our problem. I have asked Sigtrygg to watch in case they take a southern route. You must send out your scouts to watch the high passes. Have you Hersir you can send?"

"Aye, I have. They may not be Ulfheonar but they are warriors I can trust as you trust Haaken and the others."

"Good. If you see them early enough then I can bring every warrior we can muster and defeat them but it is twenty miles to my home. It would take longer for a message to reach us and longer to arrive here. Your vigilance is the key."

"I see that now. This land seems perfect. The fields yield much and we prosper but at times like this I see that the sword has two edges and one can cut."

"Aye. Cyninges-tūn is harsher and harder to farm but Old Olaf protects us." He nodded. "I know that Bjorn Bagsecgson sent you arrows and spears. If you have not enough then send for more. Our archers may make the difference."

The next day I rode with my son, Haaken, my grandson and eight of Wolf Killer's oathsworn. Garth had been desperate to come but there was too much danger for that. He was still young and the rocky wasteland that was Shap was perfect for an ambush. We rode towards the stone circle of Shap and the high passes. "This is Beorn Long Sight. He is my best scout."

Wolf Killer pointed to a lean looking warrior who wore leather armour and just a short sword. Hung from his saddle was a bow. He bowed, "I am honoured to meet with you, Jarl Dragonheart."

We were ascending a track which led from the valley bottom alongside the tiny deserted farmstead of Low Borrow. "Do you know this land well?"

He pointed to the farm. I was born there and lived there until the Danes came and slaughtered my family." I waited for he had not finished. He answered my unspoken question. "I was away hunting. I followed those that did this and killed them all. It took a month but my family was avenged. It was then I journeyed west to serve your son. I know this land."

"You will need to keep a close watch on the high passes. Are there others who have your skills?"

He gave me a serious look, "That is not for me to answer, Jarl. If I say no then it sounds as though I am arrogant. There are others who can scout but you ask me can they stand amidst a field of Danes and remain hidden as I can then the answer must be no."

"I have a scout like you. Snorri is his name. I am fortunate that he has another who is almost as good. Then you, Beorn Long Sight, will need to teach the other scouts your skills."

"I will do so but I think the gods gave me these skills where he gave others different ones."

We rode in silence on the road which followed, roughly, the Roman Road which had once stood here. There was little other evidence that those ancient builders had left much of a mark on this land and it was both hard and unyielding. After Low Barrow, we saw no sign of human habitation until we came to the Raven's Stone. Here we saw a shepherd's hut but no sign of the shepherd. We stopped for we had come as far as we could in one-half day.

Wolf Killer looked east, "So they would come across here." He pointed to the sky. "Already it is becoming colder and soon the snows will fall."

Haaken said, "I do not think they would come this way."

"It is the most deserted part of the land. If they wished to reach us unseen it is their best route."

"And that is the very reason that Ragnar Ruriksson will not come this way. He has a large army to feed. On what could he feast? If the snows came then where would he shelter?" Wolf Killer suddenly saw the sense in Haaken's words. Haaken turned to Beorn Long Sight. "If you wished to attack Elfridaby and you came from Eoforwic which route would you take?"

"If I wished to stay hidden then this way. If I wished to be fed there are two southerly routes. One comes over the big Roman Road which is longer. It has many farms along the route and some hamlets too. The shortest way is to the south, closer to the land of Sigtrygg Thrandson. It is the road which passes through Sedde's Burgh."

Wolf Killer whipped his head around, "But that is just ten miles from my home!"

"And who farms there Beorn Long Sight?"

"Seddes died many years ago. It is a mixture of our people, Saxons and a few who come from the old times."

"They have no hersir?"

"No, Jarl. Sigtrygg Thrandson and your son are the two nearest jarls. The burgh was destroyed by the Danes when they last came through. There are walls no longer. They have been raided so many times that the people there flee at the first sign of an enemy. They are a fearful people. You cannot blame them."

We turned our horses and headed home. "Then, my son you need to ride to Seddes' Burgh on the morrow. It seems to me that if you had men there they could warn you quickly and, perhaps, hold up an enemy. I think your scout is right. If that is the shortest route and if there are farms along the way then they will use that route." He nodded, "How far would you say it was to Eoforwic from Seddes' Burgh?"

Beorn was a scout. He did not know Roman miles. He looked over his shoulder and said, "A warband could march hence in three days or ride in two. There is a road and there are farms and animals there. They could be fed."

"They will not have enough horses to ride. They will march. We have less time than I thought. I will stay this night and then Haaken and I will return to Cyninges-tūn. We all have much to do."

Wolf Killer said, "Aye. Beorn Long Sight, take your men tomorrow and ride towards Eoforwic. Keep watch on the road. I need to know in advance when they come. Stay hidden and return as soon as you see a sign of their scouts."

"Aye Jarl."

"If you have someone who can pass for a Dane then they might gain information from within their walls."

"I will ask my men but I doubt it."

I wondered if I should have sent Snorri and Beorn. Wolf Killer smiled as he read my thoughts, "You must trust others father. The Ulfheonar cannot do it all. Let my men emulate yours."

Little did I know what I set in motion. We returned to Elfridaby feeling as though we had achieved something. My son and I were a little closer and knowing what the danger was somehow made it less fearful. By the time we returned to the warmth of Elfrida's fire we had guessed that our enemy would come one of two ways. To get to Wolf Killer and to me they would both have to pass through Seddes' Burgh. That insignificant huddle of huts suddenly became as important as Lundenwic. It was so close that none of us had seen its importance. It was thanks to a lean and hungry warrior that we had.

Chapter 5

Samhain was not one of our rituals and festivals. It belonged to the old people who had lived in this land since before the Romans but we respected it. The passage of the dead and the change from harvest to winter were both important in our year. We noted it because the days began to become perceptibly shorter and the nights longer. The feast helped us to mark the change in our lives. It was three days before Samhain that the warband struck.

Raibeart had had no luck in finding the enemy and that was a good thing. It meant they were coming across the land. He did have my Saami bows and a boatload of warriors sent by Gunnstein. They were the men who had fought alongside us in the recent wars. They had asked to fight and they were more than welcome. We left them, and their drekar, in the river at Úlfarrston. But of the horde who hunted us, there was no sign.

Through riders who crossed from Elfridaby and Cyninges-tūn we learned that neither Beorn nor his scouts had returned and, as with Raibeart's lack of news, we too took that to be a good omen. It was Sigtrygg and his men who brought news of the disaster to us. It was fortunate that we were close to Elfridaby else the disaster would have been even worse. As Raibeart had not brought news of ships we had our men mounted and riding towards Úlfarrston. Asbjorn and his men, as well as those we had raised from Cyninges-tūn, were all mounted. Sixty warriors rode down the Water. Snorri and Beorn were well ahead and it was Beorn who galloped back.

"Jarl, it is Sigtrygg and his men. They are riding hard towards us. I fear it is not good news."

I cursed myself for not having Aiden with us. "Let us ride to meet them then."

We met them by the farm of Nib at the southern end of the Water. He held a hessian sack up. It was bloody. "Jarl, we have kept watch towards Seddes' Burgh as you asked. Yesternight we came upon some Frisians heading for the road to Úlfarrston. We slew them all." He shook his head. "I am getting old. I should have questioned them. I am sorry."

I was impatient, "That matters not. What could they have told us? That Ragnar Ruriksson and his men are here? Their presence told us that." I pointed to the sack. "What is in there?"

"They had eight of them. We brought just one in case you knew who it was."

He reached in and drew out the skull of Beorn Long Sight. His eyes had been gouged out and his tongue removed. Even so, I still recognised the earnest young scout. "I know him and that explains..."

"Jarl! Look!"

Olaf Leather Neck pointed east. There the beacon flared.

I nodded, "That explains why we had no warning and why the beacons were not lit until now." I turned, "Einar Audunsson, ride to Úlfarrston and fetch the men of Dyflin. Bring them to Elfridaby. We will meet you there."

The young warrior whipped the head of his pony around and headed south.

"Will Wolf Killer be there, Jarl?"

"I doubt it. We have to make sure that my son's family is safe but I have a feeling they will still be at Seddes' Burgh. Wolf Killer was going to fortify it. I would rather we fight far from our homes; this was not how I planned it. We waste time. Let us ride!"

As we rode I wondered if I should have left Gruffyd at home. His small pony was tough but it would struggle to keep up with us. We had twenty miles to ride and the only consolation was that we would be riding over flatter ground than had we left from Cyninges-tūn. We would make good time. Sigtrygg and his men were suffering more than we for they had ridden hard already. Their horses might make my son's hall but no further.

I was relieved to see the walls of Elfridaby standing yet. The gates were whole and my son's standard flew. We galloped through the sturdy entrance. It was a small garrison which greeted us. Elfrida came out, smiling. It was a smile which masked her fear. "Your son and Ragnar rode out when they saw the beacon from the south. You have made good time. Did Aiden work his magic?"

"No, it was luck or perhaps it was *wyrd*." I turned in my saddle, "Sigtrygg. You and your men stay here. Your horses are exhausted and I want the garrison strengthened. Gruffyd, stay with Elfrida and guard Ragnar's sister."

He bit back his reply and nodded.

"Keep a good watch. The men of Dyflin will be here soon." I leaned down to Elfrida. "We have been surprised and Wolf Killer's scouts have been killed. You must command here with Sigtrygg."

"I am the wife of a warrior, Jarl. I know what I have to do. Do not worry about me or your son. He will be safe here."

I smiled at Garth, "Today, grandson, you begin to become a warrior!"

He took out the seax I had given him and flourished it. "I have named it Fox Bite!"

As I led my sixty men east I was grateful that Gunnstein Berserk Killer had sent his men. With Sigtrygg's and the garrison Elfridaby would be safe; for a while at least.

We met the first of those fleeing our foes close by the tiny mere a mile from the town. They were not warriors. They were the frightened people who lived in the farms. They cowered fearfully in the ditches when we approached. I spoke to them quietly. "Tell me what happened."

An older man with a badly gashed head said, "Barbarians came from the east. We had some warning of their coming for others fled before them. We ran but they had mounted men and they rode us down. We did not understand their words. Many were killed but the Allfather smiled on us. We fell down a steep bank and they thought we were dead." He held his hand to his head. "I nearly was. We spent the day making our way west. We knew that the Jarl at Elfridaby would give us shelter."

"Did you see him?"

He nodded, "We used logs to float down the Rawthey and we heard them. They are fighting in the rebuilt burgh."

"Keep heading west. You will find a welcome at Elfridaby." As they hurried away I said, "Snorri and Beorn, I need to know the disposition of the enemy."

"Aye Jarl." The two of them whipped their horses and disappeared ahead of us.

Asbjorn, bring your men. I will take you and the Ulfheonar. The rest of you dismount here and make a shield wall. We will bring the enemy to you. Cnut Cnutson, you command."

"Aye Jarl."

I drew my sword and raised it. "We ride!"

Galloping down the gentle slope to the burgh I wondered if we would be in time. My son could have no more than forty men with him. Ten boatloads of our enemies could be as many as two hundred warriors. My only hope was that there were some still strung out on the road from Eoforwic. Snorri met us. He was dismounted. I could hear the clash of arms ahead.

"Jarl the outer wall is breached. Wolf Killer and his men are outnumbered. They are fighting their way back through the huts. That is the only thing preventing them from being overwhelmed. The enemy can only bring a few warriors to bear but they have horses and soon they will outflank your son."

"Dismount! Asbjorn, go with Snorri and outflank them from the north. Beorn, lead us to the south." I swung my shield around as my tiny band of Ulfheonar tried to do the impossible; we would try to convince a larger army that we were a larger force than we actually were.

47

We left the road and headed across the fields to approach the enemy from behind. We kept low and our wolf cloaks disguised us; they hid the metal of our byrnies. Haaken and Olaf Leather Neck were on either side of me. The noise of the fighting had grown. Beorn pointed. I could see the Franks. Their helmets were rounded and had no nasal. I took in that many of them did not have armour. I also realised that there were many of them. Our approach had been silent.

I waved my sword left and right. We formed a thin line. I saw Wolf Killer's standard. It flew still in the midst of his warriors but he was beleaguered. I waved my sword and we ran towards the rear of the Frankish warriors. It was strange to attack silently but I wanted as many men to die before they knew we attacked. That would add to their fear. I brought Ragnar's Spirit down and hacked across the back of a Frank. My sword jarred on his spine and he died silently. Others did not die so quietly. I stabbed the next Frank under his right arm. Twisting my sword out of his back it emerged covered in bloody gore.

There was a wail from ahead as Asbjorn and his men struck the far side of their line. As we stabbed and sliced at the ones before us the shouts and cries spread to our side. Olaf's mighty axe sliced through a warrior's back and the arm of the man next to him. A chief was spattered by the blood and turned to face me. He swung his sword backhanded at me. I blocked it with Ragnar's Spirit and our swords clanged and rang together. Sparks flew from them. I did not give him the chance to swing again. I punched hard with my shield. His helmet had no nasal and his face took the full impact of my metal boss. His nose and mouth were struck and I heard bone and cartilage break. His eyes were streaming when I plunged my sword into his bloodied throat. He fell at my feet, dead. I sliced and stabbed three more warriors who tried to turn to face this new threat. My Ulfheonar had slain three lines of Franks and it proved too much. They turned and ran.

"Turn and face them. Form a shield wall! Asbjorn, bring your men!"

As the Franks were funnelled back through the gap, Asbjorn and his men stood behind mine to make a stronger wall. I yelled, "Wolf Killer! Take your men up the hill to my standard! Rally there!"

I did not hear a reply and I did not turn. Although the Franks were falling back some of the younger warriors sought glory and hurled themselves at our line. It was a mistake. They died. We were a solid line with warriors who knew how to fight on foot. The Franks were horsemen. The biggest danger we faced was tripping over the dead beneath our feet. I saw many of the warriors Wolf Killer had led from Elfridaby lying dead. Their swords were in their hands. They would be in Valhalla. We moved back through the congested body littered huts.

Suddenly out of the darkening gloom of dusk I heard a horn. It was a Frankish horn and it was rallying our enemies. Soon they would reform and attack. The survivor had said that they had horses. We had to be away before they charged. Frankish horsemen were good!

There was no one before us and I shouted, "Back to the standard! Run!"

I was the last to reach the horses. Wolf Killer, blood pouring from a gashed arm, stood with the twenty men who had survived. I saw that Asbjorn had also lost six men. "Mount. Those without horses ride double. We have but a little way to go. Cnut Cnutson waits with a shield wall." I mounted Storm Rider. "Rolf Horse Killer, you and Olaf Leather Neck form the rearguard. Listen for danger!"

"Aye Jarl."

I rode next to my son. "What happened?"

"My men were surprised. The enemy appeared without warning. My men were still building the wall when their scouts fell upon them. They managed to light the beacon and I came as soon as I could. By the time we reached the burgh, there were but two men left and the outer wall had fallen. I know not why Beorn Long Sight did not send me a message."

"I do. He and his scouts were captured. Their eyes were removed along with their tongues."

He closed his eyes and then opened them. "I am sorry, Beorn, for cursing you." He shook his head. "It is fortunate that you came so quickly." He suddenly started. "My home! I left few guards there!"

"Fear not. Sigtrygg has his men there as well as a drekar crew of the men of Dyflin. Your home is safe." I was missing something. "Why do you worry about your home? The enemy are behind us."

"This is not all of them. Another band, with Frisians and Danes, are heading there now. The Franks were to pin us down. The only hope we have is that they are afoot. We are mounted."

We reached Cnut just as Rolf shouted, "Jarl! Horsemen!"

We stood no chance on horseback against Franks. "Dismount. Form a shield wall!"

Riding around the rear of Cnut's double line I dismounted and pulled four men who just had leather armour from the rear of the line. "Hold the horses."

Handing my reins to one of them I pushed my way to the front of the shield wall. Olaf and Haaken joined me. We stood with Cnut in the front rank. Haaken said, "Your father's spirit will be watching us Cnut Cnutson. He would be proud."

We could see little ahead. Darkness was falling rapidly. We could, however, hear the hooves of their horses as they galloped up the road.

My hope was that they could not outflank us. There was a ditch running along both sides of the Roman Road. When they hit us, however, it would be hard.

Olaf Leather Neck shouted, "Shields!" We locked ours at the front. Those in the second rank brought their shields over our heads and warriors did the same at the side. We were a solid wall of wood and metal. Those with spears poked them out, The ones in the second rank added their weapons to ours. Blades and spearheads bristled from the wooden wall. We were as prepared as we could be.

Once the shields were locked in place Olaf Leather Neck shouted, "Brace!" We all stepped forward on our left legs and awaited the crash when the horses hit us.

We saw a moving shadow at first which quickly became a line of horses. They had spears and long oval shields. What they did not have was armour on their legs. I saw a glimmer of hope in the dark of night. The Franks had stiraps. They could punch with their spears. We could do nothing for their spears were longer than our swords. The first ten hit our shields. I heard a scream as one of my men was speared. His shield had not been locked. It was a mistake but a costly one. The men in the front rank were largely the men from my home; they followed Cnut Cnutson. They were not Ulfheonar.

I heard Snorri shout, "Let me in!" as he took the dead man's place. The one death appeared to be the only one. Many of the spears had broken. The ones who remained tried to find gaps in the shields. We waited. Olaf, Haaken and I had done this before. As the Franks before me poked their spears at the shields I took the opportunity to stab forward with my sword. The tip was sharp. It pierced the warrior's leg and went into the side of his horse. The man roared in pain and involuntarily pulled up with the reins. The frightened and wounded animal began to thrash. Its hooves clattered off our shields before it overbalanced and fell back against another two horses.

Olaf Leather Neck darted from the line and swung his axe. It hacked through the neck of a second horse. As its rider fell at our feet Cnut hacked off his head with his sword. In a heartbeat, we had reformed. The Franks were in disarray. Two dead horses and three dead warriors now blocked their path. We heard another horn and the riders fell back. As they did so I shouted, "Ulfheonar, become the front rank. Wolf Killer, take your men and ride back to your home. We will follow."

One of the horses was not quite dead. Olaf stepped forward and slit its throat with his seax. "You died well!" We did not like horses to suffer.

I heard Wolf Killer's voice, "Take care Dragonheart! This enemy is cunning!"

I did not answer him. Already I knew that! We heard the hooves of our men recede into the darkness. I said, quietly, "Beorn, see where they have gone." I heard a whisper as he left the line. Feet shuffled and his place was taken.

Haaken said, "We will hear them if they come again, Jarl."

"You are right. Unlock shields but stand ready in case they come again."

I laid my shield on the ground grateful that I no longer had to hold it. I kept Ragnar's Spirit in my hand. Stepping forward I cleaned it on the cloak of the dead Frank who lay before me. He had been crushed by the dying horse. His face showed the agony of his death. I took his sword from his scabbard. It was longer than mine. It felt well balanced. I unclasped his baldric and strapped it around my own waist. I sheathed the sword. Who knew when I might need a second weapon?

Haaken said, "Should we call you Garth Two Swords now?"

I laughed. It released the tension I felt. "It might stop me being singled out for death by my enemies."

Olaf Leather Neck said, "They do not need your name to single you out, Jarl. They see you and they know you. All of our faces are marked. As soon as a warrior dons a wolf cloak then he becomes the target for ambitious young warriors. It is why that Saxon, Coenred, challenged you. He wished the glory. All know that a Viking cannot refuse a challenge."

A short while later Beorn ran back. "They have gone to the burgh and they are fortifying it." He lifted a skull from behind his back. "I took this from one of their sentries." He took a spear from the ground and jammed it into the side of the road. He placed the head upon it. Then he went to the dead warrior who had had his head taken by Cnut and did the same on the other side of the road. "They may be Christians but I doubt they will wish to cross such a warning."

"Well done, Beorn. Mount up. Those who do not have a horse, ride double."

We headed west, following my son's path. We would not reach Elfridaby until dawn. The horses and the men were weary. Wolf Killer would be there soon enough. If Ragnar Ruriksson attacked there would be a garrison.

"Beorn, how many Franks were left?"

"Hard to say but I estimate sixty or seventy. Most had horses."

I rode in silence wondering how many Frisians and Danes they had. The Franks were obviously from Neustria. It explained why they had boarded at Boulogne. They had brought their horses by the shortest sea crossing they could. They must have needed twelve rather than ten ships.

51

It also gave me a little hope for it meant they had fewer Frisians. The Frisians were fierce warriors. If the Danes came from Eoforwic then the slightest obstacle might send them racing home. The Frisians, however, were more likely to fight to the death. I did not want to lose any warriors.

"You are quiet, Jarl. Is there something on your mind?" I remained silent. "You should be relieved."

"How so, Haaken One Eye? What can you see that I cannot?"

"Before they came you worried that you did not know where they would land. Now you do. Raibeart can bring his men over and join us. We have a larger garrison in the burgh than we had before. We just have to work out a way to defeat them."

"There are Frisians, Haaken! They take some killing."

Olaf Leather Neck spat, "And we are the ones to hew necks! Fear not, Jarl. It will be a bloody day but the men of Cyninges-tūn showed today that they can stand in a shield wall and face charging horsemen. I have known other jarl's oathsworn who could not do that."

It took us longer to reach Wolf Killer's home than we expected. We had wounded and we had to tend to their wounds. Our horses had also suffered and it was mid-morning before we viewed Elfridaby. It was surrounded! I saw Wolf Killer's banner flying from the tower and knew that Wolf Killer and my grandson Ragnar had made the safety of the walls. They were, however, surrounded. The campfires of the Frisians and the Danes were dotted haphazardly around them. I could see that Elfrida had released the water from the dams and there was a veritable lake around the stad. I relaxed. There was no way that Ragnar Ruriksson could breach the walls before the waters had subsided.

"Snorri, ride to Úlfarrston. Fetch Raibeart and his men. Beorn, ride to Windar's Mere. I want every man they can spare. We meet at Underbarrow."

They galloped off. Underbarrow was a small hamlet of five huts. It lay less than a mile west of Elfridaby. More importantly, it was on a hill. Not a large hill but one we could defend should the Frankish horsemen pursue us. I led my men around the camps of our enemies to the hill. They thought the Franks had dealt with us and the watch to the west was weak. The homes were empty. Their families were safe within the walls of my son's stronghold.

"Olaf. We will camp here. Send scouts out to gather food. Have a ditch dug."

He asked, "We wait here?"

"Do you think that they can capture the stronghold any time soon?"

He smiled, "No lord. It would take weeks."

He left and I dismounted. I felt the weariness in my legs and my back. I was too old to campaign. I dared not take off my mail. We were still in danger. I handed my reins to Leif. I found a patch of shaded earth beneath a chestnut tree. Taking off my helmet and my weapons I lay down.

Haaken approached, "Any orders, Jarl?"

"Aye. Take charge until I wake. I am weary!"

I was asleep before I knew it. Perhaps it was my weariness of the Norns, I knew not, but I dreamed.

I was on my drekar and I sailed west. No matter how much I turned the steering board I could not change our course. Wolf Killer cried out to me to turn the drekar and I could not. I saw the edge of the word and it raced towards us. Its savage teeth seemed to champ and to grind. Suddenly we reached it and the drekar plummeted over the side. We fell. We fell a long time and yet we did not reach the bottom. We landed in the middle of a forest. I was alone. I heard my son crying out for me and I ran. No matter how hard I ran I could not reach him. I discarded my helmet and my mail and forced my feet to move. Then I saw him. He lay on a table and a warrior with a full face mask stood over him. The warrior turned to me, laughing and then swept his sword down to take my son's head. I leapt forward with Ragnar's Spirit drawn to avenge him and I found myself falling into a deep, black hole.

"Jarl! Jarl! You were shouting!"

I looked up into Rolf Horse Killer's face. It was late afternoon. The young warrior could face down charging horsemen without flinching but after hearing my ranting he looked terrified. I smiled, "I was dreaming, that is all!" I put my dream from my mind. I could not afford the luxury of working out what it meant. That would have to wait for Aiden and Kara. "Have the reinforcements arrived?"

Rolf pointed to the three new camps. "They arrived just after noon."

"Fetch my Ulfheonar, Asbjorn, Arne Thorirson and Raibeart to me."

"Aye Jarl."

I made water by a large tree. I had noticed that I needed to do so more frequently these days. Age. I walked down to the small stream and threw water on my face. It felt better and I headed towards the camp again. I saw that it had been well organised. It was neat and ordered. Bushes and young saplings created a natural-looking barrier around us so that we would be hidden from our enemies. Of course, a close inspection would reveal us. In a few days, the leaves would die and we would not be hidden. However, by that time, this would all be over, one way or another.

I gathered my Ulfheonar around me. I nodded to Raibeart, "How many men did you bring?"

"Forty of my people and then the men of Dyflin."

"It is not enough. Arne?"

"Another fifty although only ten are shield wall warriors. The rest are brave and willing but..."

I nodded. They were sword fodder. "Have they brought their bows and slings?"

"Aye lord."

"Good. That will suffice. Snorri, have you scouted our foes?"

"Aye Jarl. There are almost two hundred of them. The Frankish horsemen arrived during the morning. The Frisians are hewing saplings and brushwood to make a causeway across the water and the mud. Your son's archers are slowing down their work. If they continue through the night then they will be ready to attack the walls by noon tomorrow."

"We are too few to attack the whole camp. Raibeart, send a rider to Ketil and to Ulf Olafsson at Thorkell's Stad and then you will take charge of the camp. I need the men from the north. We need to whittle down their numbers. Asbjorn I want you to rejoin the Ulfheonar this night. The Franks and Frisians do not know us. Tonight we become wolves. We will spread terror in their camp. I hope it will slow down the work on the causeway. As soon as Ketil reaches us then we can begin to take the battle to our enemy."

"Ulf will take longer to reach us."

"I know Haaken but they will be reinforcements. Our enemy has none. That is why we slaughter as many as we can. Snorri and Beorn I want you two to hamstring as many of the enemy horses as you can."

"Jarl, it might be better if we drive them off or capture them. Horses do not like the smell of blood; especially their own. If we start to hurt them then they will make a noise and panic. This way we weaken the enemy and we gain horses."

"You can do this?"

"It will be easier than cutting them. We kill the guards, untie the horses and then drive them west."

"Then drive them to Cyninges-tūn and bring back any men you can... and Aiden." I saw the relief on the faces of my men. They were always happier when we had the wizard with us. "Now we eat our rations and prepare for the night. Raibeart, keep the fires burning brightly and I want one man in four on watch."

Raibeart and Arne Thorirson had both brought supplies with them. We ate dried fish and cheese. The ale skins were soon emptied. We prepared for the night attack. I laid down my shield. I would not need that. I took off my new Frankish sword. It was too long for what I had in mind. I sharpened my dagger, my seax and my sword on my whetstone. When I was satisfied with the edge then I put them in their scabbards. Some men did not bother with scabbards or sheaths. It was a mistake in my view. This way our weapons kept an edge longer and there was no risk of metal scraping on metal when they were drawn. We needed silence. Finally, I donned the red cochineal around my eyes. Once my helmet was on I would be almost invisible. If I was seen in a flash of firelight then I would be an apparition from the underworld!

I headed towards my men who had gathered in the centre of the camp. "Work in pairs. If one falls the other brings the body back."

They nodded and Rollo Thin Skin said, "We howl?"

"At the first cry from the enemy we howl. When the horses run away we howl and then we disappear. There are too few of us to throw our lives away." They nodded and each one touched the golden wolf I had given them and which they wore around the neck. I touched my dragon. It had not been made; it had been sent and as such was as valuable to me as my sword.

"Haaken you will be with me."

"Of course! Where else would be your finest and oldest oathsworn?"

The others smiled at his arrogance. They knew it was banter.

We headed down the valley towards the river which led to my son's stronghold. The enemy were on the far side but we would be hidden from sight. As we wore our wolf cloaks and moved silently I did not fear them seeing us. Their eyes would be on the walls of Elfridaby. I had no doubt there would be sentries which was why we moved in pairs and we kept as low as we could. Our wolf cloaks and black armour made us hard to see. My sword was sheathed but I carried my seax. The shorter blade was easier to use for what we intended. We walked in the river shallows. As we approached the camps we heard the mumble of chatter. Drawing closer we heard the work on the causeway. There was an occasional shout and cry as one of the defenders managed to strike one of those toiling in the swamps with a well-aimed arrow. Wolf Killer had plenty.

Snorri and Beorn kept going. The horse herd was to the east of the camp. They would have the furthest to go. Rollo and Rolf Horse Killer were the youngest and they followed. Haaken and I found ourselves alone. We crossed the river. The water, in the middle, came up to our chests. It was cold. As we reached the other bank I heard conversation. I did not understand the words and I guessed it was either Frisian or Frankish. Either way, it meant there were men ahead.

We flattened ourselves into the bank and began to crawl up the side. As we peered over the edge we saw, just four paces away, two sentries.

The two were being lazy. They sat and they did not watch the west they looked out over the camp. After taking in that they sat on their shields and had their cloaks wrapped tightly about them I looked beyond to the flickering fires of the camp. There were many men. Most appeared to be sleeping. I could hear the work on the causeway. That was five hundred paces north of us. We were on the edge of the camp. Already the fires were dying to a glow. Soon we would be able to move among them, bringing death.

First, we had to eliminate these two sentries and take their place. The fact that they were seated made it easier. I nodded to Haaken and we crept forward. The art of such movement is to make it smooth and slow. It is sudden disturbances which catch the eye. Sometimes, if you move slowly enough a man, can look at you and not see you. You are a shadow. We were shadows. I had fought alongside Haaken so many times that we did not need to speak. We both reached up at the same time. I pulled back the Frisian's head and stabbed my seax up through his throat into his skull. He died instantly and there was little blood. I laid him to one side and then sat upon his shield. Haaken did the same.

It had happened so quickly that it was impossible for any to have seen us. We became the guards. Any conversation we had would be a mumble to those below and would be expected. Haaken whispered, "There are many fires."

"Aye." I nodded to the nearest. It was almost eighty paces from us. There were four men asleep. "We take those four first. We will stand when the fires are dampened a little and don the Frisian cloaks."

"Frisian?"

I nodded, "I recognised one of their words. It is the same as fret. We share some words with them and none with the Franks." I turned to untie the cloak from the dead Frisian whose body lay behind me and a little way down the bank. When I tugged it free I put it, loosely, around my shoulders. As I did so I saw his purse. After donning the cloak I took out the coins. It was hard to see but I could feel that there was a face on them. That made them Frankish. Their Kings liked to do that. When this was over the Neustrians would pay for this raid.

"Ready, Haaken?"

"Aye. The guards would be ready for a stretch."

We stood and began to walk slowly to the four sleeping men. I silently drew my sword and held it at my side. I looked at the camp and saw no one nearby who was awake. I could still hear the noise of brush and branches being laid upon water. They were busy building a causeway. I sank my sword through the neck of one of the sleeping men. His death noise was a hiss. My left hand went to my dragon. The man had no sword in his hand. His spirit would wander. I moved to the next man. Haaken's victim gave a soft sigh and the man I stood over opened his eyes. He saw me. He was fast. His hand went to his sword as he opened his mouth to scream. I rammed the sword through his open mouth, pinning his body to the ground. He died but his spirit went to Valhalla. He held his sword. Haaken disposed of the last man and we headed towards the next fire.

It was at that moment that we heard the howl of the wolf. I looked at Haaken and we both howled too. The sound of wolves howling spread through the camp. When I heard the drum of hooves I knew that Snorri and Beorn had succeeded. The Danes, Frisians and the Franks jumped to their feet at the disturbance. It actually helped us for we did not look any different to those we saw. Haaken and I ran through the camp. I drew my seax as we ran. Those we met were looking east to the sound of the horses. The first four men we met died without knowing we were there. We ghosted through the camp slicing and stabbing with our weapons. Men died screaming and shouting. Friend looked at friend and wondered if it was a foe. There were Frisians and Franks and they spoke different languages. It made for confusion and chaos.

We worked our way towards the river, at the southern end of the camp. There were just two fires between us and the river when we were spotted. There must have been a chief amongst them for he spied us and pointed his sword at us. The seven men ran purposefully with drawn weapons. I headed towards the chief; he was leading the others. He held a Frisian axe in his hand and he wore mail. Haaken would watch my right. The chief ran too and he swung his long axe at me. I swept Ragnar's Spirit backhanded. That was the problem with an axe. It was a powerful weapon but once it began to swing it had a life of its own. My sword caught the haft and deflected it. The head dropped harmlessly to my right and I rammed my seax through his mail into his ribs. I tore it out sideways.

As his body tumbled away, I ducked as a spear was thrust at my head. It caught the top of my helmet but Bjorn had made it well. I punched the spearman in the face with the hilt of my sword and as his head fell back ripped across his throat with my seax. Two men attacked Haaken. I swung Ragnar's Spirit sideways and cut one warrior through to his spine. I dragged my blade out and felt it grate along the bone. I felt a blow to my shoulder. I whipped my left hand around blindly. As I turned, I saw a warrior with a sword reeling back with a look of disbelief on his face. He had expected to kill me with the blow. Beneath my wolf cloak and over my mail I had plates along my shoulder. I thrust forward with my sword, "You should have gone for the neck!" I pulled my sword from his chest as he slumped at my feet.

"Come, Jarl. We must run!"

I saw warriors racing back from the causeway. We hurried to the bank and slide down into the river. We scrambled to the top and rolled down the other side. I crept back to peer through the bushes. They were searching the other bank for us. We crept down the slope and headed back to the camp. If they were searching for ghosts, they could not build the causeway and we had bought some time.

Chapter 6

We had not escaped unscathed. Erik Eriksson had a gashed leg. Rollo Thin Hair now had a new scar along his face but we all lived. Snorri and Beorn arrived back just after dawn. Behind them rode Ketil and his men. Snorri said, "We drove the horses to the stronghold in Windar's Mere rather than Cyninges-tūn. It was closer. We met Ketil."

Ketil dismounted and clasped my arm, "We came as soon as we got word."

"How many men did you bring?"

"Half of my warband. I have thirty." He looked at me apologetically, "The peace holds but I worry about my people."

"I know. Thirty will be enough. Rest." I shouted, "I hold a council of war at noon! Raibeart, send out scouts to spy the enemy dispositions."

Haaken came over. "Here Jarl, let me look at your armour. That was a mighty blow you took."

We took off my wolf cloak and helmet. I turned my head and saw that the metal plate which Bjorn had fitted over my mail was dented and cracked.

"I think I will need a new one when we return to Cyninges-tūn but it served its purpose and saved my life."

"There is little point in taking it off. If we tried to repair it then it would break."

"When we fight later I will have my shield and we will be in a shield wall. My back should be safe."

"You have decided our course of action then?"

"They will be shaken. The Franks have few horses left and they will have to fight on foot. We have fresh warriors who have yet to fight. We will use Raibeart and Ketil's men as our hammer. If we can weaken them enough then Wolf Killer can bring his men from the flanks."

"How will he cross his own swamp?"

"I have no doubt that there is a path there. Wolf Killer is no fool. It will be hidden from his enemies but he and his men will know the route they should take."

"Are you gambling, Jarl?"

"You gamble each time you don your mail and raise your sword. This is calculated. We fight hired swords. They may owe allegiance to their own Hersir and Gesith but they are not one people. We are. Have you noticed that the Danes have kept from the fighting? Last night we found mainly Franks and Frisians. We use that to our advantage."

I lay down to rest. I would not sleep but my body just needed to be at one with the earth and so I lay down on the soil of the Land of the Wolf. I held my dragon in my hand. We had found it beneath the earth and there was a connection to the land and to my ancestors. The Warlord of Rheged had touched this and now I did. *Wyrd.* The earth and the dragon soothed me.

When I felt at peace I rose and rinsed my face. I took out the whetstone and sharpened my sword and seax again. Today they would be called upon. This time I would be facing mailed warriors who had skills. This would not be a night attack using surprise. They would see us coming and they would be prepared. I found my shield and checked the straps. It had not suffered much in the fighting of two nights since. The leather covering was damaged in a couple of places but the metal studs and the boss still held firmly. I placed my dagger in the sheath I had on the inside. Finally, I took my new Frankish sword and sharpened it. That would be the weapon I would begin the fight with. It was longer than Ragnar's Spirit. I could have used a spear but I preferred a sword. Its longer reach would give me an initial advantage.

My jarls and hersir gathered around me. "My plan is to make a boar's snout. Ketil and Raibeart your mailed men will be the point. Asbjorn and his men will be behind Ketil's and my Ulfheonar will be behind Raibeart. Cnut Cnutson your men will be behind Asbjorn and the Ulfheonar. Arne, I want your men in two warbands on the flanks. You will use your bows and slings. If you are threatened then retire behind the wedge. Your ten shield wall warriors are the reserve, they fill the gaps. We attack the Frisians. I wish discord amongst our foes. The Franks and the Frisians have done most of the fighting. We slew Franks and Frisians in the night. We have driven off the Frankish horse. I want them to see the Danes untouched."

"Is that not a danger, Jarl? The Danes are fierce fighters."

Olaf Leather Neck snorted, "No Arne Thorirson, they are not. Since they took over Eoforwic they have become lazy bandits! The Jarl is right. The leader of this band is a Frisian. He is the paymaster. If he is threatened then the Danes may decide to flee rather than fight."

"Erik Eriksson, you cannot stand in a shield wall. I want you mounted and watching for Ulf Olafsson and our reinforcements. When they come I want them to spread out to make a long line and for them to make noise. Leif the Banner will fight alongside me this day. You will keep my banner and you will unfurl it when the reinforcements arrive."

Asbjorn asked, "Will he get here today? He has far to travel."

Olaf laughed, "If he has to carry his men on his back my old friend will get here. He knows the Jarl needs him and he is Ulfheonar still."

"We attack before dusk. We will not fight in the dark but I want them to think that we do as we did last night and attack them in the night. It will be late afternoon when we advance."

We used the river to allow us to approach unseen. We rose as a mighty mailed line from the river and I saw the consternation in their camp. The Danes were still close to the walls of Elfridaby building the causeway. They had men with shields protecting those building. As soon as we rose from the river they ran back to their main camp. The ones who were closest to us fled towards the standards and the banners which marked Ragnar Ruriksson and the other leaders. We had not seen them before for it had been dark. I saw that the largest was a skull on a red background. The one with the rearing red horse on a yellow background had to be the Franks.

Their flight allowed us to quickly organise into our wedges. We were six rows from the front. My Ulfheonar formed the rear rank of one half of the right-hand wedge. Behind us were Cnut Cnutson and the men of Cyninges-tūn. Raibeart and his men would have to bear the brunt of the initial fighting but if our foes thought they were our best they were in for a shock.

The enemy formed one large line three men deep. It would overlap ours. Or it would were it not for the river to our right and the swamp to our left. They had the Frisians in the centre. The Franks faced us and the Danes, the largest contingent by a long way were closest to the walls of Elfridaby.

Olaf Leather Neck began banging his shield with his axe shaft. He chanted, "Dragonheart!" The rest of the wedge took it up.

I shouted, "March!"

The chanting and the banging were not just to frighten our enemy. It was to help us to walk in a wedge. It was like the rhythms of the oars. It was almost hypnotic. The enemy were three hundred paces from us. They waited. They were not one clan. They had no chant. They were bought men and they jeered and hurled insults. It was a waste of breath for we heard them not and we marched steadily across the deserted camps.

Ketil would have the most difficult of tasks. He would be facing the Frisians. That was planned for Raibeart had less experience. The Franks were the weaker of the two bands. When we were ten paces from them I shouted, "Charge!" As we did so Arne's men loosed their arrows. We had held our secret weapon until the last moment. We caught many by surprise. The men of Windar's Mere might not be shield wall warriors but they could release three flights of arrows in the time it took to raise a shield. Many of the enemy failed to raise a shield and they died. Those

61

that did so were not looking to us and Raibeart and Ketil struck a line which was distracted.

As the first swords clashed and clanged, sliced and stabbed at the enemy I heard a horn from my left. I did not need to turn around to see what it meant. I knew. It was my son leading his three warbands to attack the Danes in the flank. As I had thought there was a hidden path through the boggy ground. I was on the right of our line for it was the place of honour. As Raibeart drove through the dispirited and dismounted Franks so we closed with their flanks as they tried to overlap us. Arne's archers raced behind us to avoid being caught. The hiatus allowed the Franks to close with us. It was a brief respite for the archers soon rained death again. Franks are confident when they charge into battle on their horses. They had forgotten how to fight on foot. Their long spears were harder to use on foot.

I swung my long Frankish sword sideways. It tore through one warrior's side for he had raised his shield to protect himself. The swing took the long blade across the shield of the second warrior. It was a powerful strike and as the man reeled so Haaken One Eye ended his life. Stepping forward I stabbed a surprised Frank in the face. As he fell back I saw that there was no one behind him. We had managed, somehow to outflank the enemy. The archers had cleared the flanks and the enemy were packing closer together in the middle. It was restricting the ability of those in the front rank to swing.

"Ulfheonar! Now is our time! "

Haaken and I led the charge. We were attacking Franks who were already unhappy. As the archers rained death on the rear ranks we hacked and slashed our way through them. One warrior, braver than the rest, tried to face me. He looked in disbelief as I brought the long Frankish sword overhead. I smashed into his shield which shattered. Pulling my arm back I stabbed forward for his middle was now unprotected. As the sword entered him he grabbed hold of it and, dying, tore it from my grip. I took out Ragnar's Spirit and raising it yelled, "Ragnar's Spirit! The sword touched by the gods!"

I heard the men of Cyninges-tūn roar as they pressed behind us. It was like a mighty wave pushing a drekar along. It had a life of its own. We found ourselves swept towards and through the Franks. It proved too much and they fled. Those who had survived the arrows and our blades now ran and we turned to face the Frisians. Ketil was beleaguered. I saw his banner as the battle swayed back and forth.

It was then that Olaf Leather Neck went berserk. It was not the madness which made him charge into the midst of the enemy it was the joy of battle. He dropped his shield and, wielding his axe two handed, he ran into the heart of the Frisians. Rolf Horse Killer had an axe which had once belonged to Olaf and he hurled himself after his friend. The two axes carved a passage through the already shaken Frisians. The Ulfheonar do not let their comrades die easily and we poured through the gap they had created. I used my shield as a weapon as I stabbed and chopped with my sword. It had a freshly sharpened blade and tore through both mail and leather. The men we fought were already reeling from the shower of arrows and the relentless pressure of our wedge. They had the panicked look of animals who are cornered and as such were dangerous.

A Frisian axe came towards me. I blocked it on my shield and stepped forward to stab at the Frisian. He countered with his shield and I brought my head forward to butt him in the face. His round helmet offered no protection to his face and his head jerked back. I punched again with my shield and he fell beneath my feet. I stabbed downwards and pinned him to the ground. Olaf and Rolf were carving a path towards the skull banner. I heard a wail from those ahead. I risked a glance behind and I saw Erik Eriksson with my banner. The reinforcements had arrived. Ulf Olafsson and the last of the men of Cyninges-tūn had reached the battle. It proved to be the final straw. The skull banner and the horse banner began to move east. Ragnar Ruriksson had gambled and he had failed. He was extricating himself from his men. They were hired, men. I saw warriors protecting him as they fled. They had red and white skulls painted on their shields. I had not seen them fight yet and knew they must have been a reserve. My enemy was saving himself with this reserve.

Ending a battle sometimes takes as long as winning a whole battle. There were dead and dying leaders whose oathsworn fought to retrieve their bodies. There were others fighting for honour. Their deaths bought the time for Ragnar Ruriksson to flee. By the time the killing had stopped the survivors had escaped. We were exhausted and many of our men lay dead yet the whole army of the Land of the Wolf began to chant, "Dragonheart!" over and over. We had won. The threat was gone, at least for a while.

There were many men who were badly wounded on both sides. Aiden himself would not have been able to save them. Those of our men whom we could save we took within Elfridaby's walls where the women of the town cared for them. Aiden arrived with Erik Eriksson. He had come with the handful of reinforcements which had been mustered. Snorri had sent a rider to fetch him and it was good that he had. Aiden saved lives. His hands saved far more than died of their wounds.

There were prisoners. Ten Franks, two Frisians and eight Danes were captured. Some had taken head wounds and recovered. Others had had wounds which prevented their escape and six of the Franks surrendered. Blood was running hot and Olaf Leather Neck wanted me to execute them as did Wolf Killer who was still smarting from the loss of his men at Seddes' Burgh.

"We have never had the luxury of prisoners before. The Weird Sisters have sent them here for a reason. I will decide their fate and I will not do so now. The blood of battle still courses through our veins. Let us clear the field and find Ragnar. Snorri, mount twenty men who can ride. Find where Ragnar Ruriksson has gone."

"You want me to slay him?"

I smiled, "I doubt he will be alone. I saw mailed warriors with skulls on their shields. They had not fought and looked to be his protectors. The men you take will not wear armour. When I have put my land in order, I will seek him out and pay him back for this raid. I do not want him loose in my land."

"Aye Jarl."

As he left Wolf Killer said, "I thought it was over."

Shaking my head, I said, "We defeated him through a trick. The handful of men Erik Eriksson led were not enough to win the battle. Had he stayed and rallied his men then the battle would have gone the other way." I waved a hand at the dead. "This is not the army we routed. He has enough to cause damage but the Danes and the Franks will be reluctant to follow this Frisian." I smiled, "That is why I need the prisoners. All that we know of this Ragnar Ruriksson is that he is the son of Rurik of Dorestad. We need to know more."

Wolf Killer saw the wisdom of my words, "You are right, Jarl. Forgive me."

"There is nothing to forgive. Our sons?"

He smiled, "They did well. They both used those new bows you gave them. Gruffyd and Ragnar slew Danes." He pointed to the walls. "And Garth stood with them. He held his new seax and was eager to slay any who came over the walls. He is a wolf cub and has a courage beyond his years."

"Good. They are now blooded. Their mothers will be less than happy for when a boy begins to become a warrior they are lost to their mothers."

I sent back Ketil, Sigtrygg, Ulf Olafsson, Arne, the men of Dyflin and the men of Cyninges-tūn. Ulf, in particular, was reluctant to return home having done so little but it was necessary. Wolf Killer's home could neither feed nor house such a host and their own homes needed protection. I kept just the Ulfheonar and Raibeart's men. Half of Raibeart's men had gone with Snorri. We made pyres of the dead and burned them before we retired behind Elfridaby's walls. I felt as though I had not slept for a week and we had had so little food that I feared turning into a wraith. Yet I needed Aiden's counsel.

We sat in my son's hall and ate a hearty stew of butchered horses taken from the battlefield. We found plundered ale in the Frisian camp and we drank well. My son and grandsons were allowed to sit with the Ulfheonar, Raibeart, Aiden and Wolf Killer. They had earned the right. They said, however, nothing but took in all of our words.

"This man is still a threat." Wolf Killer wiped the foam from his mouth. "He showed skill to attack where he did and achieving such surprise. A large army is hard to hide."

"He is for he still has many men at his command. He can raise another army if he has coin enough." Aiden had said little. I saw him frowning. "Speak galdramenn. Your thoughts and advice are never wasted."

He nodded, "This is no magic, Jarl, but I have been distanced from the danger and had time to think. All of you around this table have been reacting to the danger and fighting for your lives; even the youngest here." I saw my son and grandsons sit up a little straighter at the praise. "It is a forest and you are within. You see the trees but not the whole forest. I have been peering at this problem. Has Neustria so much coin that they can afford to fund such a large army? If they do then perhaps we ought to relieve them of it."

Haaken nodded, "Then they would be less likely to do so again."

My Ulfheonar nodded. Prevention was always better than a cure.

"And those Danes. They are a bigger threat now than they once were. King Eanred allied with us very easily. I would speak with his son as soon as I can for I wonder if it was the threat of the Danes which made him jump into bed with us. It used to be Northumbria and Mercia who threatened us. Thanks to your diplomacy and victories, Jarl Dragonheart, those threats are no longer there but the Danes? They grow like a pustule on your back. You know it is there but you can do nothing about it. It grows and it grows. They are now our nearest neighbours. Ragnar Ruriksson proved that by getting here so quickly." He looked at Wolf Killer. The road from Eoforwic ends here. This will ever be in danger."

We all looked at Wolf Killer. "I will not run."

Quietly I said, "We neither ask nor expect you to. The question is how can we prevent a repetition of this?"

It was Erik Eriksson who came up with the suggestion. "Seddes' Burgh could be defended. It seems to me that it was only taken by surprise when Ragnar Ruriksson attacked. Your men had not been there long."

"It needs a Jarl there. It needs a strong leader. I have not been there but from what I have heard it is a rich land and yet exposed for there is nothing to the east but the land of the Danes."

Aiden's words rang true. "Sigtrygg is close by and could help but he would be loath to leave the land of his father." I looked down the table at the ever-dwindling numbers of Ulfheonar.

It was Haaken who spoke for them all. "None of us wish that honour, Jarl. You saw how reluctant Ulf Olafsson was to leave here and returned to his stad. We have spoken of this. We are your oathsworn. There are others like Ketil and Raibeart and Arne who can be made jarls. We need to look amongst them."

Aiden said, "Karl One Leg? He does a fine job at Cyninges-tūn."

Once again Haaken poured cold water on that idea. "Karl is one of us. He guards the stad because we have our home there. Seddes' Burgh is new land. He would not go."

He was right. "Someone like Jarl Gunnar Thorfinnson would have been ideal."

"No Jarl. The Norns have other plans for him. Whoever the Norns have in mind for Seddes' Burgh is hidden from us. We have to fortify the burgh and hope that it is not attacked until we have found a Jarl who can rule for you. There are few, outside this hall, who could be trusted with such a task."

I nodded, "Aiden is right. We have no answers, Wolf Killer, but perhaps we have hope. Winter races towards us and we know that, soon, the high passes will guard you and your people. It is when the feast of Eostre approaches that there will be danger. On the morrow, we will question the prisoners. Their answers may well guide our plans."

Long after the others had retired I sat in the hall with Aiden. "There were things you did not say, Aiden. Speak now."

He smiled, "As you get older Jarl so your mind becomes sharper. Kara and I have dreamed. The danger to you lies in the Danes. There you are right. Our hope lies in strong walls and well-armed warriors to defend them."

I frowned, "We do not build such walls."

"Then perhaps we should. I have read as well as dreamt. The Romans and the ancient ones held on to this land long after the Emperor summoned the legions home. King Coel held back the Saxon hordes longer here than anywhere. In fact, they held it for a short time. You drove them hence."

"So? I do not see what you mean. It sounds like this land is meant to be ours."

"It is but we must be as the Romans and build stronger walls."

"Do you have the skills to do that?"

He shook his head. "I could try but it would not be what we needed. We need to find someone who can build."

"A mason? Do any exist now?"

"Aye, Jarl, and we have seen their work. Miklagård." It always came back to Miklagård. The Norns had woven our threads with that Eastern Empire. I nodded. Aiden said, "But it would cost us. We would need to hire a mason and then find the stone."

I waved a hand towards the north. "We have stone a-plenty."

"But if we have slaves and your men building then they will not be able to raid. We need gold and silver. We invest in walls and ensure the safety of your son and his people."

I stared into the dancing flames of the fire and reflected on his words. I could see the threads which attached me to the past and those who were my ancestors. They had built of stone. Was that my purpose? Was I the thread which tied the Norse to the Old Ones? The witch on Syllingar had said that I would be forgotten but Hrolf son of Gerloc would sire a dynasty which would change the world. Was I here to keep this land safe?

I saw Aiden watching me. "Do we have enough coin?"

He shook his head, "We are rich but not that rich. Your men would need to find a vast Viking treasure. We have enough to hire a mason."

"And you have a plan for that."

He nodded, "You will not like what I am going to say but Kara and I have spoken of this. We would travel with Ylva to Miklagård."

I said nothing but I bit my lip to stop myself shouting down my galdramenn. I respected him too much to dismiss his ideas so easily but I knew that such a voyage would be fraught with danger. The three of them were as dear to me as Brigid and Gruffyd. I looked him in the eyes and tried to see inside his head.

He smiled, "Thank you for your patience, Jarl. I can see from your face what it is costing you. Kara and I have both dreamed of this city. Ylva will learn much from it and she has gifts that we can only dream about."

"But they follow the White Christ and not the old ways."

"They do but they have books there. Ylva can read as can Kara. We can learn more about the old world; the world before the White Christ. In ancient times they worshipped the old gods and their writings will help us. I know you fear the dangers but this is *wyrd*. You know that."

I nodded, "You have both thought this through. How would you get there?"

"Erik Short Toe and the *'Weregeld'*. He has spoken to me often about visiting Josephus' family."

"He wishes this too?"

"He does. It was he who planted the seed in our heads. Last winter he asked for my advice. He wondered if you would allow him to trade in Miklagård. If we sail now then we can be back before the new grass grows. He is a good captain and he knows the waters. We have all of Josephus' charts."

"I am not happy about this but I owe all three of you too much to refuse. You have my permission."

Chapter 7

The next morning, we began to question the prisoners. Some of them held their tongues preferring death to the dishonour of revealing what they knew. I admired that. Those that did so would become thralls. They would slave in our mines. The ten that refused to speak were fitted with a thrall's yoke. After a year of servitude, their yoke would be removed but if they attempted to escape then they would be hamstrung. We had many slaves who worked for us and none were hamstrung for we treated them well. Some were even given their freedom. The life of a miner appealed to some warriors.

The ones who spoke helped Aiden to build up a picture of our enemies. Neustria was, indeed, rich. Their land was fertile and, generally, had peace. It was our coming which had disturbed that peace and hence their hatred of us. The taxes were gathered in the spring of each year and delivered to Paris for midsummer day. That information came from four men. Each one knew a part and it was Aiden who pieced it together. The crucial information was that they used ships to transport it up the Issicauna. What we did not discover was when it would sail. That most vital knowledge was missing. We would not be able to attack the ships at sea for we knew not when they would sail.

We learned more of Ragnar Ruriksson and the Danes, however, for most of those who offered information were Franks who were unhappy about the loss of their horses and the way they were abandoned by their leader. They were happy to supply information about the Frisian and the Danes whom they called treacherous.

Thegn Rædwulf appeared to be the key to the Danes power. He was the thegn appointed by Eanred to collect the taxes from that city. A relative of Osbert and Aella he was also related to Coenred whom I had killed. It explained much. I had wondered how the Danes had so much power and freedom in the city. They protected Raedwald.

Rurik was a different story. He had learned his trade fighting for the Count of Neustria. He had a reputation as a vicious and cruel warrior. He had the backing of a band of warriors who appeared to be like my Ulfheonar. They must have been the skull warriors. He was one of the reasons for the success and riches of that land. It told us why he had been backed by the Mayor of Neustria and why he had so many Franks under his command. His Franks believed that he would have returned to Neustria. In return for their honesty, I granted them freedom. I gave them their horses and a short sword each. They were grateful for their lives and swore that they would return home and never again attack the Land of the Wolf. I believed them and after they left, I never saw them again.

Snorri and his weary warriors arrived the next day in the middle of the afternoon. They had horses laden with armour and weapons. The men walked in.

Taking off his helmet my scout said, "We found stragglers in the road and we hunted them down. Ragnar Ruriksson did not head towards Eoforwic as I thought he would. He took the road south. Once it became clear where they were headed we turned around for we saw Mercian horsemen. I did not wish to break the peace with King Coenwulf."

"You did right. The question remains where would Ragnar Ruriksson go? Mercia or Wessex?"

Snorri ventured, "Perhaps he will go to Lundenwic. That is where the road ends. There he could take ship back to Neustria."

"That may be but he is no threat to us for the moment and we have winter to gain more intelligence."

We headed back the next day. We had not achieved all that we needed but we could not create a jarl from nothing. Wolf Killer would have to build up his warband again. I promised to send who wished the chance to serve on the frontier. Aiden was not hopeful that we would find many. Raibeart travelled with us as far as the southern end of the Water.

"I would have you take *'Red Snake'* to the seas this winter."

"Not *'Weregeld'*?"

"No for Aiden will use my knarr. I would have you escort him as far as Syllingar. Then return north to visit with the Mercians. The peace should still hold. Find out what goes on in the nest of vipers that is Man. Speak with Jarl Gunnstein Berserk Killer. Go to Ljoðhús. Thorfinn Blue Scar still exerts much power there. Return by Yule."

He nodded, "Have I permission to raid?"

"Of course. Raid wisely. Choose those we do not wish as friends in the future."

"Aiden, when will you be ready to sail?"

"A few days only. I will ask Erik Short Toe to prepare the knarr."

"He will be your captain?"

"Aye, he will."

"Then you will and the knarr will be in the safest of hands!"

Brigid was relieved when her husband and son returned intact. She examined Gruffyd from head to toe. He did not enjoy the inspection. When she took him off to bathe him I visited Kara and Ylva. I did not doubt Aiden's words but I wished to be certain. It was a bold and dangerous move. The seas were dangerous.

My daughter and granddaughter seemed to know my thoughts. Kara hugged me and then Ylva sat on my lap and began to plait my beard. "I can see, father, that my husband has told you of our plans?"

"Aye and if you read me aright then you know I am unhappy."

"I can see why you would be but the spirits are happy for this and Ylva and I need to see this wondrous city. My brother, husband and father have all been there and I know it changed all of you. My husband gained knowledge and he has made that into power. We would do the same."

Ylva finished plaiting my beard and said, "I wish to see the world grandfather. Just because I am a girl does not mean I have to be afraid."

I hugged her, "You are old beyond your years my little she-wolf."

"I have had my first dream. I have spoken with my grandmother. She approves."

She spoke not as a child but as a young woman. It terrified me and I have to confess I was a little jealous that the three in this hall could all speak with Erika, my dead wife, and I could not. I was now resigned to them leaving but I would not let them leave without giving them sage advice. They could ignore it but I would feel better knowing that I had tried. "Miklagård will seduce you. I saw warriors who were enchanted by it and it took battles against the moors and Barbary pirates to break that spell. You will wish to linger longer. I pray you do not. The Land of the Wolf needs you. I need you."

Kara and Ylva hugged me. "Do not fear father, we will return and we will be empowered when we do so!"

Cyninges-tūn seemed empty when the three of them left. Brigid chastised me for scowling all the time. "You have a family here! How do you think it makes us feel if you mope around the hall all day? It is no wonder that Wolf Killer lives so far away."

She was right, as always. "I am sorry. I will stir myself."

I went with Gruffyd to visit Scanlan. We needed to ensure that we had enough supplies for the winter. If we did need money for building work then he would have to increase the ore that we mined. My former Saxon slave was now a grey beard and, like me, a grandfather.

"Fear not Jarl. The Gods have been kind this year. We have made good trades. The seal skin boots we make are much sought after and our weapons are now the equal of Saxon blades. Gold will continue to pour in."

"And people?"

"Aye, there are still settlers. They are not all Norse."

"I know but I trust your judgement. We need no spies."

"We watch all the newcomers."

"Good for my son needs his lands filling with warriors and families."

"There are some already who are ready to leave. The prime land is already taken. Few wish to farm the fells or Olaf's slopes."

"Good."

Now that Samhain was over the weather had begun to deteriorate. It began with day upon day of rain. The ground became a muddy morass and the halls were filled with the damp smell of drying clothes. When the rain stopped the winds began. We were lucky that we had turf walls and roofs for they withstood the winds better. My thoughts were far out to sea for I feared for my family. Was Ran watching out for them? Finally, as the winds subsided then the weather grew colder. It was a slow process but the muddy ground became harder and harder until you felt the ruts through your boots as you risked the icy air outside the warmth of the hall. Not long before Yule, we awoke to see the ground covered in a thin layer of white and the air filled with snow. Winter had arrived.

I took Gruffyd and, wrapping up against the cold, rode down to visit with Coen ap Pasgen at Úlfarrston. I was anxious for news from his brother. It was not only news of my family I sought but also news of the world around us. We were cut off from much of the world and news was often as valuable as gold.

We had just entered the forest south of the Water when, in the distance, we heard the distant howl of a wolf on the eastern fells. Gruffyd looked towards the east. "Will warriors hunt the wolf, father?"

"Some may but not until they have to. Men hunt the wolf because they wish to be Ulfheonar or because they are taking people. We are the brothers of the wolf. He serves a purpose as we all do. Men who hunt for the sake of hunting do not serve the Mother. The land has a balance and we must keep that balance. We only hunt the fox when they take too many chickens. We fish only that which we need. We take iron and stone but never all. We are the shepherds of the land and the waters."

He nodded and I saw him taking in the information. He was a thoughtful child. Wolf Killer had not had the luxury of a peaceful childhood. Kidnapped whilst barely a boy and then hunted by our enemies he had grown up far quicker. Gruffyd would have the chance, as I had, to learn about the land and how to be a warrior. I would be his Ragnar.

The forest gave us shelter from both the wind and the driving snow. It had not yet lain as deeply on the forest floor as it had in the open. The paths and trails could be ridden. Soon we would be cut off from Úlfarrston and only a determined man would be able to get through. It was another reason for my visit. I took the fact that I had had no news as good news but without the vision of both Aiden and Kara, I felt blind. I had not sensed danger and I had not dreamt. They were good signs but sometimes the Weird Sisters hid such thoughts from warriors. Was this one such occasion?

As soon as we left the shelter of the forest we felt both the wind and the sea. You could smell the sea in the air. If we were going to my drekar we would take the trail to the east but we were not. It would be raised from the water and protected from frosts. The ship's boys and the family of Erik Short Toe would watch over it, lighting fires if the weather became too cold and making sure that the winds did not cause damage. They were the guardians of our dragon.

The snow was not as deep the closer we came to the coast. We spied the fishing ship in the estuary. Coen ap Pasgen's people were braving the elements to gather food while they could. When the winter gales took hold then the small boats would not dare leave the shore. There was a heavy smell of wood smoke in the air. My blue hands spoke to me of the need for a warm fire and a roof. I knew that we would be given a warm welcome. In summer we could reach the port and be back home in one day. In winter we had to spend the night in Úlfarrston. It was not a hardship for they were hospitable and appreciated our protection.

Coen and his men kept a good watch. We were spied when we were half a mile from the gate. Raids and attacks had made sure that the ground was cleared for half a mile around the wooden walled town. The gates were opened and Coen waited to greet us.

"Jarl, you are braving the weather."

"Aye, my friend, I came for news of your brother."

He nodded and waved over two stable boys to take our horses. "I too expected him about now. He said he would return before Yule."

As we walked towards his hall I said, "I am not worried but the news he brings will be important."

"He told me. It seems you rid the world of one enemy only for two more to take their place."

"True. We were lucky, I know that. We should have been destroyed by the three warbands but the Allfather watches over us."

As soon as we stepped into his hall a wall of heat struck us. My fingers began to hurt as blood rushed back into frozen joints. A slave brought over a jug of ale and a second fetched a red-hot poker from the fire. The hiss of the metal into the foaming ale meant it would be hot and would be more than welcome. The journey had been hard for my son and soon he was curled up by the side of my chair, asleep. I spoke with Coen. Many ships called in and traded with this most ancient of people. They were given a warm welcome. The river could not accommodate large ships but knarr and other such vessels could easily navigate the estuary. As a result, they prospered and gathered a great deal of information.

"King Coenwulf has died."

My first thoughts were that it was not natural and then I remembered him the last time he had spoken with me, at the peace talks, he had looked grey then. "It was his time."

"Aye, it was. His brother, Ceolwulf, rules. It is said he plans to attack the Welsh for his father had already gathered an army for such a venture."

I breathed a sigh of relief. We had made peace with the Mercians but it had been with the king and not his brother. If his brother fought the Welsh then he would not attack us. It was another reason I had advised my captains not to raid them. There were other targets which would yield more and bring us less danger.

"Perhaps your brother will add to that news. And has Man caused any problems?"

The Vikings of Man were pirates and they preyed on the ships which plied the Hibernian sea. They were wise enough to desist from attacking our ships and those of our allies but sometimes a headstrong young captain would risk the wrath of the Dragonheart.

"We have lost no ships although we sail with other ships. My knarr are sailing now with Siggi to the northern isles. Siggi has much experience and can smell trouble."

Food was laid on the table. Coen's wife looked at my son as though to wake him. I shook my head, "He will wake when he is hungry. Let him rest."

Coen was curious about Kara and Aiden. "Your daughter has much courage. My brother said she would sail beyond the Pillars of Hercules into the Middle Sea. How can they do that?"

"She and her husband have powers we do not understand my friend but I do worry about her. The spirits watch over them. At least I hope that they do."

Despite my worries, I spent a quiet and leisurely evening with my old friend and I slept well. The next morning we woke to a sky which was blue and clear but the ground was frozen as hard as one of Bjorn's swords. There was a sheen of ice on the river. The fishing boats were already far out to sea taking advantage of the benign waters. They were still and flat. Wrapped against the cold Gruffyd and I watched all morning for the sight of a sail. We saw none. As we headed back to the palisade I said, "We will return home on the morrow. I cannot conjure Raibeart and my knarr. He will come when he will come."

"When the first grass grows will I begin my warrior training in earnest with the other boys?"

"Are you ready?"

"I am. I have practised pulling my new bow each day. Soon I will be able to send an arrow a hundred paces. Already I feel my muscles growing. I am taller, am I not?"

"Aye son, you are but there is more to being a warrior than size and weapons. You use your mind. But we shall address that over the next few months."

I spent a fretful night wondering where my captains was. We had saddled our horses and were preparing to leave when we heard a cry from the watchtower. Three sails from the west! One is a drekar!"

We had all learned to fear such sightings and I drew my sword. Gruffyd drew his seax.

"Warriors to the walls!"

We led our horses back inside the palisades. It was with some relief that we heard the cry, "It is Raibeart ap Pasgen and Siggi! Our ships have returned."

I handed our reins to a stable boy and hurried back outside. At last, we would have news! Even though it was cold we watched as the three ships tacked their way inshore. The two knarr landed first and I watched impatiently as Raibeart edged *'Red Snake'* close to shore. Coen ap Pasgen joined me; he was wrapped in a thick cloak made of the skins of squirrels. He smiled, "I am as pleased as you are Jarl. He is my little brother still."

Raibeart must have known how eager we were for news. He leapt into the shallows and hurried to us. "By the Allfather it is cold! I hope I can stay inside our halls for the rest of the winter. Ran has sowed ice in the sea!"

"Come, we will go in your brother's hall but tell me, are my family safe?"

"Aye Jarl. We had a good voyage to the land of Corn Walum. When last I saw them the knarr was flying. The journey north was less pleasant. King Coenwulf is dead."

"That we know."

"And the Mercians attack Gwynedd."

"That we did not know."

"I heard naught of Ragnar Ruriksson. Jarl Thorfinnson has had some trouble. Harald Black Teeth has stolen a drekar and left the islands with those warriors who disliked the rule of the Jarl. It is said they have joined with the warriors who fled Jarl Gunnar Thorfinnson. He now has two drekar. He told us to beware them for they have no honour."

"And that is it? There are no other dangers to our land?"

"Jarl Gunnstein Berserk Killer has a tight hold on the lands of Hibernia. None will dare raid this land from there. The men of Man fight amongst themselves."

"And King Egbert?"

"King Egbert has designs upon Northumbria and Mercia."

"Has he heard of the treaty I made with Eanred?"

"None of those with whom I spoke knew of that yet. I suspect it will come as a surprise. You have time, lord, to find a jarl for Seddes' Burgh and for us to make our land strong."

"You have done me a great service, Raibeart."

He laughed, "Lord, you let me do that which I most love." He shivered as a cold wind came from the north. "But I hope that I do not need to do so again until the new grass grows."

"I hope so too. And the rest of the world?"

"Jarl Gunnar Thorfinnson had been in Dyflin. He had raided in Austrasia. They captured a great deal of treasure there from the monastery at Jumièges. He is doing well. His younger brother sails with him."

"Good. I am happy for him. I wonder how their father fares without them."

"However there is also bad news from Jarl Gunnar Thorfinnson. Some of his men murdered one of his crew and slaughtered some fishermen. A price is now upon their heads."

"Who led these outlaws?"

"A man called Hermund the Bent."

"Then we will watch out for him. Thank you once more."

I was quiet as we headed north. I was pleased with Gunnar. I was happy for his success. He was a good jarl. I had been lucky that he had chosen to serve with me. It was easier said than done to find a good jarl. Leaders like Sigtrygg, Ketil and Ulf were rare. We lived in an unforgiving land. A leader had to fight the elements as well as his enemies. Once again I missed Aiden and his advice. We saw the Water to our right as we emerged from the forest. There was a sheen of ice upon it. It would be a hard winter. The Water had frozen over before now but it was a rare event. We paused to let our horses rest and for them to drink some of the icy water from the stream which bubbled into the Water.

"You are quiet, father. Did Raibeart say something to disturb you?"

I shook my head, "No it is just that I will need a jarl for Seddes' Burgh and it is a hard decision. The men from Cyninges-tūn would not wish to make a new home there. Their roots are here."

He nodded as he pondered my words. Eventually, he said, "My brother, Wolf Killer, should make that choice. After all, he will be the closest neighbour of this new jarl."

My son was young but his innocent eyes had seen what I could not. My son would make the jarl. It was the sort of decision he would make himself when he ruled in my stead. "Thank you, my son. Your young eyes have seen what my old ones could not."

My son and his wife sometimes came over to visit with us at Yule. This year, however, Elfrida was with child and so I took my family across the frozen land. Erika was old enough now to travel. She was a quiet child and she clung to her mother. I thought it would be good for her to visit with her cousins. Garth was her age and a little roughness would not go amiss. Ylva and she were both gentle creatures. The Yule would be a chance for her to harden up. This was not a land for delicate flowers. The wild primroses which grew on the banks by the sea were as hard as Old Olaf's mountain. The girls would need to be as hard.

Elfrida was delighted to be hostess. Wolf Killer's men had laboured to build a dividing wall in his hall so that we had privacy for the four of us. She was also sensitive to Brigid's religion. She had made a small alcove where my wife could pray. Yule was a festival for us all. The main difference would be that my wife and daughter would mumble a prayer and kiss a cross before they ate. We would remain silent while they performed the ritual. I smiled as I saw Garth look puzzled as they did so. He was about to say something and I saw Ragnar lean over and whisper in his ear. The puzzled look was replaced by one of disappointment.

The feast was a fine one. Elfrida had been keen to repay my wife for her hospitality. Brigid had brought gifts for them all. It was something her Christian family had done in Wales. It was a ritual to do with a legend of men bearing gifts to the White Christ on the day of his birth. While they did do I sat with Wolf Killer.

"I think that you should choose the jarl who will rule at Seddes Burgh." He looked surprised. "This eastern part of the land is yours. I give it all to you. When first you came here it was to protect Cyninges-tūn from the east. You have done so. This land is yours. You should choose a jarl to protect the east for you now."

"You give me a great gift on this day of gifts. Thank you. Most fathers send their sons far away to make themselves safer."

He was thinking of Thorfinn Blue Scar. He was right. Many ageing jarls had been overthrown by sons who wanted their lands. I suppose my background made me different. "If I cannot trust you, my son, then I might as well go to the cave of Myrddyn, lie down and await death. If you wish to colonise the land east of you then do so. I give you the land east of Grize's Dale."

He nodded, "I have a warrior in mind. He is the younger brother of Erik who died at Seddes' Burgh. He would have been with him but I was loath to lose two of my oathsworn and kept one with me. I see now that was a mistake. Einar Thordson shall be jarl. He has been both angry and sad at the same time since his brother died. This will give him the chance to channel that anger into something positive. The walls and ditches have been repaired. We shall select a garrison soon."

I wondered at the wisdom of placing an angry young man there but I had given the responsibility to my son and I would have to trust his judgement. "Aiden will be fetching a mason from Miklagård. When we have more gold we will begin to build in stone. We start with Cyninges-tūn and Elfridaby."

"Where will you get the gold?"

"If Neustria has so much that it can afford to hire the likes of Ragnar Ruriksson then we shall go there and find it! I intend to take my ships after the feast of Eostre. You are more than welcome to come and enjoy the raid." I smiled, "But you rule your own lands now. You make your own choices."

He laughed, "I am still oathsworn. I was Ulfheonar once. But I will see how my land lies before I desert it once more. Besides the *'Wild Boar'* needs work. I will be using what little gold I have to pay Bolli to make her seaworthy again."

I knew my son had neglected his drekar. I had mine cleaned and maintained each winter. Bolli and his shipwrights would, even now, be making her as good as new for the next year's raid. In my view, it was coin well spent. We headed home after the days began to grow longer and we knew that the new year was beginning. The weather relented a little and the air was not as cold as we rode back. It had been good for Erika to play roughly with her brother and her cousins. There had been tears and even a bloody nose but that was like life. It did not always run smoothly.

Once back in my home at Cyninges-tūn, we awaited the arrival of Kara and Aiden. He had said they would spend Yule in Miklagård. They would be leaving for home sometime soon. I knew that I would not be able to settle until they were heading back up the Water.

Chapter 8

A month after Yule had passed and there was still no sign of my family. I went with Haaken and Gruffyd down to the shipyard on the river to see how Bolli was coming along with my ship. It was an excuse to be close to the sea in case news came. It was foolish but now that I was getting older my family was becoming increasingly important. Gruffyd did not mind my distraction. He pestered me to show him how to become a warrior and I had practised for a month with swords and bows. His strength grew daily and he had leapt up a hand span since Samhain. He had a new, bigger horse and he was keen to ride him. A trip to the south was an adventure! As for Haaken, he had had three months with Anya, his wife and his three girls. That was always too much for my oldest friend. He was desperate for the company of men.

I had told him of my decision regarding Wolf Killer. "I think that is wise. Your son is a good leader. A real Viking would not have done so. He would fear that his son would wish his title and his lands!"

"He can have both! So long as he does the job I do then my son can rule the land of the Wolf."

Gruffyd asked, "And what of me? Could I have it?"

"Ah, so you were listening eh? Then if you were listening you would know that I said if he can do the job I do. Could you fight in a shield wall and lead the Ulfheonar?"

"Not yet."

"Then when you can come back to me and ask me the same question."

"But by then you may have given the land to Wolf Killer!"

"True." I turned and looked at him, "Then what would you do?"

"I love this land." He pointed up at Old Olaf. "I love the mountain and the Water."

"Then you would have to stay here and serve your brother." He was silent. Gruffyd was a deep one and often sat pensively.

We entered the forest. In winter it felt like one of the dark churches of the White Christ. In many ways, it was our church and I always felt close to the spirits of the land as we passed through it.

Gruffyd broke the silence, "But if he did not want the Land of the Wolf and if I was strong enough to lead the warriors would you let me be Jarl?"

I looked him in the eyes. He was young but growing rapidly. He was not like me. I had had no ambition to be Jarl of the land of the Wolf. It had just happened. I could see now that Gruffyd was ambitious. "If you are ready then I would let you rule this land. But before you begin to think of that you must begin to understand the responsibilities."

"Responsibilities?"

Haaken laughed, "Aye, Gruffyd son of the Wolf! I have no desire to be Jarl of the land of the Wolf and to rule. Your father is responsible for all the people in this valley and the valleys beyond. If there is a danger it is he who must deal with it. If there is famine he must provide. If the wolves howl and take the young it is he who must solve the problem. I can just hide up in my farm and watch out for my own family. The jarl of this land has to watch out for everyone. Be careful what you wish for; it may come true."

He said no more and he thought on Haaken's words.

Even though it was cold enough to make our words freeze in the air I heard banging from the river. Bolli and his men had my drekar out of the water and were replacing the gunwale on the steering board side of the ship. It was the part of the drekar which suffered the most damage. When my men clambered from the ship they sometimes had to rush and their mail would gouge lines in it. We had to replace it every couple of years.

Despite the cold Bolli was sweating. He stopped working to approach me. "An unexpected visit, Jarl."

"This year we shall have every drekar at sea. I came to make sure that the work was progressing. My son will be asking for much work on his drekar."

"Aye, I know. It is not seaworthy at the moment. I would not sail her to Man and back."

I heard the criticism in his voice. I had to defend my son. "He lives far from the sea now, Bolli and he has been beset by enemies."

"I know, Jarl Dragonheart, and I meant not to be critical but you asked if the ships were seaworthy; that one is not."

"When will all of my drekar, my son's excluded, be ready for sea?"

"*'Red Snake'* has sailed the most and she will not be ready for a month or two. After Eostre then you can have your fleet."

It was later than I would have wished but I could do nothing about that. Bolli was right. I had had Raibeart sailing when his ship should have been in the yard. It was my fault. We spent the rest of the day examining the ship. I did not need to but it gave me an excuse to spend time in Úlfarrston. I could wait a couple of days for Aiden and Kara.

I think Coen and Raibeart understood my concerns for they encouraged me to stay. It proved to be fruitful. Raibeart was one of my younger jarls and he entertained Gruffyd and helped him to practise with his sword. *'Weregeld'* appeared two days after our arrival. The wind was from the north and we saw Erik Short Toe as he tacked back and forth towards us. It took some time and did nothing to diminish my anxiety. When my family stepped ashore I swept Ylva up into my arms. "Thank the Allfather you have returned safely."

Kara shook her head, "I told you, father, the spirits watched out for us."

Aiden turned, "And we have a mason and his family."

I looked in surprise at the Greek, his wife and three small children as they stepped from the knarr, "How did you manage to persuade him to come here from the warmth of the east."

Kara said, quietly, "He and his family were slaves. We bought them. It was not cheap but my husband felt it was money well spent. We have freed them."

"*Wyrd.*"

"Aye but I fear this cold will take some getting used to." The family huddled together, shivering in the cold air. She held her hand out and spoke very slowly, "Basil, Sophia, this is Jarl Dragonheart. He rules this land."

I saw the three children hide behind their father. They were terrified. I saw fear in the woman's eyes too. It was my appearance and that of Haaken. We were both grizzled warriors and Haaken's one eye did not help. I smiled and said, "Welcome. Tell your children we mean them no harm."

Basil looked puzzled and Kara said, "We have yet to teach them all of our words. It will take some time. They can live with me in my hall until the warmer weather comes."

Aiden said, "I fear we have little gold left for all the work we wished. They were not cheap."

"It matters not. I have heard that Jarl Gunnar Thorfinnson found a great treasure in Austrasia. Perhaps we will have as much success in Neustria. Come let us get home. Brigid will worry."

All the way north Ylva chattered like a magpie about all that she had seen. She was full of the wonders, the buildings, the books and the walls. Gruffyd pestered about the warriors and their arms. I smiled when Ylva could not answer his questions. She had not even noticed them. For her, it was about the great city. Gruffyd was just concerned with being a warrior.

The land and the weather, like my mood, began to improve with the return of Kara and Aiden. Once the ground became less frozen Basil set to work building his own home, close to Aiden's using stone. We had plenty already quarried and we had the newly acquired slaves who were put to work. He was not a quick worker but he was meticulous and I saw that Aiden had done well. He would build solidly but we would have to be patient. I realised that we had no gold yet and so, perhaps, this was the work of the Weird Sisters. The gold would buy the stone we could neither quarry nor steal. Our knarr would have to sail to distant lands to buy suitable materials.

We were at the shipyard preparing to go to sea when a rider came from Úlfarrston. "Lord Coen says a drekar is approaching."

I had my Ulfheonar with me and we mounted our horses. This was not one of our drekar! When we reached the port the gates were closed and Coen had his walls manned. I did not recognise the drekar but it was small. It was a threttanessa and it was not fully manned. Olaf Leather Neck sounded disappointed as he said, "They come not to fight or else if they do then they have the wish for death in their heads."

The drekar took some time to reach the wooden quay. A younger version of Jarl Gunnar Thorfinnson leapt ashore. "I am Gunnstein Thorfinnson!"

I smiled, "Welcome. You are brave to make this journey with such a small crew."

He nodded, "We lost men raiding in Frankia. I come here to see if there are any men of Cyninges-tūn who would wish to sail with me."

"You can ask but most of the men are ready to sail with us."

He looked disappointed but nodded, "I have gold to buy a byrnie from Bjorn Bagsecgson so my time will not be wasted and I bring a gift from my brother." One of his men carried a small chest. "These are parchments we found in Frankia. We were going to burn them but Hrolf the Horseman said that Aiden might be able to use them." He hesitated, "And that there may be a reward for us."

I smiled, "If that is Hrolf son of Gerloc of whom you speak then you are right. Rolf Horse Killer, take Gunnstein and his men to Cyninges-tūn."

After they had left Haaken said, "This is *wyrd* is it not? We should wait until Aiden has read the parchments. I see the fingers of the sisters in this."

"As do I. Snorri ride to Sigtrygg and then Asbjorn. Tell them I sail on a raid in the next month. Ask if they wish to come."

He leapt on his horse and left. Haaken said, "And your son?"

"His ship is not ready but you ride to him and tell him our news. Ragnar may wish to sail with us. He is old enough now."

Gruffyd said, "Can I go with Haaken?"

"Of course." The fitting out of the drekar was not exciting. A ride with Haaken to his cousin promised more.

The rest of the Ulfheonar stayed with me. Although Bolli had finished the hull and the sails they were busy making it more comfortable for them. Over the years they had stopped bringing aboard a chest and left one which they just used when we were raiding. We had fitted pieces of wood to hold them into place. We could still lift the deck to store booty but it meant we could row in the roughest of weather. We had also saved all the sails which had been damaged over the years. They provided covers for the deck. When we raided then *'Heart of the Dragon'* was our home. We liked to be comfortable. Finally, we began to store the barrels of dried fish and venison which would keep us fed on our voyage. Beer would be the last thing we would take for it would grow stale. We would take freshly brewed ale.

Aiden returned the day after Gunnstein had left us. He was excited, "Jarl the Gods have sent this! It is better than we could have hoped."

I had rarely seen him as excited. "Why? What can a piece of parchment tell us that will make us rich?"

"It gives us the dates when they will gather their treasure and when they will send it to Paris! A month from now it will be gathered at Rouen." I did not recognise the name. Aiden continued, "It used to be called Rotomagus by the Romans. It is a long way from the sea but Gunnstein told me that they raided as far as Jumièges and the river was navigable and wide. "

Erik Eriksson was close by, "If Jarl Gunnar raided Jumièges will they not be prepared for us?"

"Perhaps but the Jarl will be taking more ships. Jarl Gunnar had but two and one of them was small. We could have five if Sigtrygg and Asbjorn come with us."

"It is worth the risk and besides I wish to punish the men of Neustria. This will hurt them more than anything. We will raid." I looked at Aiden. "Will you come too?"

"Aye, Jarl. I would not miss this opportunity. Besides we may find more parchments and papers."

"Jarl Gunnar did well. We should reward him."

"I have given him a golden wolf to give to his brother and Bjorn is making Gunnstein's armour for nothing. I said that you would pay him."

"If this is the tax for Neustria then it will be a fortune and a suit of mail will be as nothing."

"It is more than that, Jarl. The taxes from Aquitaine are also sent both overland and by sea to Rouen. This will be the greatest Viking treasure ever when we capture it."

I shook my head, "Do not tempt the Weird Sisters, Aiden. You of all people should know the dangers."

For once Aiden looked discomfited. "You are right, Jarl, I shall make a sacrifice. I was carried away. I was thinking of the buildings we could erect with the profits."

"We have no profits until we sail home." He nodded, "Did many men wish to join Gunnstein?"

"There were some warriors who had come from Windar's Mere. The younger ones have joined him. The older ones seek berths with us."

"Good. We shall need them all."

"Cnut Cnutson will be here on the morrow with the men who will sail with us."

The son of the warrior who had been with me when the gods had touched my sword was now a fine warrior. He had been one I could have made Jarl at Seddes' Burgh but I knew that he would be Ulfheonar. He had already killed his wolf but he wished to become more skilful before he joined our ranks. It was commendable and showed that he knew what it meant to be one of my oathsworn.

A week later and we were ready to sail. Sigtrygg and Asbjorn joined us. Ragnar and some of my son's warriors also asked for a berth. Haaken told me that Wolf Killer had appointed his Jarl. He was happy. Einar Thordson was a serious warrior and Haaken was certain he would make a good jarl. Already more warriors had flocked to join my son. His warband would be soon up to strength. I was relieved my land would be protected by my son and his Wild Boars.

We had said farewell to Gunnstein who sailed to Dyflin to meet up with his brother. Our five ships made a fine sight as we sailed south. '*Red Snake*' led the way and '*Crow*' brought up the rear. We had heard that there were drekar at Man now. We sailed close together as we passed that island haunt of pirates. We were too big a mouthful for them. We kept the same formation when we sailed through the waters close to Wyddfa. The Mercians held the island but it paid to be careful. Once we were through that narrow passage we allowed a greater gap between ships and settled down to a long voyage through waters filled with enemies.

I stood at the steering board with Erik and Aiden. "Did you find any of Josephus' family?"

"We did. They prosper. I told them I would sail again at the end of the summer and trade with them. I hope I have your approval."

"You do and if this raid is successful then we will have much gold to spend in Miklagård."

"I was given some more of Josephus' charts. His family found them after he had died. They are of the waters north of the Pillars of Hercules. We used them coming home."

"Even after his death, he is proving he is loyal."

"I think it is more than that Jarl." I looked at Aiden. "I think this is *wyrd*. Remember who was Josephus' master. Rurik of Dorestad. His son reappears and these charts are discovered. Christians could not explain it but I believe it is Josephus helping us from the Otherworld."

His words set me to thinking. My reverie lasted a whole day but as we approached Syllingar thoughts of Josephus were driven from my mind. As we sailed close to those mystic islands, I found myself clutching my dragon amulet. Each time I descended into the witch's cave I wondered if it would be my last. It was like going down to Hel. When we passed you could feel the relief aboard our drekar.

The men began to row for the winds were from the north and east.

The storm was wild and the gods did roam
The enemy closed on the Prince's home
Two warriors stood on a lonely tower
Watching, waiting for hour on hour.
The storm came hard and Odin spoke
With a lightning bolt the sword he smote
Ragnar's Spirit burned hot that night
It glowed, a beacon shiny and bright
The two they stood against the foe
They were alone, nowhere to go
They fought in blood on a darkened hill
Dragon Heart and Cnut will save us still
Dragon Heart, Cnut and the Ulfheonar
Dragon Heart, Cnut and the Ulfheonar
The storm was wild and the Gods did roam
The enemy closed on the Prince's home
Two warriors stood on a lonely tower
Watching, waiting for hour on hour.
The storm came hard and Odin spoke
With a lightning bolt the sword he smote
Ragnar's Spirit burned hot that night
It glowed, a beacon shiny and bright
The two they stood against the foe
They were alone, nowhere to go
They fought in blood on a darkened hill
Dragon Heart and Cnut will save us still
Dragon Heart, Cnut and the Ulfheonar

85

Dragon Heart, Cnut and the Ulfheonar

Ragnar and Gruffyd enjoyed the song and no one sang harder than Cnut Cnutson. This was his father's song. We began to overtake *'Odin's Breath'*. I was about to tell them to slow down when we saw three Saxon ships suddenly emerge from an estuary. Another mile or two and we would have missed them for we were about to turn and head due south for Frankia. It was the shortest crossing we used. They had seen *'Red Snake'*. It must have looked like a tasty morsel for them. They had only seen *'Odin's Breath'* as a consort. She was a little bigger than *'Red Snake'*. Our speed meant we began to overhaul the smaller drekar. The Saxons were so intent upon catching the lithe drekar that they did not see us until we were less than half a mile from them. As they tried to turn away from my huge ship they were taken aback. The wind which had raced them to their prey now betrayed them and they almost stopped in the water as they tried to turn.

As we passed Asbjorn's drekar I shouted, "We will try to take them. Signal Raibeart to turn!"

This was too good an opportunity to miss. The men of Wessex would be taught a lesson and who knew what treasure we might pick up. Erik steered us directly into the wind and we used just the power of our rowers. I wanted to cut the Saxons off from the north-west. They would have to sail into the teeth of the wind. They had few rowers. Once we had passed them we would turn and Erik would use the wind. Luck or the incompetence of the captains came to our aid. Two of the Saxon ships rammed each other. Their bows crashed together and their rigging became entangled.

"Hard over, Erik! To arms!" I turned to Ragnar and Gruffyd. "Stay here and use your bows!"

I drew my sword and pulled out my seax. I would not need my shield. Erik brought us skilfully next to the stern of the nearest entangled Saxon. Our ship's boys furled the sail. Olaf Leather Neck hurled a grappling hook which tied us together and then leapt aboard swinging his axe. My men poured over the side. I landed on the deck and parried the spear thrust at me with Ragnar's Spirit. I stabbed the warrior in the stomach with my seax. He fell writhing to the deck. Asbjorn and Raibeart had managed to attack the third Saxon by placing their drekar on either side of it. We raced over the deck of the Saxon ship tethered to our own and followed Olaf Leather Neck and Rolf Horse Killer as they hurtled towards the shield wall of warriors on the last Saxon vessel.

My men had fought on ships before. The Saxons were not so experienced. Whoever had decided to attack a pair of Viking ships must have had brain fever or a death wish. Olaf and Rolf took a wide stance and lowered their knees as they swung. Their axes smashed into shields and knocked already unbalanced Saxons to the deck. Haaken and Cnut Cnutson led the rest of my warriors to smash through the already weakened shield wall. Swords flashed mercilessly. Shields were punched at terrified faces. I ran to the stern where the captain and helmsman were protected by four mailed warriors.

Finni the Dreamer, Rollo Thin Skin and Snorri were behind me and we ran to the men in mail. I think the four of them were confident that their mail would protect them. They were wrong. I blocked the sword strike with my own and then stabbed down with my seax. It had a wicked point and pierced the mail. It grated off the kneecap of the man I fought. As his weakened leg gave way I raised my sword for the kill. The Captain lunged at my side. If it had struck it would have wounded me but two arrows flew before me and struck him in the head. I finished off my wounded warrior and looked to see who had released the arrows. It was my son and grandson. The helmsman did not wait for death but jumped overboard. Those without mail joined him and those with mail threw theirs off before they abandoned their ship. The ships were ours!

Beorn the Scout shouted, "Jarl, this one is holed. It will soon sink!"

"Take what you can aboard our own drekar. Ran can have them as a sacrifice and to give thanks for her bounty!"

I stripped the mail from the warrior I had slain and took his warrior rings. He had a good sword, seax and a pouch with coins. I would give the mail to one of the younger warriors. I did not need it. The sword I would give to Ragnar and the seax to Gruffyd. I had no doubt we would find more bounty in Neustria. By the time we boarded our own drekar the two Saxon ships were low in the water. Our last two drekar had joined Raibeart and Asbjorn. The last Saxon ship was aflame. We did not leave drifting ships of the dead to haunt these waters. We would send them to the bottom.

My son and grandson awaited me, "Thank you for your arrows. Here are gifts for you."

They took them gratefully. I watched as the holed Saxon ship sank beneath the waves. It was still entangled with the other and with a flurry of foaming water, it too followed its consort to the bottom of the sea. Perhaps some of the crew would make it to shore and tell the other Saxons of the disaster but more likely it would remain a mystery.

We had taken shelter, when we came south, in small isolated bays. We could not do that this close to the land of Wessex. They would be watching for us. We rowed due south all night. The wind helped us. Instead of having two men to an oar we had just one and the other slept. The crew swapped over halfway through the night. We would lay up close by the small islands which the Romans called Caesarea and Sarnia. People lived there but there were so few of them that they presented no threat to us at all. Most importantly they were just a few hours from the Breton and Neustrian coasts. There were over twenty of them but only six had people who lived upon them. I had wondered if these had been the islands which Jarl Gunnar Thorfinnson used but his brother had told me that it was a single island and was much further south. Perhaps one day someone would colonise these and make them Norse. They would make raiding the mainland much easier and they would be easy to defend.

I slept and Aiden watched. He would help Erik to navigate. At night time we changed the order so that we led and kept a lantern at the stern to guide the others. I awoke to find us at anchor. We had reached an island. There was just a deck watch. I sent Aiden to bed and roused Haaken and Snorri. They had had a long sleep. We went to the prow. We were facing east.

"Aiden says that it is about a hundred miles to the mouth of the estuary and then eighty or so along the twisting river. Jarl Gunnar did the river part himself and his brother told us of the dangers. We leave tomorrow at noon. There are two small ports close to the mouth of the estuary. One is to the north and one is to the south. We can do nothing about them. If we are spotted then so be it. I want us to row along the river during daylight. I will not risk a drekar being sunk. That way we can attack at dawn. Snorri you and Beorn will be landed five miles from Rouen. Aiden's charts are accurate." I smiled, "The parchments showed the distances. We need to know if the tax ships have left. They should not have but it pays to be careful. We rely on speed to take them. We do not need to tackle the town. It is the ships and their treasure that we want."

"Are you certain they will leave it on board? If it was my gold I would keep it in my hall, guarded!"

"Aye Haaken, you would think so but the parchments say that the gold will be kept in the holds and there will be guards at the gangplanks."

Snorri nodded, "It is easier to guard one entrance to a ship rather than a whole hall."

"I will use the men of Cyninges-tūn to shift the treasure. Asbjorn, Sigtrygg and Raibeart can take the ships. We will use Cnut Cnutson and the Ulfheonar to stop reinforcements. We have spears and the ship's boys can use arrows."

Haaken chuckled, "You are gambling, Jarl. I like that. We are throwing the bones and hoping for as many spots as we can. The Allfather likes such bravery."

"You are right Haaken we do gamble but I want just one raid this year for Ragnar Ruriksson is still out there. We have him to deal with. When we do I would not leave our land undefended. We seek him with one crew; mine!"

"And then you build from stone?"

"And then we build from stone. The walls at Seddes' Burgh would not have fallen as easily if they had had a stone base and stone gates. Gunnar Thorfinnson told me that they have stone towers at their new home of Olafstad. If they can make such a tower then our Greek mason should be able to build something much bigger and better!"

As we waited for the sun to come up I wondered if the Weird Sisters would allow us to make it as easy as that.

Chapter 9

'Ulfheonar, warriors strong
Ulfheonar, warriors brave
Ulfheonar, fierce as the wolf
Ulfheonar, hides in plain sight
Ulfheonar, Dragon Heart's wolves
Ulfheonar, serving the sword
Ulfheonar, Dragon Heart's wolves
Ulfheonar, serving the sword'

We sang for the first part of the voyage. It raised our spirits. We needed them raising for the dawn had been a murky mist and rain-filled one. It made it harder for those on the shores to see us but as we would be passing the two towns at night that made little difference. It meant we had to sail closer together and we would have to rely on the ships' boys warning us when we sailed too close to a neighbour. The Weird Sisters were not making our voyage simple.

We sailed at the head of the column. Erik had the sail furled and the mast placed on the mast fish when darkness fell and we were just ten miles from the mouth of the estuary. We wanted to be invisible. With no mast and a low freeboard, we would be hard to see. The loops on the river meant that a sail would not help us anyway. We would be better off relying on the oars. It was uncomfortable as we bobbed up and down in the swell. Taking down the mast and putting it on the mast fish took time. We had ten strong warriors on the oars keeping us bow on to the estuary.

When that was done Aiden and a pair of ship's boys were at the bows watching for breakers. It was a wide estuary and so long as we stayed in the middle we would be safe enough. The dragon of **'Odin's Breath'** almost touched Erik's hand, we were sailing so close to each other. This was where the closeness of our warriors helped for we all had the same rhythm. Once we had entered the estuary we had Aiden passing instructions down through a line of boys. For the first few miles, it was nerve-wracking. The river, although wide, twisted and turned. As dawn broke it became easier, for Aiden could see better. However, we could also be seen. Gunnstein Thorfinnson had told us that there were few signs of habitation until we passed by Jumièges. That had been destroyed by Jarl Gunnar but Aiden was convinced that they would have begun rebuilding it. The parchments told us that the King of Frankia himself had endowed the monastery. It was a sign of his prestige. It would be rebuilt and there would be armed warriors, probably mounted, to ensure that the work was not disturbed. That was one place where we would have to be especially careful.

It was hard going, rowing against the current, and we had to change rowers frequently. I took to taking around the ale skin for it was thirsty work too. We were seen from the banks. It would have been strange had we not. Fortunately, it was peasants and thralls working in remote fields by the river or lone fishermen who spied us. They fled when they saw us. I had no doubt that our presence would be reported but who would think that we would dare to attack Rouen? As the day wore on our progress became slower. The river twisted and turned like a dragon's tail. There were times we came so close to the bank that I gripped my dragon amulet and prayed to the spirits to keep us safe. I promised Icaunis that I would make a blót if we survived. I knew not the name of the god of this river but I prayed that Icaunis was a brother.

The afternoon wore on and there was still no sign of Jumièges. I went to the bows to speak with Aiden. He was exhausted but he still peered at his charts.

"Is there any sign of the monastery?"

He shook his head, "We are here." He jabbed a finger at the squiggles on the parchment. It meant nothing to me save that it was not near the cross I could see on the bend of the river. "It could be a good sign. We might pass it after dark."

"And that would mean that we would have further to travel to reach the ships."

"Aye, it is thirty odd miles to the ships from the monastery."

"That could take two or three hours of rowing."

Aiden looked at his charts and said, "We could do it but we would have to go in blind. We would have to forego our scouts."

"Then that is what we will do." It was a luxury we could not afford. The threads of the Weird Sisters were, indeed, complicated and intricate.

We headed up the wide river watching the banks for danger. There were neither towers nor burghs along the banks. The river was too wide for bridges. Perhaps that explained the lack of people along it. Darkness fell and, as we turned a bend in the river, we heard the sound of a bell tolling to our left. It was the monastery. I hoped that the sound of our oars softly cutting through the water would not be heard. As the bell receded in the distance I peered to the northern bank. I saw nothing. I estimated that we would reach the ships while it was still dark. I went down the banks of oars and said. "When you change rowers then don your armour. We are going straight in."

Snorri asked, "No scouts?"

"Let us see if our luck holds. We go in fast and we go in hard. We will tie up next to the last ship we see and cross to the land from its decks."

When I reached Erik I told him what I intended, "I hope that I can turn around or we will have a problem."

"We will try to get you the time to do whatever you need." I turned to Ragnar and Gruffyd. "Your task is to guard Erik here. You have both shown that you can use your bows. On the morrow, we will see if you can stand when enemies attack! When we leave this ship it will be up to you two and the ship's boys to ensure that my drekar is not taken."

Ragnar nodded, "We will not let you down Jarl Dragonheart! We will show that we have earned the right to serve you."

I nodded. I had served Prince Butar when I had been little older than Ragnar. I knew how frightening it was to face grown men in battle. The steel in Ragnar's voice gave me confidence.

As I put on my cochineal and my mail I was more concerned that my men would be exhausted by the time we had to fight. It would be a test of both their strength and skill. It had been a long row from the sea. We saw the glow of fires as we sailed silently along the river. There were houses there. That might cause a problem when we had to sail back down the river. They would be alerted. I kept thinking that if two small drekar had done it then we had a good chance of doing so. Then I realised that we were further upstream than Jarl Gunnar Thorfinnson had been. I touched my dragon amulet and asked for the help of my ancestor. This was one time where Aiden's skills as a wizard could not help us. This would be down to the warriors I had brought from the Land of the Wolf. I had confidence. We were the best warriors. The enemy would only defeat us if they had overwhelming numbers. I saw my men donning their armour as they changed rowers. Each one of them had their own ritual. It was important for a warrior to use the same routine. It was part of being a warrior. We sailed in silence.

Guthrum Arneson, a ship's boy, came racing down the middle of the drekar. "Jarl, Aiden says it is around the next bend. He can smell the smoke from their fires."

I donned my helmet and walked down the gangway. "Ulfheonar, to the bow. The rest will follow when we are tied up."

My men followed me. Even as we walked down we saw dawn begin to break. We had barely made it in time. Guthrum stood next to me with a rope. He would have to leap aboard the Frankish ship. I peered over the dragon prow and saw that there was an island in the middle of the river. We had passed one already. The town was on the northern bank. A wall encircled it. The river was a hundred and more paces from the wall. As with Lundenwic the ground between the river and the wall was a sprawl of huts and crude halls. There were a number of ships on both sides of the river. The ones on the south were small. Far more were on the northern bank than the southern. Amongst the small boats, I counted four long, narrow ships tied up to the quay. They were more like barges than ships. Each had a mast. It was set further forward than on ours. They had to be the vessels which would transport the taxes up to Paris. I spied hope for they were lower than we were.

"Ready Guthrum?"

"Aye, Jarl."

"Do not worry. We will follow you aboard. You will have the best bodyguards!"

Suddenly a bell began to toll in the town. As the sky lightened I spied movement along the walls. We had been seen and recognised. A drekar's prow can be nothing but a danger. Erik put the steering board over as he shouted, "In oars!"

The last push from the rowers bumped us next to the end barge. The line of barges rose and fell as the rest of my drekar did the same. The Vikings had arrived!

"Go, Guthrum!"

As the boy leapt down I followed him. The flat deck was two paces beneath our gunwale. I saw the deck watch race towards Guthrum who did as he had been ordered, regardless of danger. He was securely fastening our drekar to the barge. Rollo Thin Skin swept his sword to hack into the side of the first guard who came close to Guthrum. The main danger came from the six mailed men who guarded the gangplank. They turned to face us.

Raising my sword I yelled, "Ulfheonar!" I ran at them.

They had small shields and spears but they were encased in lamellar armour from shoulder to knees. Their round helmets were like the ones the Frisians had worn. Holding my shield before me I ran at them. I trusted that my men would be hard on my heels. This was not like fighting on a drekar. The deck was flat and there was little movement. We were many miles from the sea. The six warriors braced themselves. Holding my shield before me with my shoulder behind it I hurtled into their shields. They did not expect it but I was not gambling. I trusted that my shield would be stronger than their spearheads and that my helmet would protect me. I felt the spears as they struck my shield and glanced off my helmet. It was like running into a wall but I heard wood snap as some of the spears broke.

My sword had been held behind me and, as I lowered my shield to allow me to see better, I brought it over in a sweep. I was within a sword's length of two whose spears I had shattered. My blade came across the side of the Frank's helmet. The metal held but the blow was so powerful that I saw the Frank's eyes roll back into his head as he fell. A sword from my right struck the second spearless guard as Haaken One Eye joined me. The two of us were suddenly pushed forward as the Ulfheonar put their shields into our backs and used us as a battering ram. The weight of ten men was too much for the remaining four. They tumbled over the side. Three fell between the barge and the shore. The weight of their armour would kill them. The last rolled down the gangplank. Snorri leapt down the wooden gangplank to sink his sword into his throat. We followed.

I could hear the noise of men leaving the town. "Shield wall! Follow me!"

The muddle of huts and warehouses had two or three narrow passages leading from the town. One was wider than the rest. I led my Ulfheonar to it. I could see men running towards us. I planted my feet and stood in the centre. Haaken, Olaf, Rollo Thin Hair and Rolf Horse Killer flanked me. The rest stood behind me. We locked shields and placed our left legs forward. The Franks did not run at us in a wedge. They saw a handful of men and each one thought to send us hence. These men did not know us. They had not fought Vikings. They saw us and thought to sweep us back into the river. They were in for a shock.

As one we raised our weapons above the shields. Haaken and I had the centre. Swords appeared over our heads to protect us and we felt the reassuring pressure of their shields in our backs. The warriors who raced to meet us carried a variety of weapons from spears to swords and hand axes. Some had armour but I could see that most had not. It was the town watch. Only our heads peered over our shields and when the leading Franks saw our red-eyed faces and wolf cloaks I saw the terror in their faces. Were they facing men or monsters? It was that terror which made them hesitate. I plunged my sword into the throat of the first Frank as Olaf's axe took the head from the second. The third was looking at his headless comrade when Rolf Horse Killer hacked his axe into his arm and side. The ones who followed stopped as they saw the bloody bodies.

"Charge!"

We ran slowly up the narrow lane towards them. They ran. I did not intend to follow them far but I wanted my men to have enough time to empty the chests from the barges. Halfway up we stopped. I had a sudden idea. I turned to the men behind us. "Fire the huts. You three will guard the passage with me!"

Haaken grinned, "I had wondered if I would have a song to sing. Let the Franks come and I will tell the tale of the four who held off an army!"

The Weird Sisters hear all. Our threads were spun but they could still cause mischief. Perhaps they saw Haaken's words as a challenge. I heard a horn and then spied the horses which appeared from the gate of the distant town. They had long spears. Olaf growled, "One day, Haaken One Eye, your boasting will get us killed!"

He laughed, "Then let us hope it is not this day!"

"Rolf, today you live up to your name!"

Four men with shields could fill the passage but only two horses would fit into the same space. The men who charged were forced to ride in pairs. The two riders were almost touching and that meant they could not ride as fast as they might have hoped. I had faced horsemen before and knew that horses can be trained to kill but it is not in their nature to do so. With left-arm braced, I held my sword behind me with the blade next to my ear. The two spears were jabbed towards us. Neither came near me but I heard a grunt as one struck Rollo. I stabbed forward with my sword as the horse's hoof struck my shield. My sword entered the beast's eye. It reared in pain. The rider was thrown from its back and I heard his cries as the second horse trampled him. The dying horse rolled back to form a barrier. Olaf Leather Neck hacked into the throat of the second horse as Haaken thrust his sword into the Frank's side. He fell from his dying mount at my feet. I ended his life.

Smoke began to pour from the buildings behind us and I heard Finni the Dreamer shout, "Jarl! Fall back!"

I saw that Rollo was hurt. The spear had penetrated his shoulder and he was bleeding. "Rolf! Help Rollo."

We moved back. The horses could not pass the two dead horses. They might have been able to leap across but they needed a run up to do that and there were too many crowding the narrow passage. As we moved backwards the smoke erupted into flames. That decided the horsemen. They could not make their horses pass fire. We had bought some time.

When we reached the river I saw that not all of our men had had the same success as we. There was a shield wall which spread from *'Heart of the Dragon'* to *'Red Snake'*. Cnut Cnutson and the men of Cyninges-tūn held the northern flank.

"Get Rollo to the drekar and ask Aiden how long we need."

"Aye Jarl."

The ships' boys were sending arrows over the heads of the shield wall to break up the Frankish attack. We needed to have a smaller perimeter. It would give those fighting better protection. "Four steps back! Double shields!"

The Ulfheonar were already in that formation. Finni and Erik Eriksson stepped forward to take the place of Rollo and Rolf. I saw Asbjorn to my left. He grinned, "Eystein would have enjoyed this, Jarl!"

"Aye, he would. We will tell him of it when we next see him." Asbjorn nodded. A Viking was always ready to go to Valhalla... it was just we did not expect to do so!

The Franks saw the movement of our line and took it for weakness. They rushed at us thinking we retreated. Our line was solid and when they ran at us they were met by a wall of wood and deadly swords which were wielded by swordsmen hardened over years. They had not met our like before and the wall of dead men was a lesson to them.

The horsemen had ridden around the flames and now twenty of them formed a line behind those on foot. I knew what was coming. Rolf Horse Killer ran up. "Jarl, Aiden has almost finished. He has placed kindling on the barges. He said to fall back whenever you are ready!"

That was easier said than done. The horsemen would charge if they saw us trying to reach the barges. Glancing over my shoulder I saw that they were just fifty paces from us.

"Fall back slowly. The horsemen will attack soon!"

We had almost made it when disaster struck. Cnut Cnutson was leading his line backwards when a spear jabbed into the chest of one of the horses. This one fell across two men and the horsemen poured through the gap. I saw that the other drekar crews had made their ships. They would be slaughtered if I did not help.

"Ulfheonar!" I led my oathsworn as we hurled ourselves into the side of the horsemen who had seized the opportunity to fall upon the lighter armed men of Cyninges-tūn.

I swung my sword at the leg of one warrior. It severed it. Bright blood spurted out as he fell from his horse. We hacked and stabbed in the midst of them. I do not think that, as horsemen, they had ever been attacked so ferociously by men on foot before. We did not fear their horses and we did not fear their long spears. The Franks were used to fighting men who would give up when their lives were threatened. We were their worst nightmare. If you threatened any who were our kin then you risked the wrath of a Viking. When six horses had been slain and four riders lay dead they pulled back to reform.

"Cnut, get your men aboard and the ones who are wounded." My men formed a line behind me as I shouted, "If you come near then you will all die! We are from the land of the Wolf! Fear us!"

They would not understand my words but they would understand my defiance.

Haaken said, "Jarl, It is best we get aboard. I have spied a large warband coming up along the river."

"Aye, we have gambled enough! Fall back!"

The wounded and some of the dead had been carried aboard the drekar. As we crossed the barge and climbed aboard *'Heart of the Dragon'* Aiden pointed downstream. "Jarl, they have dragged a chain across the river and they have landed warriors on the southern bank. The chain goes around a tree and is secured to the northern bank. We are trapped!"

"Not yet we are not. Tie the barge to our stern. Warriors to your oars!"

As I ran down the length of the drekar I saw that the chests of treasure and the wounded littered the decks. That was no good. We had to row. I reached Erik. He looked worried, "Jarl, we cannot turn around and they are bringing more warriors. If they use flames we shall burn!" It was every warrior's worst nightmare. A wooden ship could burn in a heartbeat.

"We are not dead yet. Lead the ships upstream and turn around the island. We will tie up between the island and the southern bank. We need to store the treasure and clear the decks. I want the masts raising."

He knew me well enough not to question my orders. He shouted to Guthrum to tie the barge to the stern rail.

I turned to the warriors. "Row like you have never rowed before." Putting my shield by my feet I took a chest next to Erik Siggison, a young warrior from Cyninges-tūn. "Let us see if an old man keep up with you, eh Erik?"

Haaken began the chant.

> *'Ulfheonar, warriors strong*
> *Ulfheonar, warriors brave*
> *Ulfheonar, fierce as the wolf*
> *Ulfheonar, hides in plain sight*
> *Ulfheonar, Dragon Heart's wolves*
> *Ulfheonar, serving the sword*
> *Ulfheonar, Dragon Heart's wolves*
> *Ulfheonar, serving the sword'*

It was some years since I had had to row but you never forgot how. I leaned into each stroke. You had to clear your mind of everything save the pull on the oar and the rhythm of the river. At first, it was as though we were hardly moving for we towed a heavy barge. I should have had someone steering it. I had forgotten. Then we started to move a little faster and the air which washed over my face cooled me. I sang as lustily as any and I could hear the pride in Erik's voice as he shared an oar with the Jarl Dragonheart. I felt us slowly turning. Once we faced downstream then it became much easier. We had barely covered a ship's length when Erik shouted, "In oars! Rest!"

As soon as the oars were laid inboard the crew began banging on the deck and chanting my name. I shouted, "We cheer when we are home! Raise the mast and store the treasure. Put the wounded at the stern. Aiden come with me!"

The ships' boys had moored us to the shore and we leapt on to the island. I ran towards the other drekar shouting, "Counsel of war!"

The four leaders joined me. I saw that, although bloodied, none were badly wounded. "They have used a chain to stop us leaving and they have reinforced the southern bank. I have no doubt that other warriors will be coming. Have your masts fitted. We will sail down the river. I want six men from each crew, including yours Raibeart. They should be the best that you have." I smiled, "Not you, of course. I need you to command your ships. We will board the barge and sail her down to the chain. I intend to cut the chain and defeat the warriors. We will sail through on the barge after you have safely passed."

Sigtrygg said, "Jarl, you take too many risks. Let one of us do this."

"I have never asked another to fight my battles for me. I got us into this and I will get us out. Obey me!"

They nodded. I turned to Aiden, "I want a fire readying on the barge. They have other ships attached to the quay. I want the barge burning and sinking in the middle of the river to stop the pursuit."

"Aye, it is a good plan." As we went back to my drekar he said, "Some of the taxes were in goods. The coin was all in the first barge. It is aboard our drekar."

I nodded. I saw that the mast was almost up. The sail would take longer. When we were next to the drekar I said, "Ulfheonar, leave that to the others. We are going to sail the barge. Cnut Cnutson, take charge of the drekar until I return."

His face came over the side, "I would rather fight with you, Jarl."

"I know but you know this drekar and you can command. You will have few enough crew as it is."

I led the Ulfheonar to the barge. "We sail this?"

"Aye, Finni the Dreamer but we do not have to row. We sail down to the chain. They have tethered it to a tree. We cut down the tree."

"And the Franks who guard it?"

"Those we kill, Leif!"

The twenty-four men from the other drekar joined us. I knew that Raibeart would be even more shorthanded but he was a good captain and he had the smallest drekar. The river would have to do most of the work until his men could rejoin him. Aiden and Haaken led the men on board and started to lower the sail. I shouted up to Erik. "Cast off the barge, Erik. As soon as you see the chain is destroyed lead the ships through. You can pick us up on the other side. Do not lower the sail until we have cleared the danger. Have the boys and archers use their arrows." Ragnar and Gruffyd's faces appeared over the side as they heard my voice, "You two can make a difference today! Make your fathers proud!"

They both raised their bows in salute.

The barge was already moving. "Olaf Leather Neck and Rolf Horse Killer, find any who have axes. They can help you chop down the tree."

"Aye Jarl."

"Aiden, you steer!"

As Aiden allowed the current to take us the three quarters of a mile or so to the chain and the ever-increasing warriors I turned to my men. "There will be less than thirty of us. We have to give Olaf and his axemen the time to cut down the tree and removed the chain. We fight in a shield wall three men deep. The Ulfheonar will be at the front. When the tree is down and the chain removed we get back on the barge. I want no heroes!"

"Aye Jarl!"

All of them showed the pride they had in being selected to stand alongside Jarl Dragonheart. If any fell then they would be welcomed in Valhalla. There was no greater honour. Each man had volunteered to come in search of riches and honour. Even if they fell their families would be rich and their memory honoured in song.

Aiden shouted, "Not long Jarl."

I turned to Erik Eriksson. He had been wounded in the battle with the Frisians. He could fight but he was not as mobile as others. Erik, guard Aiden! We cannot afford to lose our galdramenn. Not to mention our helmsman!"

"Aye Jarl."

I went to the side. Haaken, Finni, Leif and the rest of my Ulfheonar waited. The small boats were still ferrying men across the river. They had, however, no horses. These would be Franks fighting on foot and we already knew that they were not as confident on two legs. There were just forty of them but their numbers were growing. An idea formed in my mind. This was not a time to be defensive. I needed to be bold.

Turning to Haaken I said, "We drive them into the river. Let us show them that we are men to be feared!"

He grinned, "Aye Jarl. You have no shield, remember."

I took out my seax. "I need no shield!"

As the barge bumped next to the bank we leapt out. We were held there by the bank. Aiden had the steering board hard over so that the bow was caught in the undergrowth of the overgrown bank. I had no idea how he would get us off but I did not doubt that he would know a way.

I moved quickly towards the Franks. I needed all of my men ashore before we attacked. The Franks had some men in half mail and some without. All had a helmet and most had a spear and a shield. They were standing, not in a line but a loose sprawl. They knew the danger and were guarding the end of the chain. They were waiting for more numbers to arrive. I glanced beyond them. Each boat seemed to be bringing ten men. Even as I watched another twenty were landed. As they were below the chain they had a hundred paces to run. We had time.

I raised my sword, "Charge!"

The Ulfheonar were next to me and we were not restricted by houses and buildings this time. We naturally formed an arrow with me at the fore. Apart from me, every warrior had a shield and they held them before them. The Frankish shields were half the size. I picked out a leader. He had mail to his knees and a helmet with a nasal and a plume. He had in his hand a long Frankish sword. It was the sort their horsemen used.

I heard him shout something to his men and he made the mistake of looking down his line. I did not need to. I knew that my men were keeping pace with me. He swung his sword at me as I ran the last four paces. I was so quick that I was able to ram my seax against his hand so that he could not complete his swing. Instead of swinging my sword I punched the pommel at his eye. I only had a small handguard but it mattered not. It still squelched against his eye. I pulled my hand across his face and the eye came with my sword. It also knocked his helmet from his head. He had forgotten to tie his thongs. I pulled back my seax and rammed it into his other eye. He would not be left blinded for the blade entered his skull and he fell at my feet, dead.

I did not pause but swung my sword at the spearman who stabbed at me. I deflected the spear and it ground against my mail. My sword caught the edge of his shield and drove across his arm. It tore into the muscle and the tendons. He dropped the shield. I slashed my seax down his face and he fell to the ground. We had cleared the tree. So ferocious was our attack that fifteen men lay dead and another four were badly wounded. We rolled on towards the ones who had just landed. They had not formed a line. We tore into them. They made the mistake of standing and they tried to stop us. We were big men. We wore mail and we had done this since we were children. It was as though we were fighting priests. They waited for our strikes. A Viking can fight with his sword, shield, head and knees all at the same time. I slashed my sword across the neck of one warrior as I plunged my seax into the gut of a second.

I heard the sound of axes behind me. Olaf and his axemen were at work. We were no longer a solid mass of warriors. Some of the other crews had paused to slay wounded men or to finish off men who still stood. It was just the Ulfheonar warband which attacked the twenty men who had just stepped ashore. I had slain so many men that the edge had gone from Ragnar's Spirit. I was now using it as an iron bar. As such it was still very effective. It could still break arms and render men unconscious. As we hurried to attack these fresher warriors I sheathed my seax and drew my dagger. It was razor-sharp and had a vicious point.

A wild warrior swung a long pole with an axe head on the top. He flailed it at me in an attempt to keep me at bay. I ducked beneath it and lunged upwards. My dagger tore him open from his groin to his gut. I sprang to my right as two Franks with swords and small shields tried to take advantage of my position. Franks do not know how to use a shield as a weapon and I blocked both swords with my dagger and Ragnar's Spirit. Stepping forward on my left leg I smashed the heel of my right boot into the extended knee of one warrior. He screamed as it shattered and his leg bent back. As his companion stared in horror I swung my sword around. It broke the skin but, more importantly, his neck too.

As I finished off the Frank with the shattered kneecap with my dagger I heard a crash as the tree fell and then Aiden as he shouted, "Jarl, back to the barge!"

The Ulfheonar were covered in blood and spattered with gore. Yet we were unbowed. The Franks who remained had retreated to the water's edge fearful of another attack. Behind me, the rest of my warriors were advancing. We had taken enough chances, "Back to the barge! That is an order!"

Before they obeyed every Ulfheonar began to howl. The others banged their shields. If anything it made the Franks recoil even more. As we made our way back to the barge I saw *'Heart of the Dragon'* as she sailed down the river. Those on board also banged the shields in time to the ones on the shore. It was an impressive display. I was the last one to board the barge. The huge chestnut tree which had been felled was another reminder of the power of my warriors. Stepping on to the barge I raised my sword, "Ragnar's Spirit!"

Chapter 10

The Frankish ships kept their distance but warriors watched us from the northern bank. Those on the south cowered as we passed. The five drekar had all managed to pull in to the bank and our men scrambled aboard. After we had lowered the sail I waited with Aiden as he turned the barge so that it pointed north to south. He turned to me, flint in hand, "Jarl, climb the rope to the drekar. You have armour. If this goes awry I can swim."

I shook my head and shouted, "Throw down two ropes and be ready to haul!" I turned to Aiden. "We will go together."

He nodded and lit the pile of seal oil and kindling. The barge was bone dry and I did not doubt it would soon catch hold. Aiden shouted, "Run!"

We ran to the stern and grabbed a rope each. With the strongest warriors pulling we were lifted to safety. Erik shouted, "Let go the sail!"

The other four drekar were heading downstream. We had no need to row for we had the current and with a wind from the south-east we would have little need to tack too often. I watched with Aiden, Ragnar and Gruffyd as the flames ran up the mast and ignited the sail. It was afire from bow to stern and began to settle in the water. They would find it hard to follow us!

I sat down on my chest. Gruffyd looked afraid, "Are you hurt, father? You are covered in blood!"

"And none of it mine. No, my son, I am just tired. I am no longer a young man who can fight all day and all night. I will just rest here awhile."

Erik did not look down but he asked, "Have you orders, Jarl?"

"Can we keep going until we reach the coast?"

He nodded, "If Aiden helps and does watch and watch about then aye. You are probably right. If we stop then we risk danger."

"Wake me if we find trouble."

"Aye Jarl."

Ragnar said, "And we will watch over you, grandfather."

I took off my sword, seax and dagger and handed them to Ragnar. I took off my helmet and gave it to Gruffyd. Then I took off my wolf cloak and placed it on the deck. I would use it as a bed. Finally, I held my dragon amulet, "Thank you Allfather and the spirits of my ancestors. You have watched over me this day."

Then I lay down and was soon asleep helped by the gentle motion of the drekar which ghosted down the river. I dreamed.

I was walking through a forest with a bow and arrow in my hand. I looked down and saw that I was not wearing mail. I was hunting. Ahead I saw a clearing and a huge stag appeared. I began to move to get closer. At first, I moved silently. I was the wolf and I was hunting. Even as I prepared an arrow I felt my feet sinking into a muddy morass. I could not move. The deer turned and its face changed to that of King Egbert. He laughed and I saw behind him was Ragnar Ruriksson. The Frisian pulled back on his bow and the arrow sped towards me. I could not move. When I went to raise my bow it had disappeared and I had paws and fur; I was the wolf. I braced myself for the arrow but it did not strike me. Instead, I heard a shout from behind me. When I turned I was no longer in the forest but upon the top of Úlfarrberg. As I looked out I saw hordes of Danes and they were heading for me. Racing to reach my home I fell. I lost my balance and tumbled over and over. I sailed into the air. It was impossible. I was flying. I tried to reach the earth but I could not. I was heading for the moon. It grew larger and larger. Suddenly it changed from a bight golden orb to a black hole and I fell deep within it. I went down and down.

"Jarl!"

I looked up into Aiden's face. I could see that he had dreamed too, "The dream. What does it mean?"

He shook his head. "I saw only glimpses. Egbert and Ragnar the Frisian were there." He shook his head, "You were the wolf. I saw that but as for the rest... I know not. I am sorry."

I took his arm and raised myself up. "These dreams are sent to warn us of the future. We must become careful, Aiden. Mention none of this to anyone until we have worked out what it means."

"Aye Jarl."

The drekar still slipped along the silent river. I was awake now and I feared going back to sleep. I saw my son and grandson curled up close by. I went to the stern and made water. I turned to speak with Erik. A ship's boy, Siggi, ran up to me with a jug of wine. We had finished our beer and the wine had been in the barge already. I suspect it had been the guard's supply. I drank. It was rough and it was a little sour. As I handed it back I said, "Add a little water to it." It would not do to give my men unwatered wine.

"Aye Jarl."

Aiden stretched, "I will walk to the prow. Perhaps I can see through the darkness of night." Turning to Erik he said, "I will relieve you when I return." Erik nodded.

Speaking quietly I said, "How goes it, Erik?"

"We have not seen any other ships or boats but I think that they have been warned about us. I have seen fires by the side of the river and heard cries of alarm as we ghosted by."

I nodded, "A rider could have sent a message downstream. I just hope that we do not meet another chain."

He laughed, "I am not sure your son and grandson could cope with you charging wildly at enemies armed with just a seax and a sword."

"Were they afraid?"

"Not afraid but it took Guthrum to contain them. They wanted to help you."

"They are good boys both."

"They are and they fought as hard as any. When they become stronger their arrows will fly further. It has shown me that I ought to bring my boys to sea."

"How old are they now?"

"One has seen six summers and the other four. Ships' boys do not cost much to feed. They do not take up much space and they have energy to spare. I began when I had seen four summers."

"Aye, I remember. Your father was slain and your mother fell to the winter cough. It was the only way I could watch over you."

"And I have ever been grateful."

"You did not wish to be a warrior?"

"There was a time when I did. Perhaps I would have been as Cnut Cnutson. He was a ships' boy when his father died but he chose the warrior's path and he is now a leader. It was Josephus who took me down this path and I think it was *wyrd*. I can fight but here, with my hand on the steering board, I feel as though I am part of the drekar and part of the water. I fear nothing whilst I am at sea. The Norns chose this path for me. I had a choice and I chose the sea."

Aiden came back, "I can see naught." He pointed aft. "The sky begins to lighten. Soon it will be day."

Erik Short Toe stretched, "Then I will sleep. Wake me when we reach the sea." He smiled, "It is hard to get lost in a river but at sea..." I took the steering board for it was a straight stretch of river.

"How are the wounded?"

"Many needed stitches. I could not use fire but the wounds looked clean. Audun Beornsson had some bones in his left hand broken. I have put a splint on them and told him not to row."

"Will his hand heal?"

"It should but bones... we shall see."

When Aiden was comfortably settled at the steering board he said, "One thing is clear about your dream; your thread is still entwined with King Egbert and now his is entwined with Ragnar."

"I did not see that. I thought that they were just two enemies."

"No, Jarl. The spirits are not haphazard like that. Besides Ragnar Ruriksson took the road to Lundenwic. The world knows how much Egbert hates you. He will be at the court of Wintan-ceastre."

"And we both know that the oath King Egbert took will not last long. He will come after us and Wolf Killer again."

"It will last a little longer. There were priests there. I have no doubt he will seek a way to find a flaw in the oath but he will not openly oppose you. Ragnar Ruriksson gives him the chance to hurt you without being seen to have a hand in it."

"And I allowed him to escape!"

"No, you did not, Jarl. From what you say he has warriors who are there to protect him. You could do nothing. The Weird Sisters began this web when you first met Rurik of Dorestad. It brought us Josephus and that brought great rewards for us all. There is a price to pay."

I pointed to the deck. "And there will be a price to pay for this treasure."

He nodded, "I know not what it will be but we both know that nothing is free. I told you of this treasure and encouraged you to find it. I am as responsible as any."

"This treasure was earned by the blood of my men!"

"True but the way we discovered it was not. It was no accident that Jarl Gunnar Thorfinnson found the parchments and could not read them. He had the treasure from the monastery. Had the Weird Sisters wished it they would have pointed him towards this treasure too. They did not. They sent it to you. I have no doubt that Jarl Gunnar Thorfinnson will pay a price for his treasure. When men follow a jarl such as you they know that there will be honour, reward and riches but they also know that there may be death." We both glanced at the cloak covered bodies by the stern. "They know that and accept it."

As the dawn slowly broke I considered his words. Suppose I had not sailed for the treasure? That was a foolish question. Suppose I had not been born? Not taken from the Dunum? Not met old Ragnar? We begin our first faltering footsteps alone but they are directed by others. We think we make decisions but we do not. When I had told Haaken that I gambled I had been wrong. I just tried to deal with the problems the Weird Sisters put in my way and hoped that I was doing the right thing. I glanced down at my young son and grandson. My thread and their threads were entwined. One day one of them, perhaps both, would have to lead our people. They would be standing, as I was, at the stern of a drekar deciding what was best and making choices which could cost men their lives. I suppose the difference was, between me and those like Ragnar Ruriksson and Egbert, that I cared and fretted about the men I led. I suspect they did not.

It was noon when we reached the sea. We woke Erik and then my men gathered for we would send our dead warriors to Ran. It would not have done to leave their bodies in Frankia; better that they lay in the sea and when we passed this point we would remember them. Wrapped in their cloaks their bodies were slipped over the side. We all spoke silent prayers for them. I saw Ragnar and Gruffyd as they saw each of the bodies, some young and some old, drop beneath the waves to the ocean floor. It was good that they did so for they had to know that our lives were filled with death as well as glory.

Once we headed north and west we resumed our formation. *'Red Snake'* led with us in close attendance. I had decided to head for Dyflin. The other drekar had no gold but goods. Dyflin's market would be the best place to sell them. Until we had more friends it was the only place to make a profit from them. Rather than risking an attack by the men of Wessex, we kept well out to sea. It meant sailing close to the islands of Syllingar but that could not be helped. If the witch wished to speak with us there would be nothing we could do about it. She did not. Aiden was silent the whole day we came close to the deadly little string of islands but when we had passed them he smiled and returned to me from the dragon prow. "She has no message for us." He saw my face, "You look disappointed."

"I had hoped she would enlighten me about my dream."

"And if she did so then you would stop thinking about it and you need to try to fathom out the answer yourself."

"You mean Egbert and Ruriksson?"

He nodded, "We need not raid again. We have lost warriors and we could not raid again; not soon anyway. We have gold to pay Basil the Mason to build. Our time in Cyninges-tūn will be occupied. You will need to turn your thoughts to the dangers from outside. You need to wrestle with the danger."

The course we took added two days to our voyage. It did, however, mean we sailed far from land. Corn Walum was far to the east and Hibernia stood to the north-west. Ragnar watched the sea to the west. "Grandfather, what lies over there?"

"Some men say the edge of the world and if you sail too far then you fall off. Others say that there are terrible seas and rocks. They grind drekar and their crews to a pulp."

Gruffyd said, fearfully, "Is that true?"

"I know not but none who ever sail west return." They both looked open-mouthed at the blue-grey water which was now, suddenly, dangerous. "On the other hand, they may have found a paradise so great that they do not wish to share it with others."

"Would you wish to sail there, grandfather?"

"I have a family. There are grandchildren and children. I could not leave them. Those voyages are for young men who are reckless and wish to have adventures which are the stuff of legend. When a man takes a wife and sires sons his world changes. One day a young jarl will sail west and he will return. Then we will know. Until then we sail as far as Hibernia and no further."

The island soon hove into view. The southern coast was a wild place and not worth raiding. The monasteries were on the west coast. It had been many years since I had raided. I doubted I would do so again. The coast on the east was now peaceful. It was Jarl Gunnstein Berserk Killer's peace. When we reached it we saw that Dyflin harbour had few ships at the quay and no drekar. This was the summer and the time of raids. That meant even greater profit for we had goods to trade and a market which would be eager for them.

Jarl Gunnstein Berserk Killer was at home. He rarely raided these days. His tight control of the wild men of Dyflin was enough of a task for one of the most feared warriors in the west. "Jarl Dragonheart, it is good to see you and I can see you have had a successful raid. Jarl Gunnar Thorfinnson had one too. The Allfather, it seems, smiles upon those who follow the wolf."

I shrugged, it did not do to make the Norns angry. "We are forced to raid in places which have not been raided yet. Soon the Franks will be as the Saxons and learn to keep their treasures behind solid walls but for the moment we are successful and lucky!"

"What do you have?"

I waved Aiden forward, "My galdramenn can tell you."

The Jarl waved over his steward and he and Aiden headed for the drekar. The other ships were unloading but my crew stayed aboard. "Do you stay, Jarl Dragonheart?"

"No, we travel back as soon as we are unloaded."

"Then I would have come conference with you." He led me to a quiet corner of the crowded quay. "I have heard rumours of Vikings attacking other Vikings and taking their drekar."

"Do we know who?"

"It may be some of Thorfinn Blue Scar's men. He had a drekar taken by some of his men who wished to raid. They are outlawed."

"Are they named?"

"They are the followers of a warrior of Orkneyjar, Harald Black Teeth." The name sounded familiar. "He has renamed the drekar and we know not what it is now."

I clutched my dragon, "He risks the wrath of the gods. You do not rename a drekar. When we captured the ship from Magnus the Forsworn we left it as *'Red Snake'*. We have prospered. No good will come of renaming a drekar."

"At the present time, he appears to be successful. He is sailing in the waters around Orkneyjar and the northern isles. He knows them well. He takes the smaller threttanessa."

"And Blue Scar?"

"He has put a price on him but the warrior is cunning and knows the islands. The Jarl lost a second drekar in a sea-fight."

"Then we will have to escort our knarr when they sail. Has Siggi been in port of late?"

"No, Jarl Dragonheart. Are you concerned?"

The hairs on my neck prickled again. I could sense danger. "Each time I leave my land undefended then some disaster strikes. I hope that Siggi is safe. I will leave now. The other four can travel back together."

He laughed, "It would be either a brave or foolish Viking who tried to take *'Heart of the Dragon'*."

"If this man is willing to risk the wrath of Blue Scar then I think he might do so."

I headed to my drekar, "Erik, prepare to leave as soon as Aiden returns." He looked puzzled but nodded. I went to the other captains who were standing on the quay buying ale from a woman who pushed a handcart. "I will be leaving soon."

"Is there a problem, Jarl?"

"There may be, Raibeart. There are outlaw Vikings in these waters preying on other Vikings. Siggi has not visited here. I am worried. Sail together and be wary of dragon ships. They may be enemies."

They finished their ale and returned to their ships. It would take some time to sell all that they wished to trade. There might even be some goods they had to carry back. Jarl Gunnstein spoke with Aiden and he hurried back. "The Jarl told me. I have not felt danger, Jarl, but my mind has been on your dream."

We were soon underway. When I told Haaken of the danger he and the weary crew took to their oars and we flew across the waters. The island of Man no longer seemed as threatening as we sailed close to Hrams-a. There would have been a time when we would have been wary of the Vikings who lived there but they would only attack solitary ships and never *'Heart of the Dragon'*.

"Sail ahead!"

"Aiden you have good eyes. See if you can identify it."

He ran to the prow. After a few moments, he shouted, "It is Siggi and he is on a parallel course to us. He too is heading for Ûlfarrston!"

We had been lucky. From now on I would send a drekar with every knarr which left our land. The pirates would not have one ship from us!

"You can take in the oars now. Siggi is safe! We will let the wind take us in."

Siggi was unloading when we edged into the small quay. He seemed surprised to see us, "Jarl I did not expect you back so soon."

"We were worried. We heard there were drekar hunting in these waters."

He nodded, "I heard the rumour when I was in Dyfed. I used the straits of Menai. I know them well. It would take a brave drekar captain to try them."

Aiden nodded, "That is why we saw them not. We kept well away from the land of the Angles' Sea."

"Then when our ships have unloaded and we are refitted with a full crew we will go hunting pirates. I will make them find waters which are less dangerous to our enemies!"

Coen strode over his face creased with worry. "Is my brother safe?"

"Of course. Why Coen ap Pasgen?"

"Our two knarr have not returned. They left seven days before you sailed. They should have been back already."

"I fear that this pirate, Harald Black Teeth, has taken them. Do not worry, Coen; if that is true we will compensate you for your loss."

He shook his head, "It is not the boats I care about it is the men. How can you replace those Jarl?"

"You are right and it was a foolish thing for me to say. I meant we will make sure your people do not suffer this winter because of their losses."

"I know, Jarl. My nephew was on one of the knarr. I have put off telling my sister for I hoped the knarr would return. You have now dashed my hopes."

I had been so concerned with the treasure that I had left my land unguarded. Who knew what calamity had struck my land too? I turned to Haaken. "The Ulfheonar will come with me now and we will get to

Cyninges-tūn. Cnut Cnutson, see to the unloading of the treasure. Bring it to my hall."

"Aye Jarl. I am honoured that I am to be entrusted with it."

"Cnut you have earned great honour this raid. Your father would be proud of you!" He nodded and turned to order his men to unload. "Erik, have the ship readied to sail in three day's time. When the other captains arrive, tell them that we hunt pirates!"

We borrowed horses and ponies from Coen and we galloped up the forest trail to Cyninges-tūn. Coen's words had worried me. Had the dream I had had been a portent of some catastrophe? The walls stood, boats fished and I saw the smithies at work by the Water. The worst had not happened. We were seen when we left the forest and the fishing boats brought the news. It meant we had an audience when we reached the gates.

I saw anxious faces. They were the families of the warriors who had sailed with us. Some of those warriors would not be returning. Those families would be the ones to whom I had to speak later on. We would ensure that they did not suffer. If a warrior gave his life for the clan then the clan took the responsibility for that family. That was our way. Kara and Ylva engulfed Aiden. Their hall was close to the gate. Leaving my horse there I went with Gruffyd and Ragnar to my home. Erika could now run easily and she raced to me. I said quietly, "Gruffyd, greet your mother!"

It was not a lack of affection which stopped Gruffyd; he did not want to be seen to show himself up in front of his cousin. Ragnar said, "Go on Gruffyd."

He obliged and threw his arms around his mother. I saw the gratitude in her eyes and then her nose wrinkled as she smelled him. Days at sea mixed with the blood of wounded warriors did not make any of us smell pleasant.

I took off my wolf cloak and handed it to Uhtric. "Come, boys, we will go to the Water and bathe. Let us purify and cleanse our bodies. Uhtric, fetch clean clothes."

"Aye Jarl."

"Thank you, husband!"

As I turned I asked, "Are Wolf Killer and his family well?"

"He is. He has sent a rider every day to inquire after us."

"Good." My fears had been unfounded. My dream was not about my home.

We had bathed, changed and eaten by the time that a weary Cnut Cnutson led my men and the treasure to my hall. He had also brought our chests. I opened my chest and took out the Frankish sword I had

110

captured. "I give this to you Cnut Cnutson as a mark of my esteem and so that others will know of your bravery. Take it and use it well."

"Thank you, Jarl. I am honoured. When you sail again in three days' time I would beg a berth from you."

"Of course."

Brigid snapped, "Three days?"

"There are pirates raiding the sea lanes. They have taken some of Coen's people. We need to scour the seas of them."

"You will not be gone long?"

"A week at most. This is important. If the waters around our home are not safe then I have let down my people."

She relented. "I would I was the wife of a simple farmer!"

"No, you do not! We would not have such a fine hall and you would not have such luxuries as those pots and the linens. Wait until you see the rich goods we have brought back for you."

"You cannot bribe me, Dragonheart! I would be happy with a simple life knowing that my husband is there to protect me."

Gruffyd said, "But he protects the land and the people. Without him, we would all wither and die."

I looked at him in surprise. "Where did you hear that?"

"On the drekar when you slept. The Ulfheonar said it so it must be true."

Further discussion was ended when Kara, Aiden and Ylva arrived. Kara made no apology. "I have come to see this mountain of gold and silver you have captured father!"

I laughed, "We have yet to count it. Do not forget that every man who sailed with me is entitled to a share."

Us too, Grandfather?"

"You too, Ragnar!"

We set to counting. The pile of gold appeared to be disappointingly small. Aiden laughed, "It would be strange indeed if there were huge quantities of gold. These taxes come from the people of Aquitaine and Neustria. How many of them have even seen gold, let alone held it."

He was right and the gold and bronze soon mounted up. The division of the spoils was harder than the counting. Aiden had kept a record of all who had sailed with us. He apportioned the coins. There would be more arriving with the rest of the drekar as well as other goods to share.

That night, as I lay in a comfortable bed holding my wife in my arms, I wondered if I should tell her of my dream. I decided not to. Instead, I spoke of how well our son had done. She listened and nodded. "Was he in danger?"

I could not lie to her. "No more than any other of the men I took with us. But he never left the drekar. I did the same when I was young."

"The other mothers seem quite happy for their sons to be in such danger. How can that be?"

"You were brought up differently to these Viking mothers. Their job is to raise warriors to defend the land. They are happy to do so."

"Happy for their children to die?"

"No, my love, but happy in the knowledge that if they do die then they will be in Valhalla with other heroes!"

"They are not Christian."

I smiled, "No, my love and that is why you cannot understand it."

She fell asleep in my arms and I looked up at the ceiling. I was not Viking born and I found the deaths of so many brave young men hard but I knew that without those deaths then the Land of the Wolf would not remain free.

Chapter 11

The mixture of joy and sadness filled my town. I sent gifts to my other jarls. They had defended my land. I sent a chest of bronze to Wolf Killer. He had kept my land safe. I sent Ragnar back to him with Snorri. I would not take either my son or grandson on my pirate hunt. There was little point for they did not have the skills necessary for a seaborne battle. I personally took coins to the families who had lost warriors. Finally, I asked for men to crew the drekar. We had more than enough.

It was four days later that we sailed from Úlfarrston. I left Aiden in Cyninges-tūn. He and Basil had buildings and fortifications to plan. I had asked Siggi to stay in port. We only had two knarr left now, Siggi's, *'Troll'* and *'Weregeld'*. Until Bolli could make new ones I would not risk them. I had spent a day in port discussing how we might trap the drekar. Raibeart's *'Red Snake'* would be the bait. We would sail between Man and Mercia and then head west towards Hibernia passing Ynys Môn. We would turn and sail north as far as Ljoðhús. I hoped that the threttanessa would prove to be a tempting target. It would also give me the chance to speak with Thorfinn Blue Scar. He was the nearest thing we had to an older leader.

We sailed ten boat's lengths from each other in four lines. Raibeart and his drekar were always in sight but sometimes was a mere dot on the horizon. We were able to test our new formation to the south of Man when, at dusk on the first day, two drekar slipped from Duboglassio to try to take it. We were like greyhounds let loose. The crews had been eager to row and they took to their oars with a will. We began to overtake the two drekar. They could not turn to return to Duboglassio for we had a line of ships preventing them. When Raibeart began to turn his ship around they were almost trapped. They were saved only by the proximity of their harbour at Balley Chashtal. There were two towers there which protected the entrance. We could have entered and captured the drekar but that would have cost us men and it was not the men of Man we sought.

We hove to between the Angles' Sea and Balley Chashtal. We had sea anchors and we rode out the waves. They were gentler than I had seen them and I took that to be a good sign. The Allfather favoured our venture. Next day we sailed west. We saw no ships but Raibeart had told us, the previous night, that they had seen many small boats and knarr but they had fled at the sight of the dragon ship. This Harald Black Teeth had become a terror on the seas. He had made everyone fearful.

We headed north, passing Dyflin. I wondered where Gunnstein
Berserk Killer's drekar had been. His harbour had been empty. I would
ask him the next time I saw him. It would not do to have us both raiding
the same places. The world was wide and there were enough sheep for us
both to shear.

I was almost disappointed when we passed the mouth of the northern
river. It was where our land began. I had hoped to find these pirates
before now. They were elusive. We sailed up along the coast of Dál
Riata. They had been our enemies once. They were still not our friends
but they had learned the folly of fighting us. We anchored in the estuary.
We would be safe there where we slept aboard our drekar. When we
sailed north we passed the island ridden coast. This would be the place
where Harald Black Teeth might hide. We kept a good watch. The seas
were rougher than they had been close to Man and my captains needed
all of their skills to avoid the rocks which were like shark's teeth
guarding the coast.

It was dusk on the fourth day when we caught a glimpse of a drekar.
We had sailed up the craggy coast slowly looking for the masts of a
drekar. If we found one then we might find more. A sea fret had crept in
with the tide making it difficult to see anything. Guthrum Arneson's
sharp eyes spotted it for he was slightly above the sea fret on the top of
the mast. "Jarl, there is a drekar. It has a winged bird for its prow."

"Where away?"

"It is north-west, Jarl. It was only there briefly. I think it was heading
north-west."

"Keep watching for it." I turned to Erik Short Toe. Sail towards the
north-west."

"The fog and the rocks are a dangerous combination, Jarl." He was
ever the captain and concerned for his drekar.

"We will take it steadily. Haaken, shout to the other drekar and tell
them what we intend."

"Aye Jarl. I shall ask for Ran's permission too. I would hate for him
to take offence!"

The tension on my ship was almost unbearable. Suddenly Karl, the
ship's boy at the prow, shouted, "Rocks, dead ahead!"

Erik put the steering board hard over and said, "Jarl this is madness.
What good will it do to rip the hull from the finest ships in the northern
seas."

He never spoke to me like that. I relented, "You are right. Let us head
for Ljoðhús. Perhaps the Jarl can enlighten us and give us more
knowledge than we have."

"I am sorry I spoke out Jarl."

"No, Erik, you are right. The weather and the rocks are a bad combination." We led my line of ships away from the treacherous rocks and headed north.

As darkness fell so the fog cleared. The rocks and white water became easier to see than they had with the fog. We reached Ljoðhús two hours or so after our near disaster. The port was a natural harbour for it was protected by two islands which gave it calm waters. There was but one drekar at anchor. It was Thorfinn Blue Scar's ship. Although as big as mine I could see, even in the dark that it had not been well maintained. There was weed on the strakes and the dragon needed paint.

Erik noticed it too, "I would not sail across the harbour in that ship. Even from here she looks ridden with weeds and weevils."

"Aye, it might explain his laxity. Anchor as close to the shore as you can." Here they had no quay but had built a jetty which jutted out into the bay. Ships tied up to it and then disembarked before the ships were anchored in the harbour. "Haaken come with me. The rest of you stay aboard."

Jarl Thorfinn Blue Scar had aged since I had last seen him. He was white and bent over. He looked like Olaf the Toothless not long before his death. Was another jarl about to die? When he spoke his voice sounded weak too, "Jarl Dragonheart, an unexpected but pleasant surprise. Come, join me in my hall."

When we entered I saw why Harald Black Teeth had got away with his raids. The hall was filled with old men. If this was all that the Jarl had I was surprised that the outlaw had not taken his land and title from him.

I sat with the Jarl and Haaken at the long table. When last we had been here the hall had been thronged with warriors. In those days Jarl Thorfinn Blue Scar had been a powerful jarl. He had ruled these waters with a fist of iron. He was now a shell of his former self. I had been silent too long and my face had given away my thoughts. He gave a sad smile, "You are disappointed in the old man you see before you." I opened my mouth and he shook his head, "Do not deny it. I have always liked your honesty no matter how unpleasant it is. You are now as powerful as I once was. I believed I would rule forever and when I fell, in battle, I would leave a land ruled by my sons." He shook his head. I had three and now I have none. Two are carving out a land for themselves and the third was killed trying to catch an outlaw who betrayed me."

"Guthrum is dead?"

He nodded, "He sailed after Harald Black Teeth. He was ambushed and slain along with his crew." Sweeping a hand around the hall he said, "I have these ancient oathsworn and one drekar crew left. They hunt the spawn of Loki, Harald Black Teeth."

"I am sorry. That is why we are here. This Black Teeth has destroyed two knarr and their crew and I will have revenge."

His eyes brightened, "Then the gods have sent you. If any can end this pirate's reign it is you."

"Does he wish your land, Jarl?" It was a brutal question but I had to ask it. If he did then I could lay a trap here in this bay.

"I think he has greater ambitions." He looked at me. "Some of my men think he wishes to be jarl of the Land of the Wolf."

Haaken snorted, "And he could do that with just a couple of drekar?"

Thorfinn Blue Scar said, "He has three drekar but he draws the scum of the seas to his banner. Every outlaw and homeless Viking flocks to his banner. He is clever, Jarl Dragonheart, and he is cunning."

I wished I had brought Aiden for he would have seen the plan of this dangerous warrior. If he thought to take my land Haaken was right, he would need more than three drekar crew. Even with me away there were still more than enough to stop him. Ketil, Ulf, Wolf Killer, all would come to my home if danger threatened. He sought me. He had drawn me out. Now I knew why he had taken the knarr. He was tempting me into waters he knew and he would find some way to ambush me. I think Haaken was becoming more like Aiden for he gave me a knowing look. I gave the briefest shakes of the head. I did not want to speak openly about my suspicions. Who knew if Black Teeth had left spies in this hall of old men?

"Who commands your last drekar?"

"My sister's son, Halfdan Larsson. He sails the islands looking for him."

Haaken said, "But if Black Teeth has three drekar is that not a risk?"

"We cannot sit back and wait for him to come."

"Where should we hunt for him?"

"Badhl to the south of here. It is called Beinn na bhFadhla by the Hibernians. My sister's son will be close by. It is a flat island with many small bays. They keep a watch from the small hill in the middle. Halfdan will use the island they call Uist. You ask how he will catch him? My nephew hopes to take one drekar at a time. He hunts the hunter."

"How is his ship named?"

"*'Storm Bird'*. It has a white bird on a dragon's head at its prow." For the first time, he smiled, "With you to aid him then my kinsman has a chance. He is brave. I would that my sons had stayed. Then this dog, Black Teeth, would never have been able to do what he did. I lost my sons. They saw what you had achieved and chose to copy you."

"I am sorry for that."

Shaking his head he said, "It was not of your doing. The Weird Sisters punished me for my arrogance. When we defeated those on the mainland I thought I was king. I was wrong. Keep your sons and children close, Jarl Dragonheart. I feared that they would take my land from me. I was wrong and now they are gone."

I stood, "Never fear, Jarl Thorfinn Blue Scar. We will aid you in this. Your sons will return. Gunnar has an island of his own now. He has captured a mighty treasure from a church of the White Christ in the land of the Franks."

"I had heard. And now my second son Gunnstein joins him. It is *wyrd*. Will you not stay?"

"No, Jarl. We came here to let you know we were in your waters. We sail before dawn. We spied a dragon ship as we came north. It had a bird at the prow. Perhaps it was Halfdan."

"Was it black?"

"I know not."

"Beware then for Harald Black Teeth sails *'Eagles Heart'*. It is a black heart!"

"We will return when we have news."

We went to the jetty and hailed our drekar. As we waited Haaken said, "He tries to trap us. That was why we saw his drekar and it disappeared. He knew the waters and hoped to tear the keel from us."

"He is clever. If he has more than one drekar then he could take us one by one."

"Even so, Jarl, there are still warriors enough in our land to defeat him. Wolf Killer and Ketil not to mention Ulf Olafsson could defeat him on land no matter how many of these outlaws he leads."

As the drekar nudged next to the wooden jetty I said, "And what of Ragnar Ruriksson? If he joined with Black Teeth..."

"And we hunt the outlaw here leaving our home vulnerable. We should go home. We can wait for him there."

We clambered aboard the drekar, "No, Haaken, I have to trust our warriors at home. They have Aiden and Kara to help them and to use the spirits. We will end this and then return."

I had Erik row us close to the other drekar and told my captains what I intended. I just hoped that Halfdan had not been drawn into danger. I needed his knowledge.

We left as the sun began to rise. These waters were too dangerous to risk at night. I had *'Red Snake'* at the rear this time. She was no longer the bait. She was fast and Raibeart ap Pasgen was a clever captain. His orders were to take advantage of any mistake our enemy made. We sailed under half furled sails. When we needed speed then we would release our dragons. By noon we were close to the island which Jarl Thorfinn had told us of. Karl was at the masthead and he shouted. "Jarl I see a drekar, no, Jarl, there are three. There is a sea-fight!"

"Where away?"

"To the south, in the next bay!"

"Erik we will sail with *'King's Gift'*. We sail directly to the next bay."

"Aye Jarl!"

I went to the other side of the drekar. "Olaf Grimsson, you will sail with us to the next bay. Tell Asbjorn and Sigtrygg to sail south and cut off the escape of the three drekar." I was aware that as we were the closest inshore only we could see the ships.

As the sail billowed and we surged forward Haaken said, "What of Raibeart?"

"He will be as our sheepdog. If any drekar escapes then he will come to our aid."

I went to don my helmet and to prepare for war. Karl's voice drifted down to me. "Jarl there are three drekar attacking one!"

Halfdan had been caught. I hoped we would be in time. Maddeningly the rocks which lay before us stopped us taking the most direct course. We were less than four hundred paces from the battle but we might as well have been four thousand. My drekar was distinctive and as soon as he saw it Halfdan put *'Storm Bird'* over and took advantage of the wind. It would take him out of the bay. We were on a converging course. What none of them could see was Asbjorn and Sigtrygg as they raced along with the following wind to cut off the escape south. As we also had the wind we were not rowing and my men prepared for battle. I saw Harald Black Teeth, or, at least, the warrior in the fine armour at the stern of *'Eagles Heart'*. He carried an axe and stared over at us from beneath a helmet with a bird of some description on the top. I assumed it was an eagle.

Although Halfdan was under attack it was only from arrows. He had outmanoeuvred the other pirates. There were, however, three of them and they were all large drekar. I guessed that at least two of them had been Jarl Thorfinn Blue Scar's once. The four ships were pulling away from us as we had to turn slightly north to negotiate a rocky promontory.

"Jarl, look at *'Red Snake'*, she has the wind."

I watched as Raibeart deftly handled his lighter threttanessa and overtook us. He would be the first to reach Halfdan. He was too brave for his own good. I saw that the three ships of Harald Black Teeth were almost upon Halfdan. All four ships were using their oars but the arrows from the three drekar had thinned out the crew of *'Storm Petrel'*. They would catch him.

"Where are *'Crow'* and *'Odin's Breath'*?"

"They are tacking around now Jarl. The ships cannot escape south."

My captains were doing as I had asked but now I needed them to sail north. They would obey me and block the southern passage. It was up to me and the drekar of Ulf Grimsson. One of Black Teeth's drekar caught *'Storm Petrel'*. I saw the ropes snaking over. The other two sailed alongside the pirate drekar to use it as a bridge. At last, we could turn and Erik put the steering board over. I saw the rocks less than ten paces from us. We were that close to ripping out our hull. Raibeart had turned quicker and he laid his drekar alongside *'Storm Petrel'*. We now had a chance but Raibeart had the smallest crew. There had to be over a hundred and twenty warriors upon the three enemy drekar!

"Erik lay us beam on to the bows of *'Storm Petrel'*. We can use the stern of *'Red Snake'* to board."

I turned and shouted, "Tell Ulf to lay his drekar on the steer board side of *'Red Snake'*!"

Raibeart deserved his courage rewarding. We would support him. I led my men to the steerboard side.

"Shorten sail!"

As the sail was furled we lost way and bumped gently into the stern of *'Red Snake'* and the bows of *'Storm Petrel'*. I saw that Halfdan and his oathsworn were beleaguered at their stern. Raibeart and his men had formed a shield wall around the mast of *'Storm Petrel'*. I jumped to the steering board of Raibeart's ship. The ship's boys stood there with bows in hand. "Support your captain! Ulfheonar to the mast."

Raibeart was a popular warrior. Despite the fact that he was not born Norse he embodied everything my men admired in a warrior. Olaf Leather Neck led the charge across the deck. He and Rolf Horse Killer did not use their shields but swung their axes two handed. Normally this was dangerous, especially on a ship, but here they carved a path through the two sets of Black Teeth's men. Until the men from Ulf Grimsson's drekar boarded we would be outnumbered. Olaf's charge had cleared a space so that we could form a wall of warriors.

We were fighting against warriors who, like us, knew how to fight on a drekar. These were neither Franks nor Saxons and they fought hard. I had my shield and I blocked a blow from a hand axe. Ragnar's Spirit sliced down and bit into the shield of my opponent. Perhaps he was taken aback by my grey beard but he looked surprised at the power. I ripped it out and as his hand came forward I jerked my tip into his throat. More of my warriors followed us and I felt Cnut Cnutson and the men of

Cyninges-tūn add their weight to our back. The extra power pushed the enemy towards the gunwale. My men were fresh and they were strong. Warriors tumbled over the side as they fought to keep their balance.

Then I heard a shout, "Jarl the steering board!"

I glanced to my right and saw that Harald Black Teeth had moved his drekar and was now piling his men over the stern. Halfdan was now completely surrounded. We had to do something quickly. "Push!" I held my sword above my shield as did Haaken, Finni, Leif and Rollo. As our warriors pushed, the men whom we faced could not avoid the points of steel. They tried to move their heads out of the way but their feet slipped on the blood-covered deck and soon the last of those before us tumbled over the side.

"Cnut, support Halfdan. Ulfheonar, let us board the enemy!" The only hope we had was to threaten their drekar.

We leapt down on to the deck. Now that Harald Black Teeth had gone to the stern there were just two drekar to deal with at this side. Although more men were clambering across to us they were not the mailed warriors whom Harald Black Teeth led. We were reckless and we were wild. We swung our swords and axes before us as we moved quickly across the deck. I blocked a sword with my shield and brought my own weapon up into the gut of a warrior. I tore my blade out knowing that the edge had ripped through his stomach. I stepped across his body and dropped my head as a wildly swung axe came close to decapitating me. It glanced off my helmet. The uncontrolled swing left the warrior open to my sword. I stabbed him so hard that my sword came out of his back.

Sometimes men get lucky. Finni the Dreamer slipped on the guts of the warrior I had slain. As he did so a warrior with a spear darted forward. Finni might have been slipping but he had the reactions of a fox. He turned his head so that the spear clanged against it, stunning him. Before the warrior could strike again I swept my sword down. It sliced through his right wrist and his left forearm. Bright blood spurted and made the already slippery deck even more treacherous.

"Erik Eriksson, help Finni back to our ship." Finni the Dreamer had taken a hard blow and he was dazed. "Leif the Banner, guard my back!"

"Jarl! It is *'Crow'*!" Snorri pointed to the south where Sigtrygg was bringing *'Crow'* to our aid. Asbjorn still obeyed my orders and blocked the route south.

Then I heard a cry, it seemed to come from far away, "Jarl! We need help!" It was Cnut Cnutson.

"Back to *'Storm Petrel'*. Sigtrygg can deal with these." Although there were two drekar we had slain many already and with a fully crewed drekar, Sigtrygg would make short work of them. I hurried back to the *'Red Snake'*. It was too late for Halfdan. Even as Leif and I climbed back aboard the threttanessa I saw Harald Black Teeth as he slew the brave warrior and take his head. He flourished it before hurling it into the remains of the crew.

It enraged me. With my Ulfheonar I attacked the press of warriors who had surrounded Cnut Cnutson. I saw warriors who had come from Cyninges-tūn. They lay dead. Even as we closed with them the crew of *'Eagles Heart'* began to return to their ship. They had seen the approach of *'Crow'*. Harald Black Teeth would fight another day. Even as we slew the last of the men who remained on the deck of *'Red Snake'* I saw Harald Black Teeth laughing as his ship headed north and east. He could not flee south but he had the whole of the wild seas of the north in which to hide. I hacked down at the Viking who cried for mercy. He held his sword still and I sent him to Valhalla.

"Kill them all!" There was no point in keeping any warriors alive. These were the sweepings of every outlaw in the Isles of the North and beyond. They were treacherous killers with no honour. Harald Black Teeth had deserted them. They deserved nothing better.

By the time it was over the two drekar were charnel houses. We had just begun to strip the armour from the dead when Erik shouted, "Jarl, we are drifting on to the rocks!" I could see that the wind and current had taken us alarmingly close to the rock-filled shore.

"Men of Cyninges-tūn, back to our ship. Ulfheonar, we will stay and help the crew of *'Red Snake'*." Raibeart's crew were in a bad way. He had lost warriors and others were wounded.

I went across to the next drekar. Sigtrygg stood there. "I am sorry we were late, Jarl. We obeyed orders."

"You did right. Let us see if we can save these drekar for Jarl Thorfinn Blue Scar."

In the end, we simply did not have enough men. We salvaged *'Storm Petrel'* but only twelve crew remained. With Asbjorn's help, we saved another of the jarl's captured ships, *'Dragon'*. Harald Black Teeth had renamed it *'Serpent'*. The last one which had been called *'Whale of Ljoðhús'* had been renamed *'Scavenger'* it was not a good name for a ship and she had ripped her hull out on the rocks. Erik Short Toe said she had done it to avoid the shame of her new name. We spread the few men we had to each ship. We would have to rely on the winds to return to Jarl Thorfinn.

The battered fleet headed north, back to Ljoðhús. Our enemy grew ever more distant as he fled north. He would not risk these seas again.

Erik asked as the lights of Ljoðhús hove into view, "What will he do, Jarl?"

"I am guessing he will sail around the coast and head for Norway, Denmark or Frisia. As Thorfinn has kin in Norway I would say Denmark or Frisia. Perhaps he will go to Eoforwic. Who knows. He will have gold for he has taken many ships. He did not strike me as the kind of jarl who would share his profits. I think he will buy another drekar and find more men like the ones who now lie at the bottom of the sea. There are many such leaderless men. We have not seen the last of him but our waters will be safer now."

Jarl Thorfinn Blue Scar was happy to have his ships returned but it did not compensate for the loss of his men. "Halfdan was like a son to me." He shook his head. His eyes were red and hollow. He had the smell of death about him. "If you see my children say I beg them to come home. My hearth is empty as is my heart. I have built a land but it is not a home."

I looked around the deserted warrior hall, "Have you enough warriors to fend off an attack?" I knew he had many enemies.

"We have young men and boys. We are old but we can train them. You have taken away the danger to us. The Pictii do not like to risk the sea. We will survive."

"I will have my drekar keep watch on your sea lanes. If you need help then send to me. I am your ally."

"I know, Jarl Dragonheart. I know."

We stayed for six days ensuring that the ships, all of them, had suffered no damage and sharing out the mail and the weapons. The forty young boys and youths who were being trained by the old men would be well-armed. I hoped that they would have time to gain the skills which might save their lives.

As I boarded my drekar Jarl Thorfinn Blue Scar came to see me off. It would be the last time I would see him for he was dying. I think he knew that but I did not; I just suspected it. He clasped my arm, "As one father to another I tell you to hang on to your children. I used to believe that it was *wyrd* for them to fend for themselves. Now I do not think so. I would give all of my treasure for one of them to be with me now."

I nodded, "They may return. Who knows?"

He shook his head, "I shall die alone with my old warriors for company and soon we will be a name, a distant memory only."

Chapter 12

We had lost almost as many men fighting the outlaws as we had in Neustria. Our aid to our friend had hurt us. We still had enemies out there and they had been increased. I knew that Harald Black Teeth would remember me and seek revenge. As we headed south through stormy skies and seas I thought about the Jarl's words. They were a warning but surely I had heeded them already? I kept my family as close as I could. Even as the thought flitted into my head I knew that it was not true. Wolf Killer and I still had a problem. If I was dead I could not resolve it. The Jarl's words made me promise myself that I would spend time with my two sons and grandson. Who knew how long I had left in the Land of the Wolf.

I would send a message to the Jarl's sons. They should know how he felt. I owed it to him. They were successful and he was now alone. Was one the price you paid for the other? Would I pay a price for my Viking treasure? Time alone would tell.

Coen ap Pasgen was delighted with our news. Raibeart and his battered crew would rest awhile and repair their drekar. I suggested that they use *'Weregeld'* if they needed to trade. Raibeart nodded, "When I am certain that the repairs are almost finished I will trade with Dyflin and then visit Blue Scar." He shook his head, "It is sad to see a man grow old so quickly."

Haaken said, "Mayhap that is why it is better to die young with a sword in your hand."

As we headed back to Cyninges-tūn I was not so sure. I am not Norse born and I had had to learn the way of the warrior. It seemed to me that it was better to live as long as you could if you could for death was forever. I could barely picture Prince Butar now and Old Ragnar was just a ghost who flitted in and out of my dreams. When I thought of Olaf the Toothless it was the mountain which came to mind and not his toothless grimace.

Aiden and Kara both knew that something had affected me when I trudged through the gates of Cyninges-tūn. I found it easier to talk to the two of them rather than my wife. She was Christian and understood nothing of the way of the warrior and even less about the chasm between my son and me. I sat and told them all. Ylva plaited my hair for me and listened. She was growing quickly and was thoughtful. What else could be expected from the child of a volva and a galdramenn? Her time in Miklagård had matured her.

When I had finished Kara nodded, "You are right, father, spend time with the boys. Aiden has told me your dream and I think it is to do with all four of you. I cannot see how yet for there are too many parts I do not understand. As for Jarl Blue Scar, it is sad but you are not him. What you have built here will endure long after you are dead."

"That is not what the witch in the cave said. She told me that Hrolf's legacy would live on but not mine."

"You were not listening father. She said that his line would create kingdoms. That is not the same."

I knew that she was sweetening the witch's words to make them more palatable. I did not argue. I was weary and I needed my home and my wife.

Winter came far quicker than we could have expected. It came with the news that Jarl Thorfinn Blue Scar was dead. I did not need to send a message to his sons now. It would only upset them to know that they had not been with their father at the end and that he had needed them. It also caught our new mason, Basil, by surprise. He found that the slurry that turned to stone would not set in the cold. He had never experienced that. Miklagård did not have snow and frost. Luckily Aiden knew how to do so and the two of them worked together to make the process work. The new gatehouse was finished before the winter set in. He promised that he could lay stones in winter unless the ground was frozen. That had made Scanlan laugh for the ground was always frozen.

Aiden wagged a finger at him. "Then we shall keep the ground from freezing!"

Poor Scanlan was terrified, "You will use magic!"

"Of a sort. We will lay hay on the ground and that will keep the top pliable. There are such methods written in the books we found in Miklagård. My time there was not wasted."

And so my town became stronger. The stone gatehouse would be a strong point if we were attacked. Eventually, we would have a stone wall all the way around. We were safe and even more settlers arrived. They came from remote hillsides subject to bandits or they came from further afield having heard of this land of promise. We had peace and we had prosperity and those with skills sought work while others sought land and we had both. As winter approached I took Gruffyd and headed for Elfridaby. The ground was frozen but the snows had not arrived. The trees all had the gaunt look having just shed their leaves. I knew from Brigid that their black skeletal shape in the gloom of dusk terrified Gruffyd. I sensed his nervousness as we passed through Grize's Dale. I could not remember what had frightened me when I had been his age.

Then it came to me, wolves. That fear had disappeared when I had slain my first wolf. Gruffyd could not so easily dispel his fear.

"How is the bow coming along? We might be able to hunt with Wolf Killer."

"It is more powerful than the one I am used to. I can pull the string back but not as far as I should. Snorri has been teaching me. I can aim better now but I do not have the range the bow is capable of."

I was impressed with his knowledge of his weapon. He had been learning.

"You are young and you will become stronger. When we hunt I will let you eat the heart of the first animal we kill. You will gain its strength and part of its spirit will be in you."

"The Ulfheonar eat the heart of the wolf."

I nodded, "We are its kin and it is why we are the most feared warriors."

"My brother killed a wolf and I would too."

"You are not old enough nor are you strong enough," I said it flatly for there was little point in building up his hopes.

"I know. I tell you this, father so that you know I will work hard. I watched when Ragnar and I sailed with you. We both learned. Men follow you into danger which would terrify most men. I would lead men as you do."

I remembered Jarl Thorfinn Blue Scar and his regrets. When Wolf Killer had said the same thing I had dismissed his words. I would not make the same mistake twice. "Good, then you must watch but do not watch me only. Haaken leads in his way as does Olaf Leather Neck. Snorri is the master of scouts and all defer to him and his skill. A good leader knows how to use the skills of those who follow him." He nodded. I smiled as he jerked his pony's head up. His pony had a tendency to try to eat from the berry bushes. He did not allow it. "And a good leader must have a heart of ice. He cannot lose his temper nor can he fight wildly."

"Haaken said you went berserk once."

I felt myself reddening. Sometimes I cursed the songs of my friend. They highlighted my mistakes. "I did not go berserk. I fought hard to protect my oathsworn."

"Olaf Leather Neck goes berserk. I have seen it."

"No, you have not. You have seen Olaf lose his temper. That is why he would not make a good jarl but if you need a warrior to face overwhelming odds and not flinch then have him lead your men."

"Did you choose your men or did they choose you?"

My son's questions showed that he had been thinking. "At first I fought alongside those who were Ulfheonar and we followed others. Haaken and Siggi are two such. Then it was the warriors who became Ulfheonar."

"No, I mean others like Ketil and Raibeart. Many jarls would not make them leaders."

"How do you know?"

"Raibeart told me. He said you were the only Jarl who would have made him a jarl and Ketil said the same."

"I judge all men as I see them and how they act. Sometimes I make mistakes and that can be costly."

"Like Magnus the Forsworn."

I shook my head. He had heard all of these songs on our last voyage. "Aye like Magnus the forsworn. If you are a leader then men lose their lives because of such mistakes."

I was grateful as we crested the rise and saw, in the gloom of dusk, Elfridaby. I would have some relief from the interrogation. Ragnar ran out to meet us. I had not seen him since we had returned with the treasure. He had grown again. Garth followed behind.

"Grandfather! I can send an arrow two hundred paces!"

I saw Gruffyd hang his head. He could not manage that yet. "Good. You must show Gruffyd how to do that. He is younger than you but he is catching you up."

Ragnar grinned, "Of course cousin!"

Garth said, "And I have learned to use a slingshot, grandfather."

"Excellent! I have three young warriors to serve me!"

Ragnar looked up at me. "Do you stay long, Jarl?"

"I have no reason to hurry home."

"Good, then we can hunt! Father has new men and there are some good hunters amongst them. They are like Snorri and can smell game!

"Then we shall hunt!"

Elfrida was no longer the waif-like girl who had been taken from King Egbert. She was now a woman grown. She had been the best wife that Wolf Killer could have chosen. I thanked the Norns and their threads. They had woven well. She waited outside her hall for me. When I dismounted she threw her arms around me. "Thank you, Jarl for looking after my son. He has not stopped talking about the raid and how brave you were." She lowered her voice, "You showed no favouritism to Gruffyd and I think he appreciated that."

I looked at her, "He is my grandson. He is of my blood. I treat them all the same."

She looked up as Wolf Killer approached and mumbled, "Not all see it that way."

Wolf Killer inclined his head, "I was sorry to hear about Jarl Thorfinn Blue Scar."

"Aye, he was treated badly by some of those who were supposed to serve him. A jarl must choose his men wisely."

"I know I have learned that to my cost."

Elfrida put her arm around Gruffyd and said, "Come, let us go and see where you shall sleep this visit."

She knew that her husband and I needed to talk. "Ragnar says you have new men."

"And you are wondering if they can be trusted?"

"Let us say I worry having seen the results of a single bad apple. Magnus the Forsworn, Harald Black Teeth and Hermund the bent are three such."

"And I have been cautious. The frontier is now Seddes' Burgh. Einar Thordson is master there. His men have to constantly watch for enemies. I sent the new men to serve with him. He had two slain whom he thought were not to be trusted. There are six of whom he approves. I intend to bring three of those into my hall for my warriors are fewer in number these days."

I nodded, "That is wise. Ragnar says that there are some good hunters amongst them."

"There are. They are the three I would have here for they remind me of Snorri. There is a forest to the south of Seddes' Burgh and we have hunted there."

"I would hunt with you and Gruffyd too but I would not travel that far. My bones feel the cold more than once they did and I do not relish sitting astride a horse for that long."

"You need not. When I was told that you were coming I invited Einar Thrandson to visit. He will bring the new men. He has not sworn an oath to you yet."

"He is your man."

"And I serve you, Jarl Dragonheart. I know that we butt heads sometimes. That is in the nature of fathers and sons. I see that now with Ragnar. But I serve you and know that I would have nothing if it were not for you. You rescued me when I was a child and you helped me take my wife. I am loyal."

"I know, I know."

He led me into his hall. He had improved it over the years but mine was both bigger and more comfortable. Perhaps I was getting old. The fire, however, burned well and I warmed myself beside it. A slave took my cloak and Wolf Killer poured us some ale. "Is Aiden not coming?"

"No, for he and our new mason are busy making our walls stronger. He is turning them from wood to stone. The attacks by Ragnar Ruriksson made me look to my own defences. I do not have the swamps and low lying land that you do. I have the Water and the mountain. It will not be cheap to make us stronger but it will be worth it."

"Have you heard where the Frisians fled?"

"The last we heard he was heading for the court of King Egbert. I do not think we have heard the last of him."

"Einar has made the walls of Seddes' Burgh harder to scale. There is a double ditch and a step for archers to use. These new men who have come are good archers. Two of them are the equal of Snorri."

"That is high praise indeed."

"I know. I hope they can teach Ragnar when they join me."

"When will that be?"

"At Yule, if the roads are still open. So far they have always been passable even in the worst winters but I know that it is a mistake to make assumptions."

"You are learning my son."

The four of us went hunting before Einar and his new warriors arrived. We went with Siggi Flat Nose. He was the most senior of Wolf Killer's oathsworn. He was to Wolf Killer what Haaken was to me; his oldest and most trusted warrior. I noticed that he viewed Ragnar almost as his own child. His wife had been taken by the coughing sickness before they could have children and he had never remarried. He was rarely more than three paces from Ragnar all that day.

We hunted deer. This was the time of year to do so. When winter came and food was scarce some deer would die. It was better that we take the weaker, slower ones now so that the herd would be stronger. We did not hunt for the pleasure. It was to hone skills and to find food. The more skilful the prey then the better it was for us. A man was a harder beast to hunt. Wolf Killer had a large forest to the north and west of his home. We had passed through part of it on our journey. The trees were close together and hunting would be challenging. Two of Wolf Killer's men held our horses as we entered the wood.

I allowed my son, Wolf Killer, to lead for this was his land and he knew the trails. Ragnar went by his side followed by Siggi Flat Nose. I walked behind Gruffyd and Garth who held his slingshot. I had hunted enough in my life. If I did not kill then it would not be something which would worry me. I did not need my skills improving. This way I could watch my young son and his technique. I saw him and Garth watching

Ragnar and emulating him. Ragnar, in turn, watched Wolf Killer. They placed their feet. They did not step. When Wolf Killer stopped and sniffed they did so too. I smiled. They would not know yet how to use their noses but when we spoke of this later we would tell them what they had smelled. We carried our bow and an arrow in one hand. The other we held out before us. That way we used the sense of touch.

I was slightly to the side of the others. My fingers touched a wet leaf. I smelled my finger. A stag had marked his territory. I clicked my tongue. The others stopped and turned. I rubbed my finger and thumb together and sniffed. I pointed at the leaf. Wolf Killer nodded and began to angle more to the left. I had the trail. They moved through the trees. I moved my bow and arrow into my left hand. I had to be ready to knock an arrow and loose in a flash. There were not just deer in these woods; wild boar roamed too. I had had to deal with wild boars before. I had a son and grandson to protect.

Wolf Killer stopped. He had the scent of something. He readied his bow and Ragnar and Gruffyd did the same. Garth put a stone in his slingshot. Siggi and I watched, not ahead, but to the side. The hunt was for the young ones. We watched them. The small herd had been behind a stand of elder. They must have caught the scent of man for they leapt. It caught both Ragnar and Gruffyd by surprise. Their arrows flew and struck the older hind but they were not mortal wounds. Garth was more accurate. He managed to catch the deer on the side of the head and it staggered as it fled. The deer took off through the forest leaving a trail of blood as she ran.

"Follow her and end her misery." Wolf Killer's voice was harsh. The three ran and we followed.

"Do not be harsh on them, Wolf Killer. They had little time to react."

"You taught me to be silent and ready, father. Should I not do the same?"

I said, quietly, "And you have forgotten when you did the same on the slopes of Snaefell? When Snorri had to chase after the doe and finish her off."

I saw realisation strike his face, "I was young."

"As are these two. The third had but a slingshot but he did not flinch and hit the prey. Praise what they do right and not what they do wrong!"

When we reached them we saw that they had found her and Ragnar had slit her throat to end her suffering. Siggi nodded his approval. "Now take her heart. You two slew her, you should share in the victory."

The two cousins looked at each other. I saw the apprehensive looks on their faces. They did not wish to make a mistake. I took out my hunting knife and handed it to Gruffyd. "This has a good edge. Cut her open and find the heart."

He nodded and took the knife. It was sharp and, as he ripped up her middle the intestines and guts flooded out. I saw his face as he gagged but he bit back and carried on. The smell would be vile but it was a rite of passage. When he had opened the beast Ragnar took his own knife and said, "Thank you, cousin. I will find the heart." He put his hand and knife inside and with one slice brought out the heart.

He was about to bite into it when Siggi said, kindly, "It will be better if it is cooked. The heart of the wolf you eat raw but not the deer. I will get a fire going while you take out the rest of the guts. We will leave those as an offering to the forest."

As they did so I smiled, "Olaf Leather Neck would think it a waste to let such food go back to the forest. When Olaf hunts then nothing remains."

Once the deer was gutted and the fire was going the heart was speared on a branch to cook. Wolf Killer and I found a sapling which we cut to carry back the deer. Wolf Killer smiled. "You are right, father, they did well. I had forgotten Snaefell and the deer. That seems a lifetime ago."

"As does my time in the mountains with old Ragnar. We seem to have lives which we live and then move on to another life."

As they watched the heart being cooked Garth said to me, quietly, "My stone hit the deer too, grandfather. Can I not eat of the heart?"

I realised that he had been overlooked. "Of course you can. You boys share the heart with young Garth here. He too hunted."

Ragnar grinned, "Of course, little brother. Come and join us. Three is a lucky number anyway!"

The boys enjoyed the cooked deer heart more than they would have the raw variety. All three swelled with pride as they ate it although I noticed that they did not eat it all. We let them carry the carcass back to the horses and with it slung over the back of the spare mount they led it back to the hall.

Einar and his ten warriors arrived three days later. We had hunted in the meantime but not had any success. Sometimes it happened that way. We had had some success and the boys were happy. Einar and his men had walked from Seddes' Burgh. I was intrigued by that. We rode whenever we could.

I had met Einar but that was before his elevation to jarl. He had a short mail byrnie and an open helmet. His sword was shorter than mine. His shield bore a device; it was a wild boar with red eyes. He had been one of my son's Wild Boars and taken that device for his own. That was good. He was young; about the same age as Raibeart. That too was as it should be. He could gather young warriors around him. That had been the way with Prince Butar and Jarl Thorfinn Blue Scar. He would make mistakes but so long as he survived then he would learn from them.

He dropped to one knee before me and bowed his head, "I come, Jarl Dragonheart, to be oathsworn. I serve your son and I would serve you."

I took out my sword. I saw the eyes of his men widen as they saw the legendary blade. I held the hilt for him to hold. "Then swear on this, Jarl Einar Thordson. It is Ragnar's Spirit but know that the sword holds all oaths as binding."

"Like you, lord, I swear I shall never be forsworn." He grasped the hilt. "I swear to serve Jarl Dragonheart and to give my life for him!"

I reversed the sword and held it aloft, "And I swear that you shall be of my clan and we will protect you and yours."

He stood and beamed. It gratified me that he was pleased. This had not been done for effect. He had meant it. "Let me introduce my new warriors. These are three of those who would serve my lord, Wolf Killer." He gestured and three warriors stepped forward. "This is Ulf Blue Eyes." I could see where he had got his name. His eyes were the blue of the Middle Sea and were striking. "This is Oleg the Wanderer." His face had something of the look of the Rus Vikings about him. He had high cheekbones and slightly narrowed eyes. "This last is Erik Sigtryggson." Erik was the youngest of the three. The other two both had fine mail and swords but Erik had just a metal-studded leather byrnie and a short sword.

"I look forward to hearing your stories this night." They nodded, "Tell me Einar, why did you walk rather than ride?"

His face became serious. "We found the trail of warriors not far from the burgh. They went over rough ground and it would not have suited horses."

Wolf Killer asked, "Did you catch them?"

"No lord. They took the high pass east and went over rocks where we could not track them. Oleg and Ulf are fine trackers but even they could not follow over rocks."

I smiled to myself. Snorri and Beorn would not have lost them. Their heads would now be planted on spears as a warning to other transgressors.

"We will ride east on the morrow and see if we can spy them. I like not strange warriors this close to my home."

That evening we had a fine feast. We heard stories from the three new warriors. Ulf had served a Viking of Orkneyjar, Harald Iron Hand. I had not heard of him but then I had rarely journeyed north. I would ask

Siggi about him. Oleg lived up to his name. He had been a Rus Viking and had been down to Miklagård. I lost track of the jarls he had served and how he came to serve my son but the story was interesting. Erik had served Hakon the Bald in Dyflin. When he said that I became wary. Many of the men who had served Hakon the Bald were men without honour but as his tale unfolded I saw that he had left before we had scoured Dyflin of the rats. He had ended up in Dorestad and taken passage on a knarr which had brought him to Eoforwic. He had not liked it there and headed west. He had done well to travel the high lands alone and safely.

I enjoyed their stories as did Ragnar and Gruffyd. Their adventures and the places they had seen made them even more eager to go A-Viking again. The next day the weather turned stormy. What began as rain soon became sleet. I went to my son and Elfrida. "I think Gruffyd and I will return home. I like not the look of this weather."

"But I was going to go hunting again. Einar and his men are good hunters. It would do my brother and son good to see such hunters. They will be disappointed."

"There is another reason, Wolf Killer, the news of warriors in the eastern fells worries me. If they were followed and they lost their pursuers then who knows where they are. I will get home and organise a hunt for them."

"Then bring Brigid and your family here for Yule. We often come to you but if you come here then we can go hunting again. Perhaps we will hunt the wolf. There are many in the eastern fells."

"Very well then we shall do so."

Einar and his new men also tried to persuade us to stay. They all seemed very eager for us to see their skills. I was touched that they wished to spend longer in my company. As we headed west, wrapped in our cloaks against the sleet which began to turn to snow Gruffyd asked, "Why could we not stay? I liked those new men and I would hunt with them."

"And I wanted to stay too but there is danger in the land and I am Jarl Dragonheart. I cannot sit back and enjoy the hunt. I must act."

"I thought being a jarl meant you did as you wished and answered to no man."

"It is the opposite son; you answer to all men for as much as they serve you then you serve them."

We rode in silence for a while and then he held out a piece of bone he had taken from the deer. "I shall carve this into a wolf when I get home. I would have had a second if we had hunted."

I sighed, "We will hunt at Yule. You will be stronger then and we will be prepared for the inclement weather."

It was a full-blown blizzard and it was dark as we rode through the gates. Winter had come in one day. My son was blue from the cold and I received an even colder blast from my wife's eyes. I had shaken my head, "He is to be a warrior. He will have to endure much worse when he is older."

"If you keep him out in a blizzard then he will get no older! You have not the sense of a chicken sometimes!"

The thought came into my head that being a jarl counted for little in his own home. I suspect even Uhtric would be spoken to more civilly than I.

Chapter 13

Most of my men were in their homes preparing for the winter. They stayed there behind well-made walls and with roaring fires. The blizzard we encountered on the way home was just the first of a series which lasted six days. We were forced to stay inside our homes. The first day that they relented and we just had empty grey skies I went abroad. Since I had returned from Elfridaby I had had a prickling sensation at the back of my neck. When I mentioned it to Aiden he told me not to ignore it. Snorri lived just on the other side of the Water with his new wife, Seara. They had married when Snorri returned a rich man. He had cleared a place in the forest and they had a fine house. It was close to where I had my first hall. I took Cnut Cnutson and Rollo Thin Hair with me.

"Snorri, Einar Thordson tracked some men to the eastern fells and then lost them on rocks." He gave a smile. "I know you would not have lost them. Since then the snow has come and covered whatever tracks they might have left but I would know if they were still in my land."

He turned to his wife. She had been Eystein's widow and was a hardy woman. She nodded, "Will you be away the night?"

Snorri shook his head, "We look for sign. There are but four of us. I will be back before dark."

"Then I will have a stew ready for when you return."

He mounted his pony and pointed to the east. "If they came from Elfridaby and wished to stay hidden then they would avoid the Water. Did you see any signs as you came through Grize's Dale?"

"I confess I did not but Gruffyd was questioning me."

"Then we start there." He rode with his head leaning forward. We three were almost superfluous. He needed us not. He suddenly stopped, halfway up the trail which headed to the ridge above the Water. He knelt and then rose. "They came this way."

"They were heading for Cyninges-tūn?"

"Perhaps. We will backtrack a way and see if we can see further sign."

Rollo was inquisitive and could not help asking, "How did you know they had been here? I see nothing."

Snorri pointed, "Do you see how the snow is shallower here? Men walked along it and then the snow fell a little deeper. There were a number of them else it would not have been so obvious."

"Could it not be men from our town?"

He pointed to his own house hidden by the trees but just two miles up the valley. "Had they come in daylight then I would have seen them and they would have called in to speak to me. This was someone who wished to remain hidden. I have dogs and they bark. They have not barked at night. Someone made sure they were well away from my home."

He remounted and we went quicker for he could now see the track. I was more aware of it but had he not identified it then it would be hidden still. We dropped down to the other side of the ridge and the air became colder. The ground was still frozen here in the lee of the ridge. We came to a clearing and Snorri dismounted and, using his seax, chipped the snow away from a particularly flat piece of ground. We dismounted too and we saw the black shape of a fire begin to appear. He continued to clear it away as he said, "They camped here. It was after the first snow, the blizzard when you returned to Cyninges-tūn, Jarl. This other snow has fallen since." He raked his seax through the blackened fire. "They ate squirrel." He walked around the edge of the clearing. Occasionally he would kneel down and scrape away. Suddenly he jumped up and went to a bramble bush, now devoid of its leaves he spied something clinging to the shrivelled uneaten berries. He came back to me holding a tiny piece of cloth torn by the bramble thorns. "Well, Jarl, unless I miss my guess this came from a Danish cloak. It is the red cloth they like and which is made in Eoforwic."

I looked at it and he was right. He had had sharp eyes to spot it. "How many?"

He looked at the ground and said, "No less than eight and no more than twelve." He saw me phrasing my next question. "They went north. The second blizzard was worse than the first. They would seek shelter."

"That could be anywhere. There are many farms such as yours, Snorri. No one travels the roads and trails now. They could be anywhere."

"Not quite Jarl. My neighbours are old Einar down towards the Water and Sven who lives above my farm. I visit them each day and they call in to see my wife. Unless they have taken three or four farms then they will have to be somewhere more remote." He looked at Rollo. "Your father Audun Thin Hair lives at the Rye Dale. No one lives within a mile or more of him."

"That is half a day from here and is not close to Cyninges-tūn. Why would they go there?"

"I know not but eight to twelve Danes loose in this land cannot be good."

"Rollo you and Cnut go to see your father. You can spend the night there. Even if they have not been close it is good that he has warning. If not there, Snorri, then where?"

"Elter's farm by his Water is remote. He lives there alone with his family. It is close to Cyninges-tūn and yet far from others."

"If we ride hard we can be there by dark."

Snorri looked uncomfortable. "I would not be happy leaving my wife alone if there are Danes in the land."

"You are right. Then we will go there on the morrow."

Rollo and Cnut set off across the top of the ridge. They would tell Arne Thorirson and Harland Windarsson at Windar's Mere. Even though it was winter and few warriors would stir we still kept a watch.

I left Snorri at his farm. As he dismounted I said, "You have enough coin now to hire warriors of your own, Snorri. They could help with the farming too. I like not your wife being alone."

"She does, lord. When the door is closed and the fire banked up she nestles in my arms. She and Eystein had great plans. There will be a time when she is ready to face the world but it is not yet. I am new to this world of women but I am learning. She is like a wounded deer at the moment. She needs care and, I think, she needs me. As for the warriors. That is a good idea. Perhaps I will buy her a couple of slaves too."

I reached home before dark and told Karl One Leg my news. He nodded, "I will make sure we keep a good watch and look for anything which is unusual." He now had more warriors to watch the walls for I now paid for the old warriors who could no longer fight in the shield wall to be the watch. We also paid for some youths who would use the money to buy weapons and helmets and then they would become warriors. Karl made sure that they were well trained. The treasure might have brought unwelcome intruders but we used it wisely. No one wore golden armour! I used some of his watch to send messages to the Ulfheonar who lived close by. Snorri and I would not go alone the next day and we would go prepared for war.

Before I went to my hall I spoke with Aiden. He and Kara frowned. "We have not sensed danger. Perhaps they use magic to hide from us."

"Perhaps. We will have to find them the old fashioned way. Snorri and I will summon the Ulfheonar. The wolf hunt will be soon anyway. This will be a good opportunity for us to hunt men."

"Be careful, father. If they have magic then your swords might not avail you."

I held up the dragon charm, "But I have this and there is magic here too." I patted my sword hilt.

Aiden smiled, "True and I feel better knowing that the dragon is around your neck."

It was dark when I entered my hall. I had helped the stable slave to care for Storm Rider. He had done well. Brigid was worried when I entered, "Is there danger?"

I had learned not to lie to her. It always came back to haunt me. "There may be but the fact that we are aware of it means it is under control."

"Can I come with you?"

I looked at an eager Gruffyd, "Go where?"

"Tomorrow, when you go to find the danger!"

I was going to ask him how he knew and then thought better of it. He was a clever boy and could work things out better than any child I had ever met. "No, for it is winter and we are uncertain where the danger lies. I cannot afford to have a warrior watching out for you." I knew not if that satisfied him but he was silent and argued no more.

The weather warmed just a little and we left under a sleet filled sky and clouds scudding in from the south. Olaf Leather Neck, Rolf Horse Killer and Erik Eriksson accompanied Snorri and me. Beorn lived along the way and we would pick him up as we went. Snorri waved a hand at the sleet which was almost horizontal. "This will hide the enemies' tracks. We will have to look for other clues."

Olaf Leather neck nodded, "And you have the nose and eyes to find them." He rode, not with his normal two handed Danish axe but a shorter skeggox. He could use it on the back of a horse. We wore no mail but all had leather armour studded with metal and we had two swords each.

Elter lived by a small Water in a remote valley. I could never work out why more people did not live there but, as our horses sank up to their withers in the boggy patches by the becks and streams I began to understand why. "There will be no tracks here Jarl but I see smoke ahead. That is a hopeful sign. Elter still lives." The grandfather came out to greet us. He was a rugged old man and seemed more like a rock than a Viking. He and his wife lived there with their three daughters. All three had been widowed in wars against our foes and there were eight small children there too.

"It is rare to see you in winter, Jarl."

"I think there is a party of Danes in our land. Have you seen them or any sign of strangers?"

He laughed and pointed at the muddy legs of our horses, "If they came here they would soon turn around. This land protects me and my family. I have been hunting every day and you are the first to have visited since the blizzards began. I know all that goes on in this land. I have lived here since I first came with you Jarl. I would know if there was danger."

"I am relieved. Send one of your grandchildren for help if there is danger or if you spy anything."

"Aye Jarl."

We turned around and I began to head back to my hall. Snorri halted. "Jarl, if we ride to the top of the fell of Lough Rigg then we may be able to see the Rye Dale."

"A good idea and it will save us having to go back through that bog!" We passed the tiny tarn beneath the gaunt fells and then headed up the twisting path which led to the top of the whale-shaped hill. It was not a pleasant ride but at least it was drier than the boggy morass which acted as a moat around Elter's Waite.

It was the middle of the afternoon by the time we led our horses up the last few steps to the top of the windswept and desolate fell. We were thankful that the sleet and rain had ceased, at least temporarily. We could see across to the Grassy Mere and the Water of the Rye Dale.

Snorri had the best eyes and he said, "I see smoke coming from the farm of Audun Thin Hair. He must be safe."

Olaf took some dried fish from his saddlebags and gave us each a piece. It would keep us going. "Where else might they be Snorri? Think you they may have gone back?"

"If Wolf Killer's men saw them heading east and yet we found tracks close to Cyninges-tūn then it is safe to assume that they are determined and they seek something over here. They have skirted our walls. They are waiting for something or perhaps the sudden bad weather changed their plans."

Rolf Horse Killer asked, "Are they serving Ragnar Ruriksson? They could mean harm to you or your family Jarl."

"Karl One Leg has the walls and gates guarded. It would take a wraith to get through and with Aiden and Kara watching too then I doubt that even a wraith would manage it."

Leif the Banner spat out a bone, "Then why else? Revenge? We have hurt the Danes before now."

Snorri had been watching the east, "I would say the treasure drew them here. We have slaves in the mines who were warriors. Some were Danes. These could be kinsmen come to rescue their comrades and steal our treasure. It is known that you are generous, Jarl and that treasure is shared out. Think of the farms where they could reap a rich reward for a little work."

"Perhaps but we do not know! How can we guard every remote farm and home?"

"Over there, two riders moving towards us!"

We mounted and, drawing our swords rode down the slope to meet them. It soon became obvious that it was Rollo and Cnut. We urged our horses down the slope. We met them in the lee of a rock. The rain had begun while we were eating and was now hurtling at us from the east; it felt like ice.

"Jarl, my father is safe but his dogs barked three nights since. He found the signs of men passing to the west."

"Did he see anything?"

"No, Jarl."

I looked at Snorri, "We passed no one. Where are they?"

Snorri nodded slowly, "There is but one place. Myrddyn's cave!"

The one place I did not want to go was Myrddyn's cave. There the ancient wizard's spirit dwelt and these Danes had hidden there. I knew it now with every bone in my body. The hairs on the back of my neck prickled. I grasped my dragon amulet.

Even Olaf Leather Neck looked apprehensive, "Should we send for Aiden?"

Snorri shook his head, "They could be gone. They have sheltered there because of the weather. It is easing. They could move and we will lose them. Even I cannot track them through a bog and there is a bog between here and the iron mines. We have to face the cave." He looked at me and shook his head, "There is no other way, Jarl."

"I know. Let us go then and face our destiny."

As we headed down the slope I was just glad that I had not brought Gruffyd else he would perish along with his father and his oathsworn. The cave was a sinister place full of magic and the spirits. Aiden had warned me of the magic possessed by our enemies and I had ignored him. Would I now pay with my life?

The twisting path descended down the southern side of the fell. The cave had always been important to us. It had been there that Wolf Killer had killed his wolf and there that the spirit of the dead wizard had appeared. I found myself gripping my dragon as we descended. Men I could fight. There was no warrior whom I feared but spirits and magic were a different matter. All of my dreams had a cave in them and black holes into which I fell. This was not a dream; this was an actual black hole. The light was rapidly fading for days were never long at this time of year. I wondered if we would reach the cave before dark.

We finally descended close enough to see the cave. We had some shelter from the rain as we moved along the side of the rocky rigg. Whatever sun there had been was disappearing to the west. Snorri dismounted in a jumble of rocks and scrubby bushes. He tied the reins of

his horse to one and drew his bow. The rest of us emulated him. We had
no bows but we were all well-armed. I drew my sword and seax. Cnut
and Rollo were the only ones with their shields. They stepped forward
and followed Snorri. The wind was still coming from the south and east.
It would not take our smell to the cave. It would sweep it back up to the
top of the Lough Rigg. If the Danes were in the cave they would have a
sentry. Any sentry would wait beneath the overhang of the rocky roof,
sheltered from the worst of the weather. Snorri edged around the path
which led there.

Suddenly he stopped and he handed his bow to Cnut. Drawing a
dagger he slipped to the ground and disappeared from sight. Cnut, Leif
and Rollo moved slowly forward and we followed. Snorri reappeared and
took his bow. He waved us forward. The sentry lay with his throat cut. I
could see a faint glow from inside the cave. I knelt to examine the
warrior. He had four warrior bands and his face was tattooed. It
confirmed that he was a Dane as Snorri had surmised. If the others were
the same then these were not just a band of young warriors out for an
adventure. These knew what they were doing. These were experienced
warriors and here for a purpose.

Snorri silently entered the cave. It turned back on itself. The Danes
would be at the far end. I glanced to the left where I saw firelight
flickering off the dark black pool which stood there. That was where the
spirit of the ancient wizard had risen and I found myself pressing into the
opposite side of the cave. The rocks beneath my feet were treacherous
and I had to put thoughts of the dead pool from my mind as I
concentrated upon keeping my feet. The sounds of the wind and the sleet
abated and I could hear the murmur of conversation ahead. They were
within. The dead sentry had confirmed this but their voices told us that
they were still awake. Snorri paused and we all stopped. I sniffed the air.
I could smell wood smoke but not horses. The men had come on foot.

Snorri readied an arrow. He slid to the ground and Cnut and Rollo
stepped up to ready their shields. Leif and Olaf Leather Neck were at my
side. We moved across the stones to stand behind our men with the
shields. We could see nothing but it was obvious that Snorri could. He
stood and released first one and then a second arrow. He turned and
nodded. Cnut and Rollo ran. We followed.

There had been nine Danes. Two now writhed on the floor of the
cave with arrows in them. The others were grabbing weapons and
helmets to face us. I had no time to think of magic for we had Danes to
slay. As we ran towards them I shouted. "A prisoner if we can!"

The seven who remained stood with their backs to the fire. They
would sell their lives dearly. These were warriors and surrender would

never enter their heads. Cnut and Rollo used their shields to drive a wedge between the Danes. As a Dane swung his axe at Cnut Cnutson's unprotected right side I lunged forward and my sword deflected the axe to the ground. I stabbed at him with my seax. He brought the haft of his axe across his body to block the strike. I swung my sword sideways. His left leg was unprotected and my sword bit into his upper thigh. It struck bone and stopped. I ripped it back and he fell to the ground.

A sword came at me from my right. I sensed rather than saw it and I barely had time to bring my sword around to block it. The Dane bundled into me and we both fell to the ground. He stank of stale sweat and old seal oil. His lank and greasy beard pressed into my face. He turned his head and opened his mouth. I knew what he intended, he would bite off my nose. At the same time, he was trying to bring his sword up. It was still locked with mine and our hands and swords fought for space to slide a blade into the other. His breath stank worse that he did. I noticed that he had filed his teeth to make them look frightening. He raised his head so that he could bring it down on my nose and tear it from my face. As he did I lowered my chin. His blackened teeth struck my face mask. He roared in pain and his back arched a little. I brought my seax up and began to worm it under his right armpit. He tried to wriggle away but our swords were still locked. I felt flesh and I pushed harder. He roared again and I twisted as I pushed. It slid past a bone and my hand stopped at his armpit. I pushed even harder, driving the seax as far into his body as I could make it go. Suddenly his body went limp. I pushed him from me and stood.

Rollo was lying injured but the rest stood. The Danes were finished. The one whose leg I had hacked lived yet. His hand tried to creep across to his axe so that he could die with a weapon in his hand. I walked to him and put my foot on his hand. "Before we send you to Valhalla you will talk. Leif, tie something around his leg!" I did not want him bleeding to death before he had talked. Leif tied a leather thong he had hacked from a shield around the top of the Dane's leg.

The tattooed warrior spat out a gobbet of blood, "Just kill me and end it."

"Why are you here? Who sent you?"

He laughed although it was a weak laugh for he was dying, "You steal the greatest treasure, the tax gold of the Franks and you ask why we come? I thought you were clever. For the gold!"

Snorri asked, "How did you think you would steal it? There are nine of you."

"We managed to hide from you for half a month did we not?" He grinned. He too had blackened teeth which had been filed and stained.

"You celebrate the feast of the White Christ. Then we would have had your gold!"

"Who is your leader?"

"I am the leader. I am Sven the Merciless."

"Who is your Jarl?" He said nothing. I reached down and tore open his tunic. There he had a golden wolf such as my Ulfheonar wore. I ripped it from his neck. "Where did you get this?"

For the first time, he looked worried. "Give it back to me and end my life."

Olaf Leather Neck snarled, "What if I take your balls first and then hack off your right hand! Answer the Jarl. Who sent you?" He took out his seax and knelt next to the Dane's groin.

"Ragnar Ruriksson gave us the golden wolf and said it would protect us against your magic. It had a spell laid upon it by a witch. He told us we could keep the gold if we stole it. I have told you all now keep your word, Jarl and let me die."

I nodded. Olaf put the axe in his hand and then ripped his seax across his throat.

I turned to Snorri, "How is Rollo?"

"The cut was to his leg. It will heal."

I pointed to the fire. "Let us be certain. Use a brand to seal the wound."

Leif and Olaf held Rollo as Snorri pressed the red hot piece of burning wood into the wound. There was a hiss and the smell of burning hair and flesh but Rollo gritted his teeth and said not a word.

"We will leave as soon as Rollo can stand. We will spend the night at his father's farm. Tomorrow we will search the bodies."

Erik Eriksson came over to me and took out his own wolf. "The two are close, Jarl."

"Aye but not identical. Aiden did not make this." I took out my seax and began to scrape at the gold. Ours were made of solid gold. I soon discovered that this one was a thin layer of gold on top of iron. "This is a cheap copy."

Snorri finished bandaging Rollo's leg and said, "Yet it had enough magic to hide them from Aiden and Kara."

"You are right. This Ragnar Ruriksson must be dealt with."

Snorri rode ahead to warn Audun Thin Hair that we returned. They were ready for us with hot food and ale. Rollo's mother had prepared a bed for him. Rollo was soon asleep but we sat around the fire talking of the Danes. Rolf Horse Killer asked, "What did he mean the feast of the White Christ? Why would that be a good time to take the gold?"

Olaf Leather Neck added another log to the fire, "The Ulfheonar would all be in their own homes at the shortest time of the year. Men would not wear armour and the Jarl and his family would be celebrating in his hall. The Jarl's lady is Christian and it is known we give gifts and celebrate."

Snorri said, "There is something else, Jarl. Those Danes made for that cave. They avoided all but Audun here. They knew about the Yule celebration and the gifts that are given." He held up his golden wolf. "And there is this. Someone has examined a wolf amulet or seen one at least. When we fight they are not seen and we never leave an Ulfheonar, dead or wounded, on the field. The only time someone can see one of these is at a feast. Whoever described this to Ragnar Ruriksson has seen one."

My scout was right. When we had celebrated our victory over Hakon the Bald and King Egbert we had feasted. My Ulfheonar had worn their finest clothes and their wolves were displayed for all to see. Many men had examined the wolves with interest for they were wonderfully made by Aiden.

"Then it is someone who sailed and fought with us but now serves Ragnar Ruriksson."

Rolf Horse Killer said, "When we were in Dyflin did I not hear that some men had gone outlaw and left Jarl Gunnar Thorfinnson?"

Olaf said, "Aye I heard that. If a man murders his own clan and becomes outlaw he would end up serving a man like Ragnar Ruriksson."

Leif said little but when he did it was important, "Hermund the Bent served Jarl Gunnar Thorfinnson. He saw the golden amulets we wore. I remember he asked if it was made of real gold. It was only now that I remembered this. I did not like him." The others nodded at the memory of the man.

"Then we find this enemy when the first grass grows and we end this."

"But if he has taken shelter with King Egbert..."

I looked at Erik, "We end this. If he takes shelter in Miklagård we end it. But for Snorri's sharp eyes these could have attacked at Yule. Then it might have been our families who suffered. They could have taken the Ulfheonar one by one. If this Hermund the Bent told them about the wolf would they not tell their new master how the Ulfheonar are spread out and live with their families alone?"

"Aye Hermund the Bent knew where we lived."

My warriors took that in. They had thought of me being in danger, as I had, but then I had realised that the treasure was no longer in one place. It was spread out. When the feast was over it could have been that many of my oathsworn would be dead. I saw the eyes of my men harden. They would take any danger but a threat to their family was unforgivable.

We returned to the cave the next day. We left Rollo to recover at home. His mother would ensure he was cared for. We borrowed ponies from Audun and loaded the armour and weapons upon them. We made a pyre outside the cave and burned the bodies. It was not an act of kindness. I did not want their spirits to haunt the cave nor did I want the wolves and the foxes to descend and feast on their flesh. We sent them to the Otherworld and rode back to Cyninges-tūn; all of us were eager to see our families.

We were greeted at the gates by our families. When we had not returned they had been worried. The armour and weapons were sent to Bjorn Bagsecgson and I went into Aiden and Kara's hall. Brigid and Gruffyd were there. I took out the wolf I had taken from the Danish leader. Kara put her hand over it and then recoiled. "You are right, father, it is bewitched. There is a spell upon this. We need Bjorn's fire to destroy it."

I nodded, "We will do that soon. First I have to tell you that we will be spending Yule with Wolf Killer. He has invited us and I wondered at the wisdom of going for my hall is more comfortable but now I see that it is *wyrd*."

Kara and Aiden nodded. Brigid looked troubled, "But why? If there is danger then surely we will be safer in these walls?"

Kara put her arm around my wife, "Did you not listen to my father. They know of our customs and our rituals. If we do things the same way then we become predictable. My father never spends Yule anywhere else but here. Last year was the first time he spent Yule with my brother. The traitor would not know that. It is my father who draws the danger. I think it is right."

"But what of the feast of the White Christ?"

I smiled, "I am sure that Wolf Killer will not object."

"But Macha and Deidra celebrate with me."

Kara nodded, "Then I will ask them if they would accompany you. How would that be?"

I saw that Kara had found the solution. "Very well. This Ragnar Ruriksson is a bad man!"

I smiled, my wife sounded like our daughter. "He is, my wife, and we shall end his evil soon enough. Let us just get Yule over with and then we can plan his demise."

Chapter 14

I met with my Ulfheonar before we left for Wolf Killer's hall. My wife laid on a feast for them and their families. I began with the warnings of imminent danger so that we could enjoy ourselves later when the ale flowed like water and the food fell from overladen platters. "We have sent one party of killers to the Otherworld but we know not how many others this Frisian has sent." I pointed to the golden wolf around Snorri's neck. "He has a witch now. The enchanted copy of our wolf amulet has been destroyed but before you go Kara and Aiden will cast a spell of protection over your wolves." Every warrior clasped their wolf; it was one of the few threats which frightened my men. "Remain vigilant. I go away to be with my son and his family but also to make this land less dangerous. Make sure you visit all the isolated farms in my absence. You are the guardians of the Land of the Wolf."

Olaf Leather Neck said, "We should slay all the Danish slaves in the mines. That way they cannot be used to attack us."

I shook my head, "That is not my way. I promised them their lives. They did not ask these Danes to come here. Scanlan will watch over them. Many will be freed eventually. They know that. I have sent to Raibeart and Coen and warned them of the dangers too. All strangers must be treated with caution."

Haaken summed it up for us, "We will watch, as you ask, Jarl, but we will also prepare for war. No matter where this outlaw hides we will find him."

The feast ended well. My warriors collapsed by the fire unable to either eat or drink more. Brigid and Kara took the women to Kara's hall which did not smell as bad as the sweat and beer-filled hall that was now filled with sleeping warriors. Uhtric would have to clean our home while we were away. Gruffyd also had his first strong beer. Brigid had glared at me as I had carried him outside to vomit his meal up. I had shrugged; it was something all young men did. He would not repeat it and better to do that where he was safe with my warriors than when he was in some foreign port among strangers.

As we were taking my wife and daughter, Snorri and Beorn accompanied us along with servants to ensure our safe arrival. Macha and Deidra had agreed to come too which made my wife happy. I had to chastise Gruffyd who kept giggling as the two portly former nuns waddled on their horses. They were unaccustomed to such travel. The grey overcast skies promised more snow for the wind had shifted from the south to the east. Already banks of snow-laden clouds were building up. We rode faster. Snorri and Beorn turned around as soon as we sighted Elfridaby. They wished to be in their homes before night fell.

Ragnar and three warriors rode out to greet us and escort us the last mile or so. I saw that the three warriors were the new ones whom Einar Thordson had brought. Ragnar gave a bow, "Welcome Jarl Dragonheart. We have been waiting for your arrival with great anticipation. I have brought an escort for you."

I saw that the three warriors were grinning. I knew from the raid to Neustria that he and Gruffyd were very popular. The new warriors had picked up on that.

Brigid wagged her finger, "And no greeting for me!"

Ragnar flushed, "I am sorry. Of course, you are welcome and we have fine quarters for you." He leaned over to me as we approached the gate. "My mother is so excited that you will be with us for this feast that my father has almost lost his mind! He will be glad that you are here and the preparations can stop." He turned to Gruffyd, "Come we will find Garth. He is keen to show you his seax."

I knew that Brigid would have been the same. I was anxious to speak with my son. It was a pity that Einar was not here too. I would have liked to ask him more about the trail he had followed. Elfrida fussed over us and our horses were taken away. Wolf Killer rolled his eyes at the noise and clamour of the sudden influx of women. Deidra and Macha were full of the trials of riding while Erika was just excited to be visiting Elfrida. Wolf Killer put his arm around my shoulder, "Come, father. Let us find a sanctuary away from this gaggle of geese!"

He led me to the warrior hall. His Wild Boars were gathered there. They were his oathsworn and, as such, the equal of any warrior save the Ulfheonar.

My son smiled at the relative silence. "This is better. Karl, ale!"

A one-handed, ancient servant brought over two empty horns and his young assistant, Arne, brought the barrel. He smiled at Wolf Killer. Karl was one of his oldest warriors. His hand had been lost fighting Danes. "Here, Jarl. It is the fine black beer I know you and your father like."

"Good, Arne, leave the barrel. We will send for another when we have finished this one."

I laughed, "There was a time when I would have emptied it but these days I have to make water too many times in the night."

Siggi Flat Nose came over to join us. "Good to see you Jarl Dragonheart. Did you find those intruders or were they will o' the wisps?"

I told them what had happened and the good humour disappeared. Wolf Killer remembered the cave, "That is the place I slew my wolf."

"I remember and it is also where I met the wizard's spirit. There is something about this that disturbs me. It seems that this was a portentous omen. I fear that the people of Cyninges-tūn will be worried until we end the threat."

My son's warriors had gathered around to listen to us. "To that end, I will find out where Ragnar Ruriksson hides and when I discover that I will end his life."

"And I will join you this time, father. It is time the Wild Boars showed their teeth again."

Siggi banged the table as his men cheered. "Aye Jarl. We have many good men to avenge and the *'Wild Boar'* has forgotten what it is like to fly across the seas." He put an enormous arm around Ulf Blue Eyes. "And these young bucks can show us if they fight as well as they hunt."

I looked at them. They looked so much younger than the rest of the Wild Boars. "They hunt well?"

Siggi roared, "Only Snorri could better them and I hear he is getting old."

I laughed, "He still found a trail buried beneath the snow. I fear we will do little hunting for I could smell snow in the air."

"Then, father, we will drink and eat. As soon as the snow stops we shall hunt!"

I stopped drinking long before my son and his Wild Boars. Siggi was the soberest and we carried my son to the bed we made for him in the corner of the warrior hall. When he was comfortable he escorted me through the bodies which littered the floor. "He is a good leader, Jarl, you have raised a fine son."

"It is what a man leaves behind after he has gone to the Otherworld. He is doing a fine job with Ragnar and Garth. Have you sons?"

He shook his head. "My family was killed in a raid many years since. I have taken women and I dare say sired children but they are not mine for I did not raise them. I chose to serve your son."

"I am sorry for your loss but glad that you watch over him."

The snow had already begun and even as I trudged to the hall where Brigid, Erika and Gruffyd were sleeping I realised that there would be no hunting for a day or two. Elfrida and Brigid were still up although the children were all asleep. They were talking. Elfrida stood when I entered, "Is he well?"

I smiled, "He sleeps but I suspect he will rise late." I waved a hand towards the door. "Not that it matters. The snow will be lying thick upon the ground."

She nodded. Brigid said, "I have told her of the danger we bring."

I frowned, "We do not bring danger. Danger is all around us. Elfrida knows that better than any."

"It is true. This is a fine and fertile land. Farming is easier here than in the kingdom in which I was born yet there is danger all around us. My husband and his Wild Boars have made the land as safe as it can be. His riders patrol even in winter. His warriors protect us in our home. No home is ever truly secure but I feel safe here."

I saw Elfrida yawning. "And I feel safe too. I think, wife, that we have kept Elfrida from her bed long enough. Let us retire."

When I rose the next day I was the first. The hall was empty. Karl had been in already and brought provisions. I went to the table which was readied with freshly baked rye bread, cheese, honey and ale. I had not had enough drink the night before to dampen my appetite and I began to eat. Like a mouse, Garth appeared, shyly through the door. I smiled, "Come and join me, young warrior. We shall eat together."

He grinned and jumped up next to me. I poured him some small beer as he proudly took out his seax and cut a hunk of bread and smeared it with runny cheese. I dripped some honey upon it and we ate in silence. I finished first and watched him eat. He would grow to be a fine warrior. I was lucky to have such heirs.

When he finished he wiped his mouth with his hand and said, "I am growing grandfather," He pointed to the doorway where there were knife marks in the post marking his progress, "and I will ride to war with you one day."

"Do not be so eager, Garth. You need skills before you can face an enemy. Your brother and your cousin have only just used a bow and it will be some time before they can stand in a shield wall." I pointed to the seax. "You learn to use the seax first."

He nodded, "I have learned to keep it sharp. If enemies come I will use it."

"Good for you are a warrior's son and will grow to be a great one. I look forward to the day when I ride to war with my two sons and two grandsons. Then will our enemies flee at the sight of five such warriors!" I saw him swell with pride at my words and we spoke until the rest of the hall awoke. He told me of his hopes and of his adventures. It seemed he hunted each day with his slingshot and had felled both pigeons and squirrels. He showed me how he used his seax to gut them. He spoke of the places in the woods where he hid and played. He was learning skills which would help him to become a warrior. It was a special time. The snows which kept us from hunting drew my grandson closer to me. It was *wyrd*.

The snows fell for three days and then stopped. A blanket of white covered the land as far as the eye could see and then the cold wind turned to blow from the north and the land became frozen hard. Wolf Killer decided that the frozen ground would allow us to hunt. I was not so certain. The warm hall with its roaring fire appealed and yet my son insisted. "Ragnar, Garth and Gruffyd are all keen to hunt. My new young warriors strain like greyhounds. They have begged us to go hunting since you arrived. I think they are keen to impress you. Come it will blow the cobwebs from us and give us an appetite. Besides I have a desire for some deer meat!"

I relented and we wrapped up for the hunt. Siggi came with us as well as the three new warriors. I was interested to see their prowess. I doubted that we would find anything for the ground was hard and slippery. I was lucky for my sons and I had sealskin boots but I noticed that the three young warriors did not. We had plenty of sealskin and knew the value of such boots. With the fur on the inside, they were both watertight and warm. Their soles could grip on all but the sheerest of ice.

I did not have a bow; I had a boar spear. I had almost been killed by a wild boar before when hunting deer. The rest all carried bows. Wolf Killer turned to Ulf Blue Eyes, "Tell me where will we find game?"

"Up towards Scal Thwaiterigg is good hunting. There is a wood there for the deer and it is not far for us to walk with the young ones." He smiled, "It is good that the family all travel together and hunt together. I think we will have success today!"

His enthusiasm and that of Oleg the Wanderer was infectious and we set off with a spring in our step. It was just a mile or two to the land which rose gently to the rounded, tree-covered hill to the northeast. The young hunter was right; it would not take us long to reach it. Siggi and Erik Sigtryggson brought up the rear. Gruffyd and Ragnar flanked young Garth and my son and I followed the two hunters.

As we headed across the frozen ground I was impressed by the two scouts who led us. It could have been two younger versions of Snorri who did so. Once we reached the edge of the wood we stopped. It appeared to be virgin snow and I saw no tracks. The overcast day helped us for there were no misleading shadows. The two scouts waved for us to wait and then disappeared into the woods. We stamped our feet to keep them warm while we waited.

Ulf Blue Eyes appeared a short time later. He waved Erik forward and said, to Wolf Killer, "Oleg has found tracks. Erik, follow my steps until you reach him. I will go to the side and make sure that we are safe. If you spread out in a long line we will have good hunting."

Wolf Killer nodded but I said, "No, the three boys stay close to Wolf Killer and me. Siggi, you go to the left." I nodded to Garth who had no bow but carried his seax. He was ready to use it. "Watch your brother, Garth!" He nodded.

They nodded, "As you wish Jarl Dragonheart, but there is no danger!"

Erik eagerly led the way. With Siggi to our left and Ulf to our right, we should have been safe enough but something did not feel right. The hairs on the back of my neck prickled again and I touched my dragon amulet for good luck. Gruffyd saw me and said, "We need no luck, father! Ragnar and I have our bows and arrows knocked."

"Just be careful and do as Snorri taught you. Keep your eyes and ears open."

The trees were closer together than I had expected. I was glad that I had told the boys to stay close. Soon I lost sight of Erik and Ulf. The overcast skies meant there was little light in the forest. I was beginning to doubt the skills of the hunters; we had travelled five hundred paces and still seen nothing. Then I caught the faintest, musky smell of deer. I looked down and saw the first hoof prints. Ulf had been correct and we were on the trail of deer. It was Ragnar who alerted me to danger. He suddenly raised his bow. He had been taught well and knew not to speak. He gestured with the bow to the left. I looked and saw, lying in the snow, a doe with two arrows in her. The white snow was covered with blood. This was not right.

"Down!"

Even as I pushed Gruffyd into the snow two arrows flew from our left and right. I heard a cry as Wolf Killer fell. I turned and saw Siggi kneeling with an arrow in his shoulder. It was an ambush. Siggi, even though he was wounded, went running to his left. I shouted, "Erik, Ulf, Oleg! An ambush!"

Garth was the closest to his father and he ran towards him with his seax in his hand ready to defend him. He knelt, protectively over him. I could see that my son was badly wounded. To my horror, a second arrow pinned my grandson to my son. I saw my grandson's eyes widen as the arrow struck and then life left them. This time, however, I saw the killer. It was Ulf Blue Eyes.

"Ragnar, Gruffyd take cover by Wolf Killer. Ulf, Erik and Oleg are traitors!" I ran to my right as another arrow sped from Ulf Blue Eyes' bow. I was running crouched else it would have killed me. As it was it scored a line across my scalp. The killer ran to my left and I took off after him. He was younger than I was and fitter. I could not let him escape. So long as he was running he could not send another arrow my way.

Suddenly Erik Sigtryggson appeared. He looked to be aiming his bow at me. I did not hesitate. I had to get to Ulf even if Erik hit me I would get to Ulf Blue Eyes. In glancing at Erik I lost sight of Ulf. Even as the arrow left Erik's bow Ulf loosed one at the young archer who fell with an arrow in his shoulder. I saw then that Erik's arrow had been aimed at Ulf who had doubled back behind me. It had missed but the time it had taken to release the arrow had brought me to within twenty paces of him. I hurled the boar spear. Wolf Killer and Siggi had both been right. The young warrior had great skills. He brought his bow around to loose another arrow. The boar spear smashed into the bow, breaking it in two before he could release it. The heavy spear drew blood from his left hand.

Now I had a chance. I drew my sword and ran at him. I wondered where Oleg was. I hoped that my son and grandson were safe. Ulf drew his own sword. I could see by his stance that he was confident. He shouted, "Old man you will die as did your son and then when I have slain you I will kill your cubs! Ragnar Ruriksson will have his revenge!"

I allowed him to bluster for I wanted to be calm when I fought him. I pulled out my seax. "You are an assassin, no more. Do not try to pretend that you have any honour. You kill from cover. Now let us see if you can fight in the open! Face a warrior who can see your black heart!"

He suddenly launched himself at me. He too had a dagger in his bleeding hand. His sword was fast. It whipped back and forth. He was trying to mesmerize me. He was quick and I barely blocked his sword with my seax. His dagger sliced across my forehead. I punched at his injured hand with my sword. I saw him wince and step back. He was laughing. The blood dripped down my cheeks and nose from the wound.

"Is that the best you can do? Ragnar was right you are easy to fool. Sending you after those Danes was simplicity itself as if I could not follow warriors across stones! He knew what you would do and you did it. He directed your steps. He is the master! Soon he will have your land and will be King there!"

I noticed that the blood was flowing freely from his left hand. It was time to go on the offensive. Suddenly I heard a shout from behind. I dared not look round. If Oleg had got to my son and grandson I could do nothing about it. If I turned my back then I would be dead in the flash of a traitor's sword.

He must have expected me to turn for he feinted with his sword. I was not fooled and I lunged at his middle. He brought his dagger across to block the blow. For once he was slow. Perhaps his hand was slippery with blood. Ragnar's Spirit sliced through two of his fingers and his dagger fell. He swung his sword at my head and I instinctively brought up my seax. Sparks flew as the two blades clashed. I brought my own sword around in a sweep to his side. He had quick hands and he managed, somehow, to bring his own sword around to block it but my left hand was also quick and it darted forward to slice into the cheek and blue eye of the assassin. It was blue no longer but a red, useless mess.

He took two mighty steps back. His one blue eye glared hatred at me, "Your sons and your grandsons lie dead, old man. Oleg has finished them and even if you slay me he will kill you. You have used up all your luck this day. Oleg will carry the sword of legend."

"You talk too much." I swung both my sword and seax in circles before him. I was the one who would mesmerize now! His fingers bled still and the orb of his right eye hung down. His vision was impaired and he flailed his sword before him. I brought Ragnar's Spirit around with all the power I could muster and hacked off his head.

Turning, I ran back to my son and grandson. When I reached them I saw they lived but Oleg lay with four arrows in him. His legs also bore a wound. Ragnar said apologetically, "We both hit him but we wanted to be sure he was dead. We loosed two more."

I nodded and leaned down to look at Wolf Killer and Garth. The second arrow had killed them both. It had gone through Garth's tiny back and into his father's throat. Their blood lay in thick dark pools on the pure white snow.

"Stay here." I picked up my son's bow and headed towards where I had last seen Siggi. I followed the trail of blood. He lay with his back against a tree. The arrow was still in his shoulder and his leg was bleeding. I took my scarf from around my neck and tied it above the wound in his leg. "Hold still."

"I wounded him but he passed me. I heard shouts."

"My son and Garth are both dead. The boys killed Oleg. I slew Ulf Blue Eyes."

He tried to rise, "Then the last killer, Erik Sigtryggson lives still."

"I hope so for he was not an assassin. He tried to slay Ulf Blue Eyes. Stay here while I seek him."

I headed towards the place I had seen him fall. He lay in an untidy tangle. I could see no arrow. When I drew close I saw his chest moved albeit slowly. He lived. When I reached him I saw that the arrow had hit his head. It had been a glancing blow. The wound ran along the side of his head. It had rendered him unconscious. I dropped the bow and picked him up. I carried him to my son and grandson. "He lives. Gruffyd, keep his head to the side. Ragnar, come with me."

As we approached Siggi he smiled, "Thank the Allfather, you live young master."

"Come we will carry you to the others." Between us, we managed to carry the huge warrior back to the slaughterhouse where my son and grandson lay.

Erik was stirring. I knew not how many other killers might be around. The two had brought us here for a purpose.

"Ragnar, I leave you in charge. I know not how many other assassins are here. I will go for help. I would send you but I fear another ambush." He nodded, "You are now the master of your hall. Today you become a man."

"I will not let you down, Jarl Dragonheart."

"I know you will not." Nodding to Siggi I headed back for my boar spear. It was close to the body of Ulf Blue Eye. I spat at his body as I passed him. I wish that he had not died with a sword in his hand. "I curse you Ulf Blue Eye and swear that in the Otherworld I will find you and kill you for all eternity!"

I moved warily through the forest and I avoided our tracks. I wanted virgin snow and that way I knew that I was safe. As I headed towards the walls I heard the cry go up. I realised as I closed with the gate that I was covered in blood. The wound on my scalp whilst not deep had bled. The captain of the guard, Sven Broad Shoulders said, "Jarl what is it?"

I could not tell him before I had told Elfrida the dire news. "Get ten men and twenty horses. Meet me back here!" He hesitated, "Obey my orders!"

He flinched and then turned and ran. Brigid and Elfrida came out. Brigid's hand came to her mouth as she saw my face. I shook my head and said, "It is a scratch." I held Elfrida in my arms. "My son and Garth, they are dead. There were assassins. Ragnar and Gruffyd are unharmed."

She buried her head in my chest and began to sob. I heard hooves as Sven Broad Shoulders and the horses arrived. Elfrida lifted her head and said, "My poor chick, Garth? He is dead?"

"Aye, he went to save his father and they were slain by the same arrow. Erik and Siggi are hurt. I will go and fetch them."

Her eyes became ice as she said, "And his killers?"

"They are both dead!"

As we rode through the icy wind from the north I was oblivious to the weather. I was cold inside. My son and grandson were dead. I should have ended Ragnar when I had had the chance. I had put gold and treasure first and that was a mistake. The Viking treasure I had was my family and not the Neustrian gold.

"I am sorry, Jarl."

I looked up. "What?"

Sven Broad Shoulders shook his head, "I should have obeyed you instantly. Siggi taught me better than that."

I nodded, "He is hurt. We were betrayed by two assassins, paid for by Ragnar Ruriksson. But he will learn and I will pay him back tenfold!"

Chapter 15

The presence of Macha and Deidra was *wyrd*. We had brought them to be of comfort to Brigid but they saved the lives of Erik and Siggi. Erik's wound was worse than we had thought. They bled his skull and he began to recover. They saved Siggi's leg and managed to remove the arrow without causing too much pain. I took them to one side after they had tended the men and said, "I thank you both. Without you, we would have lost two more brave men."

They seemed uncomfortable with my fulsome praise, "It is our Christian duty, my lord."

"And I thank you."

We were all still numb inside. Their bodies were laid in the hall. Poor Garth looked little more than a baby. He had only seen five summers. The boy named after me would never grow up and yet in his short life, he had shown courage.

We buried them the next day. We built a barrow just outside the walls. Wolf Killer was buried in his armour and covered with his wolf cloak. Garth was laid by his side. I put his seax in his hand. He had been so proud of that weapon. He had died too soon but he had had a seax in his hand. Wolf Killer's amulet around his neck glistened in the thin winter sun as we laid the turf upon it. We made the barrow high enough to be visible from afar so that all would know heroes lay buried. His oathsworn and his family stood around in silence. Had Haaken been there he would have sung a song of my son's deeds. As it was we each remembered them in our own way. Ragnar became a man that day. He may only have seen twelve summers but he put aside his childhood when we buried his father and little brother. He put his arm around his mother who seemed somehow smaller than she had been.

She looked up at me with reddened, tear-filled eyes. "How can I go on without him, Jarl? He was all I ever wanted. He was not perfect, no man is, but I loved him faults and all. What will I do?"

"You will go on. You will be there for your son. I can guide him and teach him to be a warrior but you must teach him to be a leader. I know you did that for my son. Now you will do it for my grandson. You will rule this land as my son did."

"I cannot."

"You can. When Erika and my daughter died I thought I could live no longer. Kara helped through that pain. You will get through this mourning. You will never forget my son. I still speak with Erika and I visit her grave often. It does not mean I do not love Brigid but you are like me, you have a big heart. Do not give in to darkness. You are the light in this land, Elfrida and the land needs you."

"I will try for I know that it is what Arturus would have wished. He spent his life trying to be you, you know?"

"All he had to be was himself. I wanted no more from him. He was a great warrior. My Ulfheonar were proud to have him as one of their own. When they hear the news there will be great sadness. That is a measure of a warrior's greatness; not how many men he has slain but what his fellow warriors think of him. He was well thought of and he was my son. I, too, have a void in my life."

"And you will seek revenge?"

"I will have my revenge! Rurik's line will end... completely!"

I saw Elfrida recoil from my words. "You make a bad enemy, Jarl Dragonheart."

I nodded, "Where my family is concerned I am as cruel a warrior as ever lived!"

We stayed for ten days. I rode with my son's Wild Boars and made sure that there were no other enemies in the vicinity. I had wondered if other assassins were lurking nearby. They were not. I put Siggi in command of the oathsworn and made him responsible for the training of Ragnar.

He felt guilty about the two assassins. "I should have seen through them."

"Wolf Killer did not. Einar did not. I did not. Why should you be any different? They played their part well. We underestimated our enemy and I will not do so again."

Siggi had ten of his men escort us home. As I sat on my horse awaiting the women and their farewells Ragnar came to me. "How will I manage without a father?"

"I managed and remember that I am still your grandfather. Old Ragnar, after whom you are named, gave me the benefit of his mind. I will be watching over you. When you are ready to be jarl you will fight under my banner. You cannot change the past but you can shape the future. Remember that."

"I will. I will do this in memory of my father and a young brother who had life snatched away from him."

We had not told any outside of Elfridaby of the catastrophe. However, I was not surprised when Kara and Aiden came to me with concern etched all over their faces. They were relieved to see us alive but Kara said, "Something evil has happened! Tell me!"

We went in their hall and I told them both. The two had had their differences but Kara was even more upset about her brother than she had been about her mother. My wife had chosen death to save the people. Kara, like Siggi, blamed herself as did Aiden. I spoke sternly to both of them."You cannot see all. Some things are hidden. This is the work of the Weird Sisters. This Ragnar is a clever man. He duped us with his handful of Danes. I became complacent and thought we had outwitted our enemy. I will not do so again."

The Ulfheonar were not just upset they were angry. Haaken and Snorri, in particular, had helped to raise Wolf Killer and trained him to be Ulfheonar. My oathsworn took another oath and that was to rid the world of Ragnar Ruriksson and all those who served or harboured him.

I made a visit, alone, to the grave of my wife and daughter on the other side of the Water. The burned-out remains of my steam hut still stood by the Water. I had not visited since the fire. The snow-covered mound had a fine view of the Water and the mountain of Olaf the Toothless. I left Storm Rider by the Water and walked to the mound. When we had had the steam hut I had often felt my dead wife's spirit and heard her words in my head. Since the fire there had been nothing. I knelt by the barrow oblivious to the cold of the frozen white ground. I took out my dragon and held it in both hands. I closed my eyes and began to speak. When I had used my steam hut I had used my mind to speak as well as my voice. I did so again.

"Erika, our son is dead and our grandson Garth. They are with you now. Our son should be in Valhalla but he was denied that. My comfort is that they are with you. Forgive me for my failure to save him. I would that he lived and I was with you. That is not in my thread. I will have vengeance but I know it will never bring either back. Young Garth never saw the world. He was barely grown. He was a tiny sapling whose tip was barely green. He will need your care. I will watch over his family but I need to know that you and the other spirits watch over my second family. I must travel abroad and seek these foes. Watch over Cyninges-tūn as you did in times past."

I remained kneeling, listening for a voice in my head or a sign. There was nothing and I feared that I had been deserted. Suddenly I was nudged in the back. I turned and Storm Rider began to lick my face. He whinnied and raised his head. I saw the thin afternoon sun like a corona behind Olaf's head. I nodded, "I understand, my wife. I must go to Old Olaf."

Before I did so I journeyed to my boatyard. I went the day after my visit to the grave. At the river, I spoke with Bolli and Erik Short Toe. I wanted my ship ready to sail as soon as we discovered the whereabouts of Ragnar. *'Heart of the Dragon'* would need to be in perfect condition. Erik now had a family of his own and in his eyes, I saw the anger he felt. He was thinking of how he would react if his child was killed.

After I had told them what had happened Erik said, "Will Wolf Killer's family be safe there, Jarl? It is the edge of our world."

"When the Ruriksson threat has gone then I will visit my vengeance upon the Danes. King Eanred is our ally now. I intend to make Eoforwic Saxon again. They appear to be more trustworthy than the treacherous Danes."

"There is no rest for you then Jarl?"

"No Bolli. If I wish to sleep again at night I must exorcise the demons that destroyed my son."

I then went to the hall of Raibeart. He and his men lived close to Úlfarrston. He knew the news already. "He was a fine warrior and would have made a good leader once you decided to enjoy an easy life."

"I fear that is not in my thread. I see no peaceful old age for me. The Norns will cut my thread as suddenly as they did Wolf Killer. I had feared my own death and no one saw Wolf Killer's."

Raibeart nodded, "*Wyrd.*"

"Aye, *wyrd.* As soon as you can I would have you take *'Red Snake'* and find news of where he is to be found. I wish to know where Ragnar Ruriksson is hiding."

"The rumour was that he was with King Egbert. If so it will be both dangerous and difficult to find his exact location. It is better I take *'Weregeld'* and go as a trader. King Egbert still keeps the peace. Lundenwic is a hive of gossip and news. I would prefer to try that first. But you are jarl and I obey your commands."

"You are right but a knarr can be attacked. We may have scoured our seas of Harald Black Teeth and the like but that does not mean he has not moved to another part of this land."

"I will take a large crew. The raid on Neustria made my men rich. They have good armour and weapons. They are of the same mind as I am. We can trade and, if we are attacked then they will find that we have teeth. The knarr is a good ship and a fast one too. It will attract less attention than a drekar."

His arguments were sound and he was right. I had learned long ago that the men I appointed as jarls were clever and able to use their own judgements. "You are right. I am in your debt."

"No Jarl. None of us could be as we are without you. I am being selfish. I wish to continue the life I lead. I am grown used to the finer things. My men and I live like lords. Our wives use pots which graced the tables of bishops and thegns. We wear linens and cloths like princes.

We cook with spices from the far Empire. We are grateful and it is times like this that we can show that gratitude. I will sail as soon as I can gather my crew." He was about to part when he said, "I will call in at Dyflin first. Jarl Gunnstein Berserk Killer has many visitors. There may be news there."

Haaken had insisted that I have an escort to Úlfarrston. I left them when the walls of Cyninges-tūn were in sight. "I will go to visit old Olaf."

Cnut Cnutson nodded, "I will tell your daughter, Jarl."

Cnut would never argue with me. This was his way of telling me that Kara might take matters into her own hands. I smiled and turned Storm Rider up the path to the Blue Water. Storm Rider picked his own path up the mountain. When we reached the Blue Water, halfway up. he stopped and I slipped from his back. He began to drink the water and I turned to head to the peak. On my way back from Úlfarrston I had felt the wind behind me. It was a sign of change. The winds from the south would bring a thaw. Winter was not over for the days were still short but it was a hopeful sign. The skies were still grey but there were gaps which gave me hope. We were too high for a thaw to take effect and I had to be careful as I walked up the slippery, slick path. I was concentrating so hard on my footing that when I reached the top I surprised myself.

There was no one place you could stand to see the whole of my land, the Land of the Wolf. You had to walk around and look at each part. I began with the east, for that was where Elfridaby lay. The clouds had parted on the way north and I saw thin sunlight playing upon the water. Erika's grave stood clear and sharp. Elfridaby was hidden by the hogback of the Hawk's Head ridge but I could see, in my mind's eye, the new grave of my son and the manned walls.

Turning north I could see the Lough Rigg. Beyond that lay Ulf Olafsson in the stad by the Eden. He would be sad and angry when he heard the news of my son. He would raid with us. Beyond that lay the northeast and the land of King Eanred. At least he was an enemy no longer.

To the west lay Dyflin; there we would gather news. Perhaps Raibeart would hear news in that Viking crossroads.

Finally, I turned my gaze south. There was a line of enemies there from Man to Wales, Corn Walum and Wessex. King Ceolwulf was fighting the Welsh but who knew when he would turn his gaze north. The pirates who lived in my old home would just be waiting to find a weakness in my land. But it was Wessex where my most dangerous enemy lay. King Egbert would be delighted that my son had died. He had tried to kill him many times. His assassins had failed him. Ragnar

Ruriksson had shown great cunning. His plan had been worthy of a Greek from Miklagård.

'Then use your own mind, Dragonheart that was raised by Ragnar. Be the wolf. Use the night and use guile. When you strike do so swiftly. A wolf kills suddenly and silently. It only howls when it is safe in its den. Use cunning.'

The words I heard were not my own. They came into my head from I know not where. It was Prince Butar who spoke them. He and Olaf the Toothless had been close. Old Olaf had wasted and died after the prince had been slain. Now I knew why my mother had sent me here. In my mind, I had planned on taking every ship and warrior I could to fight and kill all those with Ragnar. That would be a war and too many died in war. Ragnar Ruriksson had shown cunning. He had lured me north with his Danes so that his killers could worm their way in to Wolf Killer's land. I needed to leave my land as strongly defended as it could be. I needed a small number of men. Ragnar Ruriksson had to die. Those who sheltered him would die also but there would be time for their deaths. I wanted to strike fear into the hearts of all my enemies.

I stood and took out my sword. I raised it to the sky. A sudden shaft of sunlight shone from my blade making it glow and shine. "Thank you, Olaf and Butar. Your spirits watch over us yet. I will heed your advice. I will be cunning and I will be as the wolf."

As I sheathed my sword and turned to descend the shaft of sunlight grew and reflected upon the Water of Cyninges-tūn. I saw my wife's face reflected in it and she was smiling. It was there for but an instant and then the cloud came back and it was gone. She had spoken with me.

The short days meant that it was dark by the time I reached my walls. Aiden stood, with Gruffyd and Ylva at the gate watching for me. I dismounted and handed my reins to Gruffyd. Ylva took my hand. Her tiny fingers were warm. My hands were almost blue with the cold. "You must watch out for yourself, grandfather. You should wrap up against the cold."

Her young face looked so serious. "You sound like your grandmother. She oft times chided me thus."

"I know. She has come to me at night and told me to watch out for you."

I felt my neck prickle. "But you are a child!"

She looked up at me and her eyes suddenly seemed like deep pools which went on forever. When I had fallen into the water beneath Wyddfa I had seen such a pool and then I had found the sword of my ancestor. I stared at Aiden who nodded, "She has the power Jarl. She can see into the past. She has told us things she could not have known and when we asked her she said an old woman told her in her dreams."

"An old woman, Ylva?"

She nodded as she skipped along next to me. "She looked like you and not my mother. The woman who looks like my mother is younger. She comes often. The old lady came for the first time at Yule."

The prickling sensation came again. That was when Wolf Killer had been killed. "And what did she say?"

"Oh, she said nothing. She took me flying through the air. We were like two hawks and we soared high into the sky. She took me to a mountain even higher than Uncle Olaf. We flew high and then we plummeted underground and we saw dead warriors who looked like they were sleeping. It was exciting! Then we flew over a field with warriors fighting. They rode horses and had shining mail such as you wear. A man dressed as you, with the sign of the wolf, was killed by a young boy. I did not like that for he looked sad when he died."

We had reached my hall but I wanted to know more. She had described the death of the warlord. I knew that from Aiden and the ancient writings. "But you said she told you to watch out for me. How could she do that if she does not speak with you?"

"When we flew back we came here to your hall. The old woman roosted up on the roof and I was sent into your hall. I wrapped my wings around you, Gruffyd, Erika and Aunt Brigid. Then I woke. It was clear to me. I am to watch out for you and your family. My mother and father do not need me to watch over them." I saw Aiden smile and stroke his daughter's hair.

The silence was broken by Gruffyd who said, "I do not need anyone watching out for me!"

The little girl shook her head, "We all need someone to watch for us. I have the old woman and my mother's mother. You have me." She nodded. "It is *wyrd*."

Aiden shrugged, "You will learn Gruffyd." Then he said to me. "As you have learned, Jarl Dragonheart. Prince Butar came to you." I nodded. "Good, for Kara and I worried that you would forget that you are this land. If you make war then you will break this land. The powers of evil have tried to do that. The death of Wolf Killer was as a crack. If it widens then this land will be destroyed. You must heal the crack."

"But the Frisian?"

"He will die, it is *wyrd*. You made peace with Egbert and gave your word. He has not broken his... yet. If you break your word then that will be the first time. The world knows that Dragonheart is never forsworn. You cannot break your oath."

"But what if Ragnar Ruriksson hides with Egbert?"

"You know that matters not. If Egbert had nothing to do with the death of Wolf Killer then he has not broken his oath. If he gave sanctuary to the Frisian it still does not break his word. King Egbert will break his oath. Until then he is safe." He smiled, "Is that not what Prince Butar told you?"

I shook my head, "You read my thoughts again. I have much to think on." I picked up Ylva and gave her a hug before kissing her on the top of her head. "And thank you for watching over us. Gruffyd will learn."

We put Storm Rider in the stable and I said to my son, "Do not tell your mother what Ylva said. She will not understand. She is a Christian."

He nodded, "How can Ylva watch over us? She is a child. She is not a warrior!"

"She has powers, my son as does Aiden and Kara."

"But I do not?"

"Your powers will be as mine. You have the power of the warrior. But always listen to those voices in your head." I pointed to the shadow of the mountain. "Find times to be alone and listen to your head. The voices of the spirits will speak with you. Heed them. Now come. I am ready to eat a horse, with its skin on!" Storm Rider whinnied. "Sorry boy, just a figure of speech!"

Although I was hungry and ate all that was put before me I did so in silence I was planning what to do. My original plan was gone. It was Raibeart who had planted the seed in my head. I would take *'Red Snake.'* I had to be as cunning as my foe. Everyone knew my drekar. *'Red Snake'* often sailed with Raibeart. They would assume it was him. I could take the Ulfheonar and choose the other crew from those who would be Ulfheonar. Erik Short Toe could captain. I would have my drekar, *'Heart of the Dragon'* sail the waters between Dyflin, Wyddfa and my home. Her presence would be reported and my enemy would be lulled into complacency. All I needed now was to discover his whereabouts and that depended upon my young jarl.

I went to Bjorn Bagsecgson. I needed an addition to my helmet. The facemask was effective but I had an idea for a wolf's head to be above the mask. It would add protection to the front of my helmet. The scar from Ulf Blue Eyes' dagger had barely healed. It was a reminder of how close I had been to death. The extra metal would give me more protection.

Bjorn had already offered his condolences. He had watched my son grow into a man. I knew that his favourite son was far away with Jarl Gunnar Thorfinnson. The death of Wolf Killer made him fear for the son he could no longer protect. I told him what I needed. He nodded and examined the helmet. "I can see why you need it but it is not as easy as that, Jarl Dragonheart. If I put metal here at the front it will make the helmet front heavy. There will be a tendency for it to slip forward even with leather thongs."

"You are saying it cannot be done."

He laughed, "Of course it can be done, Jarl, but it is not as simple as shaping a piece of metal and fixing it to the front. That part is not difficult but I will need to balance the back. If I attach a mail aventail to the back it will balance it. I can use the same weight of metal in the links as in the wolf."

"That will make the helmet heavier."

"A little but not much." He laughed, "Your neck is thicker than it used to be, Jarl. You can bear the weight!"

I had a sudden thought. "Could you coat the metal wolf in gold?"

"I could but if it was struck then the gold would chip off. It would be a waste."

"I can always get more gold. My enemy thought to make a wolf of iron and cover it in gold. I would mock him in my own way besides it would be effective would it not?"

"It would. I will have one of my smiths begin the mould. It will take at least seven days."

"Do not worry. I will not need it until I have news of my enemy and that will take time."

"Many men will wish to sail with you, Jarl. Wolf Killer was popular. The manner of his death angered the warriors. He was not given a chance to die with a sword in his hand."

"I know and I think that was part of my enemy's plan. He knew that if we were killed while hunting we would not have swords. He is a cunning enemy. His father was too. I should have been more ruthless and slaughtered his whole family. My kindness has killed my son and grandson. I will not show mercy next time."

Bjorn said, quietly, "You will, Jarl. It is not in your nature to be ruthless."

"There was a time when you were right but no longer. My heart will be as the steel you make. It will be hard and unyielding." I saw again, in my head, the look in Garth's eyes as he had died. That young boy deserved to be avenged. I would change my nature; at least until the enemy was slain.

I let my Ulfheonar pick the warriors who would sail with us. They knew the ones who aspired to be wolf warriors and they had fought alongside many of them. Cnut Cnutson was an obvious choice. I sat back as they debated the merits of the various warriors. The six who would be Ulfheonar were chosen first. Along with Cnut, there was Alf Jansson,

Einar Hammer Arm, Sven Svensson, Bjorn Eiriksson and Olvir Grey
Eye. The other twelve were the warriors who had the best armour and
weapons. That proved they were good warriors for they had taken the
armour from enemies they had slain. We would need to practise rowing
with them but the voyage to wherever our enemy was hiding would do
that.

When they were selected we gathered them in the old warrior hall. It
was almost empty now. Warriors stayed there only when we were
preparing to go A-Viking. For the rest of the time, they lived in their own
homes. The hall seemed filled with the ghosts of dead warriors. It was
comforting for all my warriors had died with their swords in their hands.
That thought brought pain to me again, for Wolf Killer had been denied
that chance.

"You are here because you have been chosen to sail with me to
avenge Wolf Killer and his son Garth. I order no man to go. If any
choose not to voyage then leave now. There will be no dishonour." All
remained silent and their eyes stared at me. "Good. We sail in *'Red
Snake'* as soon as Raibeart returns. He will discover where Ragnar
Ruriksson hides. We go not to make war; we go to slay a murderer and
his oathsworn. We will have to use cunning and the skills of the
Ulfheonar. Wherever this snake lies curled and hiding, it will be in a land
which is filled with our enemies. Make no mistake, this will be
dangerous."

Olaf Leather Neck said, with a lopsided smile, "If you try to frighten
us with numbers of enemies you cannot. It matters not how many we
face every warrior in this hall is the equal of five ordinary warriors. We
fear not numbers." He laughed, "My fear is that my axe will blunt before
I have hewn enough heads."

"Good. We leave on the morrow for I am anxious to sail as soon as
Raibeart returns. We will need some time to become used to the new
drekar. It is smaller than we are used to."

Cnut asked, "Where did he sail, Jarl?"

"Dyflin and then Lundenwic. He went in the knarr to avoid too much
scrutiny. If he is successful he will return in seven days or so. That is the
time we have to become one crew."

Gruffyd was keen to join me. It was Aiden whose arguments swayed
him. "Your father has lost a grandson, Gruffyd. He was little younger
than you. With such a small crew he cannot afford to have one watching
over you. It will be hard enough for him as it is."

"Will you not be travelling with him, galdramenn?"

Aiden shook his head, "Not this time. Kara and I have spoken with the spirits. This task is set for your father. The Weird Sisters wish it so. When we dreamed we did not see you on the drekar."

He nodded. If Aiden was not going then it would not be so bad. "Then while you are away I shall train every day with Karl One Leg. Soon I will sail with you and become a warrior."

I nodded my gratitude to Aiden. I would not lose another of my blood. My heart might be that of a dragon but Gruffyd and Ragnar were now all that was left to me.

Chapter 16

    'Red Snake' had been captured from Magnus the Forsworn. We had not changed her name, nor her prow. It was still painted red but we had improved her as a ship. She was now the fastest drekar we possessed and could turn in the tightest of rivers. Erik Short Toe and his crew needed no persuasion to crew the drekar. However, Erik was adamant that we had to learn her tricks and traits before we sailed. I was happy about that.

    Haaken and Olaf arranged the men on their chests. It took time for we needed balance as well as power. The oars closest to the steering board were the Ulfheonar but the rest took some time. We sailed for the first time on a blustery day. It was perfect for the wind and the waves were unpredictable and we all had to concentrate. I watched from the steering board. I began to feel the drekar beneath my feet. She was almost skittish compared with *'Heart of the Dragon'* but Erik soon had her mastered. We sailed almost to Hibernia and then turned around. As we sailed home Haaken began a chant. He chose one carefully. He chose one about our defeat of Magnus the Forsworn. That was appropriate. We sought another murderer and we sailed in his drekar. The new men soon picked up the words and by the time we reached Úlfarrston, we were roaring the song out loud enough to drown the wind.

The Saxon King had a mighty home
Protected by rock, sea and foam
Safe he thought from all his foes
But the Dragonheart would bring new woes
Ulfheonar never forget
Ulfheonar never forgive
Ulfheonar fight to the death
The snake had fled and was hiding there
Safe he thought in the Saxon lair
With heart of dragon and veins of ice
Dragonheart knew nine would suffice
Ulfheonar never forget
Ulfheonar never forgive
Ulfheonar fight to the death
Below the sand they sought the cave
The rumour from the wizard brave
Beneath the sea without a light

The nine all waited through the night
Ulfheonar never forget
Ulfheonar never forgive
Ulfheonar fight to the death
When night fell they climbed the stair
Invisible to the Saxons there
In the tower the traitors lurked
Dragonheart had a plan which worked
Ulfheonar never forget
Ulfheonar never forgive
Ulfheonar fight to the death
With Odin's blade the legend fought
Magnus' tricks they came to nought
With sword held high and a mighty thrust
Dragonheart sent Magnus to an end that was just
Ulfheonar never forget
Ulfheonar never forgive
Ulfheonar fight to the death
Ulfheonar never forget
Ulfheonar never forgive
Ulfheonar fight to the death

The last cry of '*Ulfheonar fight to the death*' was so loud that a flock of seagulls took flight. It was a good omen. We went out each day for the next three days. We sailed to Man and back. We sailed to the land of the Lune and back. Each day Erik got to know the knarr a little better. The oars bit into the scudding grey water a little smoother with every stroke. We twisted, turned and backed water. We pivoted on the spot by rowing the two sides in opposite directions. Most importantly, however, we became one crew.

After three days sailing I ordered the men to load their armour, weapons and shields on board the drekar. I intended to sail as soon as Raibeart landed. We would not waste one moment. Finally, we loaded the firkins of ale and the dried food we would take with us. It was during the afternoon and Guthrum was at the masthead when we spotted the knarr. "Sail from the south!" We assumed it would be Raibeart but we took no chances. We donned helmets and grabbed weapons. Guthrum's shout, "It is '*Weregeld*'" told us that it was not an enemy. We could relax.

It took the knarr some time to beat towards us. It was a northerly breeze and the knarr had no oars. Eventually, it bumped up against the wooden quay and Raibeart jumped onto the stone path. He raced directly to me and gave me the information he had gathered. "Jarl, I have found them. King Egbert has given them his summer palace at Carhampton. It is on the northern coast of Wessex not far from the estuary of the Sabrina. He is gathering an army. There were many drekar in the estuary."

I nodded. I had expected him to prepare for an attack. Ulf Blue Eyes had told me of his ambition to be King of the Land of the Wolf. King Egbert was suckling a viper at his breast. "How many men?"

"That is difficult to ascertain, Jarl. When we were in Lundenwic we heard that he had been given the estate and then we heard, from a different source, that he was gathering men. This time it is not just Danes he seeks; he is searching for any Viking who wishes to serve alongside him. Harald Black Teeth has joined him as has Hermund the Bent, the murderer who fled Jarl Gunnar Thorfinnson. When we reached the Sabrina we saw six drekar there already. I dared not approach too closely. There is a hilltop tower and they keep a good watch. We sailed north and then landed at the estuary. I got as close to the hall as I could."

"How far is it from the sea?"

"Less than a Roman mile. I had made a chart for you but you should know, Jarl, that they keep a close watch from the tower."

"You have a suggestion?"

He nodded, "If you land to the west of the tower, beyond the headland then you can approach across a small wood hill to the west of the town. I spied it as I sailed north. When I scouted out the King's estate I saw that there was a camp around it with the warriors who would serve Ragnar Ruriksson and the hall was guarded and watched by his oathsworn. They also keep some of the drekar fully crewed. He is careful, Jarl."

"You have done well."

Raibeart looked around, "Where are the other drekar?"

"We sail alone, Raibeart. I do not go to make war; not this raid anyway. I go to kill a murderer. We use cunning and the dark to do the deed."

"He has many men."

"From what you say they are the sweepings of every cesspit in the west. We saw when they attacked Seddes' Burgh that they have no heart. It is our decision."

"If you succeed it will make a great song."

"You would take more drekar." He nodded. "And that way he could slip through our fingers again. He would run and I do not want to waste our lives hunting him from one hiding place to another. We go to his hall and we find him there. Then he cannot run."

We sailed on the evening tide. The wind which had delayed Raibeart's arrival now helped us and we made good time as we headed south. The waters were choppy and the air chill. The men huddled beneath cloaks as the threttanessa skimmed across the waters. We passed Man and Erik took us west to skirt the island of Ynys Môn. The other news Raibeart had brought us was the King Ceolwulf of Mercia was busy fighting the Welsh. The lands to the north of Carhampton were filled with warriors. The home from which I had taken Brigid, Dyfed was not far from the north coast of Wessex but that too was filled with enemies. Raibeart's idea had merit. A landing to the west of Carhampton would be safer.

We halted by the whale island. This was a large island which looked like a whale breaching. It gave shelter and we halted there. For we did not wish to sail in daylight when we approached Carhampton. From what Raibeart had said Ragnar Ruriksson's men and ships had sailed from the east. A drekar approaching from the north would arouse suspicion. Asbjorn and a crew would be plying the seas from Dyflin to Úlfarrston. He would be seen by spies for I had no doubt that there were such watchers. They would see *'Heart of the Dragon'* and Asbjorn in his wolf cloak and helmet which was a twin of mine. They would think I was still in the north. My plan could only succeed if my enemy believed I was in my home waters. If he suspected we were close then we would not catch a smell of him.

We left after dark to sail across the waters of the Sabrina estuary. It is a busy waterway during the day but not so at night. We were only out of sight of land briefly during the middle of the night. Erik had the ability to smell the land. His charts were the best we had. Aiden constantly updated them when our captains returned from a voyage. Raibeart's new information was already incorporated. He stood us well out to sea when we passed the beach of Carhampton and then took us towards the thin shadow that was the coast and the headland behind which we would hide.

I had decided on a plan as we had headed south. When we had passed the headland I began to prepare. We would land in the dark and head up to the camp and estate after dawn. I handed my sword to Erik. "Care for this while I am ashore."

"You are leaving Ragnar's Spirit?"

"We have to get close to this murderer. I must rid myself of all that identifies me as Dragonheart." I took off my wolf cloak and donned a plain one. I swapped my distinctive helmet, now replete with a golden wolf and took one of the shields and swords we kept as a spare. We pulled into a quiet, deserted bay. We had passed one already but that had a village and huts. We had travelled further from our prey to land unnoticed. As we bobbed about in the swell I explained my plan to the Ulfheonar. None of them were happy about it.

Haaken pointed to my beard and my hair. "You can change your armour, sword and shield but you still look like Dragonheart."

I took the cochineal from the chest at the stern. I rubbed it into my beard and my hair. "I realised, when I donned it on my eyes, that it made my eyebrows appear to be red and not grey. Gruffyd noticed it. I will be Einar Redbeard."

When I had finished I turned so that my men could see the difference. Haaken nodded, "It works, at least, in this half-light. You look younger. You might get away with it. It is almost like Aiden's magic!"

We jumped into the shallow water. The drekar could get far closer to shore than could mine and was another reason we had chosen it. Once ashore we headed up the beach and struck inland so that we could approach the estate from the landward rather than the seaward side. Erik Short Toe would sail out to sea and head back in. Each night he would shelter in the bay until we returned. I hoped it might be the following night but that was out of our hands.

We skirted the next bay and the village. Snorri and Beorn led the Ulfheonar and we followed. The warriors from Cyninges-tūn were proud to have their jarl amongst and they stayed, protectively, close to me. Snorri came back and approached, "We are less than a mile from the camp. They have sentries." He pointed to the east. "The main road approaches yonder."

I nodded, "Then we will head there and wait until the sun rises. We will make them think we have marched all night to join them. It will explain why we keep ourselves apart and rest."

Haaken asked, "I am still unconvinced by this plan, Jarl."

"Who else should lead the men of Cyninges-tūn? Do you think the Ulfheonar alone can achieve the death of Ragnar Ruriksson when he is in a hall surrounded by his oathsworn? We need eyes on the hall in daylight and this is the only way I know."

"But if you meet someone that you know; what then?"

"Then I will deal with the problem. Now go. You and the Ulfheonar have a harder task than we do. You need to hide for a day. We will see you tomorrow night."

Haaken clasped my arm, "You truly do have the heart of a dragon and the balls too! May the Allfather be with you." They disappeared as only wolf warriors can do. They were there one moment and gone the next. I led the men who were left and we headed towards the road. When we found it we retired into the undergrowth to await the dawn.

Einar Hammer Arm and Sven Svensson were placed on sentry and the rest of us made ourselves inconspicuous. Cnut Cnutson spoke with me. "My father would have objected too, you know, Jarl."

"I know. He would not be happy that I left my sword behind. I confess that is the one part of the plan I do not like. But it had to be done. It can be recognised too easily. As for the rest, the helmet, the cloak and the shield they are not my own but they will do." I patted the sword. I had taken it from a Frank at Seddes' Burgh. It was not a long one such as their horsemen used but it was a good blade. Bjorn Bagsecgson had approved. "I do not want to risk being identified. If I see anyone I recognise then I will disappear. It is you who will be the leader of this band. My life is in your hands, Cnut Cnutson."

"I know and that weighs as heavy on my shoulders as does this mail."

"I have confidence in you. If you speak in a surly manner and scowl then you will fit in well."

As the dawn broke we stirred ourselves and I took my place among the warriors. I walked next to Olvir Grey Eye. Our shields were over our backs and we trudged as though we were weary from a long night's march. Snorri had told us that we were about a mile from the camp. I kept my head down as we smelled the fires as they cooked their first meal of the day. A voice stopped us. We bunched up as though we were a rabble.

I kept my head down as I listened, "Who are you?"

"I am Cnut the Fearless and we are here to offer our swords to the Jarl who raises this army. We were told in Lundenwic that Ragnar Ruriksson was taking on men."

"He is but he needs men who have their own drekar. Where is yours?"

"Lying on the rocks off Syllingar. The master was drunk and ran us on the rocks."

"You were not the jarl?"

"No, that was Thorstein Ill Luck. Thorstein the Drunk would have been a better name for him."

I risked a glance at the men who stopped us. They were Danes. There were three of them and they had expensive-looking byrnies and carried the double-handed Danish axe; their arms were laden with warrior rings. If we could get by these three then we stood a chance. I did not recognise them and that was a good thing.

"Those islands are treacherous. How did you get to the mainland?"

"We made a raft from the wreckage and the Allfather was with us. The current brought most of us ashore."

"But not all."

"No, and we came ashore with just what we carried. We are ready for food and a rest."

"We can use warriors who are so resilient and favoured by the Norns." He pointed to the beach. "Each clan has its own camp. There is plenty of space by the beach. The others do not like sand flies. You have little choice."

"And food?"

"What you can find and keep is yours. Lord Ragnar has forbidden fighting in the camp. You would do well to remember that. Any infringement is punishable by death."

Cnut nodded, "Follow me." We passed the three Danes. Worryingly they scrutinised each of us as we passed. I kept my head down. I looked around the camp. Some of the fires had more men around than others. They were obviously the crews of drekar. Others had just a handful of men around them. I estimated that there were over a hundred men in the camp. When we reached the dunes above the beach I sat and looked at the hall. It was a hunting lodge. A long low hall, it had but one entrance and that was guarded by two Frisians. The nearest campfire was forty paces from it. Ragnar Ruriksson was taking no chances.

Cnut was enjoying playing the part of a sour-faced would be leader, "Karl, Ulf, go and find me some food. I am starving. Ketil and Arne find some beer."

I lay with my back against a dune. I took off my helmet and began to examine the hall to see how we could get to Ragnar Ruriksson and still escape. Beyond the hall, there was a brewhouse. I saw a huddle of women there. If he ran this as his father had run Dorestad then the women would serve the beer and more. I hoped that the distraction might allow us entry.

I leaned over to Alf Jansson, "Have a wander along the beach and tell me what you see."

"Aye, Jarl."

"Einar, Einar Redbeard, remember? Do not call me jarl or all this will end in bloodshed; ours."

"Sorry, Einar."

Ketil and Arne came back with a small bucket of ale and six horns. "If we are here too long we will have no coins! This is expensive ale."

Cnut shook his head and said loudly, "Fear not for we shall have our fortunes made when we raid!"

I let the others drink the beer. From their faces, it was not particularly good beer. It did, however, give me the opportunity to stand and look around the other camps. There was a small camp thirty paces or so from us. We could hear them and I did not doubt that they could hear us. Karl and Ulf returned with food. They told a similar story. The food was not cheap; neither was it particularly good. The black bread was not to the taste of my men but grumbles would be expected.

Then I saw the door of the hall open. Ragnar Ruriksson did not come out but I recognised one of the men who did, it was Hermund the Bent. He had served with Jarl Gunnar Thorfinnsson. I had not liked him. He might recognise me and I was about to sit down again when the man next to him opened his mouth. He had blackened, filed teeth. It was Harald Black Teeth. I remembered him from the fight at Beinn na bhFadhla. I mumbled, "Trouble." As I sat down.

To my horror, the two of them came over to the camp closest to us. I lay back in the sand and put my helmet over my face as though I was sleeping. I could hear everything. Perhaps the darkness focussed my hearing for the words they were speaking were as clear as though they were next to me.

"Why do we stay here, Harald?"

"I have told you Hermund, you address me as Jarl now! I have earned it."

"Sorry, Jarl but I do not see why we wait here. The food and ale are like pig swill and the prices make us poorer by the day. From our words, with this Frisian Prince, I doubt that he will stir himself before midsummer. He seems not to know his own mind."

"But when he does we can reap greater rewards than you can imagine. We can plunder the Land of the Wolf. You have been there and you know."

"They have the Dragonheart and his sword. We would not survive. Let us go and raid Jarl Gunnar Thorfinnsson. He has treasure too. It is not as much as the Dragonheart took but it will be easier to steal."

A third voice piped up, "I agree with Hermund. We have two drekar now and I spoke with Ulf the Squint Eyed. He is keen to sail with you, Jarl."

"If the Norns had not played tricks with us we would have had even more drekar. How they trapped us at Beinn na bhFadhla I will never know."

"That is in the past, Jarl. Let us slip away this night. If it does not work out then we can always come back. We have time until midsummer."

Harald Black Teeth had a voice which growled and when he spoke again he sounded like a wounded bear. "We stay because Ragnar Ruriksson needs us. He has but thirty Frisians left, no Franks and one crew of Danes. Our crews are the best that he has."

"What of those with the Jarl on the boats? There are Frisians there. I have spoken with men who say that the warriors of the skull are fearsome warriors."

"I know not. Perhaps he and the Prince have fallen out. He rarely visits those ships. Why are they not off the beach with ours? Forget those men. We are the ones who hold the balance of power."

"So we wait?"

"Dragonheart will come. His son was killed. I served with his men. He and his son were close. They might have the death wish upon them. Ulfheonar are but a skin away from being berserkers."

"Then we do wait. If Dragonheart is coming then we should be ready."

"Yes, Hermund but I like your suggestion. We will go and visit with Ulf the Squint Eyed. It does not hurt to have allies. If things do not work out for us then we raid Thorfinnson!"

When their voices faded I risked removing my helmet and sitting up. Alf Jansson reappeared over the top of the dunes. He sat next to me and took the horn of ale proffered by Ketil. He spoke quietly out of the side of his mouth. "There are six drekar just off the beach. I spoke with a sentry. He said another six, those of the Frisians and a Dane are anchored in the estuary of the river. He knew not why. He believed the Prince, for that is what he calls himself, has some Frisians sleeping aboard his ships as he fears an attack by the Dragonheart. The sentry seemed afraid of the Jarl of the White skulls who appears to command at least one of the drekar."

I smiled, "It is good that we inspire such fear."

"The six which are close here do you know any?"

He nodded, "I saw *'Eagles Heart'*; it is Black Teeth's ship."

I nodded, "He was just here. Are they close in?"

"Two are beached. They could be refloated easily enough but at low tide, which will be soon then they will be high and dry. High tide they will float, just."

Nodding I took the horn from him and drank some. We would steal a drekar and try to fire the others. I had an escape plan now. When we arrived I had had none.

A loud voice shattered my plans. "Cnut Cnutson! I thought you sailed with the Dragonheart! It is me Olaf Twisted Lip."

We had been recognised. "One of the men from Black Teeth's camp came over with another warrior. Our worst fears had been realised. We had to fool them. Was Cnut up to it?

"I left him two years since. I joined a crew which raided Wessex."

The man nodded, "It is rich pickings but dangerous. Who is your jarl now then?"

"We have none. He drowned when our ship foundered off Corn Walum."

When Cnut said the word, '*drowned*' the warrior clutched his hammer of Thor. "That is bad luck. And you come here to seek work?"

"We have not eaten well and we will take any work."

Olaf Twisted Lip said, "You could do worse than join us. We could use good warriors. Even if this does not come to aught we have a certain success. Two of Thorfinn's sons have taken an island off Frankia. They have great treasure they took from the Franks. One of them is a pup and they have no walls. It will be easy."

"We will consider that but we have yet to meet this Ragnar. I prefer to speak with a leader before I make up my mind."

He was about to turn away when he asked, "Why did you leave the Dragonheart? Your father was one of his closest warriors."

"Aye well, he was always comparing me to my father. I am my own man. I wanted to make my own name. That is why I am now Cnut the Fearless."

He laughed, "A better name. I will mention to the Jarl that you might consider joining us."

"Let us speak amongst ourselves first. I would not wish to fend this Jarl."

"As you wish but if we do not sail soon then I fear he will leave in the night! And as for meeting Prince Ragnar then you have to wait to be invited. He fears assassins and he rarely leaves his hall."

Cnut nodded, "Then we will wait."

Olaf Twisted Lip waved and then he and his companions headed towards the ale and the women. Cnut sat next to me. "Did I let you down? I tried to think what was best to say."

"You did well. We were just unlucky to be so close to them. We cannot move now." I raised my voice slightly, "Two of you watch but do not make it obvious. If there is danger then whistle. We will try to move closer to the hall when it becomes darker."

I rolled my cloak to make a pillow and this time I used my leather helmet protector to hide my face. My helmet I laid next to me with my sword and shield. I was not aware of actually sleeping but I think I must have for I suddenly heard voices close by.

"If it had not been for the sword, shield and helmet I would have sworn this was the Dragonheart!"

"You are a fool. The Dragonheart is an old man with a white beard and hair. This is some warrior who wishes to be taken for the Dragonheart."

"More fool him then!"

"You awake! I wish to speak with you!"

I was going to open my eyes when I realised that they were kicking Cnut to waken him. "What is going on? Is this how you treat someone who wishes to serve your prince?"

"You were all sleeping so soundly that we could hear your snoring from the hall. The Prince would see you but it will be after dark. He is busy at the moment! He will decide if you are to join us or not. He only wants the best warriors. To be honest you look as though the Saxon fyrd could walk over you."

"I have killed men for less!"

"We shall see. Come after the sun has set. You may bring two warriors only. No shields and keep your hands from your weapons."

"He fears three men?"

"He is careful. There are assassins who will slit a throat for the price of a sword. You look desperate enough to risk that. If you do not wish to serve then leave before dark. We have a close watch after the sun has set."

"Very well!"

When their voices had receded I sat up. Cnut said, "They were Frisians. Big bruisers too. They had many warrior rings. How do we do this, ja...Einar?"

"You, me and Olvir will go to speak with him. Einar Hammer Arm can command the rest. Haaken and the Ulfheonar will take care of the sentries. You need to congregate in small groups close to the ale and the women. When we go inside see if you can cause trouble and a disturbance. Sven, Alf and Bjorn, you watch the sentries. When they move then try to enter."

"There are many ifs there."

I nodded, "And I chose all of you because you are young and can think. We come here to slay a snake and escape." I nodded to the ale hut and the women. "Already men are drunk. They have idle hands and coins. We are ready for war and they are not. They outnumber us that is all. We will try to capture a drekar if we can. I do not relish a foot race back to our ship. Let us move closer to the hall and away from Black Teeth."

In ones and twos, we stood and wandered closer to the hall and further from Black Teeth's camp. It was closer to the sandflies but we would live with that. Our new position meant we could see the guards at the hall from the side. We were almost hidden behind the hall itself.

The afternoon seemed to drag. We were further away from Black Teeth but we could still see his camp. Harald Black Teeth and Hermund the Bent returned with another warrior. They sat amidst their men and their heads were close together. They did not notice that we had moved. From the conversation I had overheard I guessed they were plotting. I would have to send a message to Jarl Gunnar Thorfinnson when we returned home. As the afternoon wore on so the crowd at the ale hut grew and the women spent more time inside pleasuring the men than serving beer. It caused some trouble. We had been told that fights were punishable by death. That meant fights with weapons. Fists and feet did not count as weapons. There were frequent bouts of ill-temper which were settled in a sudden flurry of blows, kicks and bites. Crowds formed a circle when they occurred and afterwards, they surged back to the beer. We were the only clan which appeared not to want to participate.

"Einar Hammer Arm. It is time you began to make your way to the ale hut. Buy beer. It would look wrong if you did not."

"Aye." He stood and began to walk over. Three warriors went with him. Beorn Eriksson went in a different direction with other warriors and Sven Svensson wandered, seemingly aimlessly around. It allowed Alf Jansson and Karl to head over the sand dunes down to the beach. When it was dark they would secure a drekar for our flight. I followed Cnut and Olvir to the hall. We had sharpened our weapons in the afternoon. The sun was slowly sinking into the sea to the west. The sun would take some time to set. I had no doubt that they would wait until it was fully dark to allow us in.

As we waited we watched ten Frisians leave the hall to go on sentry duty. Five disappeared behind the hall while the other five walked to where we had been interrogated by the Danes.

We walked to the hall. Cnut spoke to the taller of the two Frisians. He was broad and his nose had been smashed in a fight. He had a long knife scar running down one cheek. It had been badly stitched. He was not a pretty sight. "The Prince said he wished to see us."

"He said he wanted to see you after the sun had set. Do you see that glowing orb in the sky, that is the sun! Now go away!"

Cnut was being deliberately baited. The second one had his hand on his sword. Cnut shrugged, "You are a funny man. I suppose it makes up for the fact that you are the ugliest bastard I have ever seen. It must be the only way you get women; you make them laugh." He looked down at the man's groin. "We don't mind waiting. It is pleasant enough here. I am upwind of you."

The ugly Frisian's hand went to his sword. His companion said, "If they do not satisfy the Prince you can have him as a plaything, Guthrum. Be patient. The cocky ones always cry out!"

As the sun dipped down below the horizon Cnut went to enter, "Wait until you are sent for."

Cnut turned, "Perhaps I will take my men and find a better leader."

The one called Guthrum laughed, "If you try to leave at night you will be slain! You wait!"

We waited. The noise from the ale hut was even louder. Another fight broke out and the two sentries looked over as one of the Danes we had met earlier smashed his fist into the face of a Norse Viking. His nose erupted like a ripe plum and he tumbled towards us, unconscious.

The bruiser who had spoken to Cnut came out of the hall. He frowned as he saw the huge Dane kick the unconscious Norse between the legs. He said to the sentry, "Guthrum, go and tell Magnus Oakshield that the prince would like his warriors to be able to row. If he carries on like that he will be punished."

"Aye."

"You three follow me and keep your hands where I can see them."

He pushed open the door. The air was foul. It smelled of ale and vomit. I saw three women lying on a pile of furs. The Frisians had obviously been pleasuring themselves with them. I recognised Ragnar Ruriksson. He looked young but I saw his father's cruel eyes in his head. He had a fine and well-made sword across his lap. It was not in a scabbard. Two bodyguards stood behind him. He sat on what I assumed was King Egbert's chair. It was on a raised dais. I could see that he had delusions of grandeur. He wanted to be King. This elaborate show was to make it seem as though we were in the presence of greatness. It did not work.

I made sure that I stood behind the other two. The light was poor and my disguise had been effective so far but I did not wish to gamble.

Ragnar spoke, "You wish to join my venture, Cnut the Fearless?" He laughed, "You do not seem particularly fearless to me."

"Why, do I look afraid? I do not feel afraid. Should I be?"

Cnut was doing exactly what I wanted him to. He was buying time for my men outside to distract the guards and for my Ulfheonar to slip into the hall. We were a ruse, a human smokescreen.

I could see that he had annoyed this would be Prince. "I could have you slain for such insolence."

Cnut spread his hands wide and said, "What insolence? I asked if I looked afraid. I can assure you I am not. I think we have made a mistake in coming here. We have waited all day for this audience and now we are being questioned. Perhaps we shall leave. Do you want swords or not?"

Ragnar's voice rose as he shouted, "No one leaves at night! I will have you put to death."

Cnut laughed, "Then we will leave in the morning but so far I have not seen any that I fear." He looked at the two bodyguards, "And that includes these two."

Just then there was a loud shout from outside. Ragnar shouted, "Go and see what that is! A man cannot think in here." He turned back to Cnut, "You are cocky. These two don't say much, do they? You, the one hiding at the back, come closer. Are you afraid of me?"

I stepped forward and the light shone on my face. In the half glow from the fire and the darkness, my red beard was not obvious; the light made it seem grey. He shouted, "Dragonheart! Treachery!"

Chapter 17

A number of things all happened at once. The three of us drew our swords and seaxes as the two bodyguards stepped forward. Those who were not drunk and not copulating, all four of them, went for their weapons. Ragnar tried to get out of the way and then Olaf Leather Neck burst into the hall swinging his might axe and roaring, "Ulfheonar!"

I lunged at the nearest Frisian. My sword plunged into his throat. Cnut slew the second while Olvir used his seax and sword to fend off two drunks who staggered towards him. Ragnar Ruriksson pushed the chair over as he ran. I knew that he would have another exit from this hall. He was too cunning to be trapped by a single door. I was ready as he ran towards the women and warriors who lay on the animal furs. Cnut and Olvir had killed their opponents and they followed me. Flanking me they hacked and chopped at the Frisians who tried to help their master. As I had expected there was a hidden door at the back. I suspect King Egbert had had it placed there so that he could leave without being seen. From the outside, it would have been invisible for there was no handle to mark it.

Ragnar burst out into the dark. I was three paces behind him. I shouted to my men, "Go right and left!"

I could hear the clamour from the camp as my men made a nuisance of themselves. It would mask the sound of the Ulfheonar in the hall as they slew the oathsworn of Ragnar Ruriksson. I saw the footprints in the dunes. He was heading for the beach. Alf and Karl waited there. I stepped over the body of a Frisian sentry. An arrow stuck out of his neck. That would have been Snorri. As I crested the dunes I saw my prey. He was running towards the nearest drekar. It was one with a longboat attached by a rope to the stern.

I heard him shout, "Guards! Assassins! Help me!"

I wondered, as I pounded across the harder sand after him how men could have followed such a pathetic excuse of a warrior and then I realised, he had surrounded himself with tough warriors. He did the thinking and they did the fighting. I was catching him but he would reach the drekar before I did. He was thirty paces from it when Alf and Karl stepped from the shadows of the drekar. The bodies of the watch lay in the surf. I heard Alf shout, "Do we kill him for you, Jarl?"

"No. Alf, I shall have vengeance myself."

Ragnar turned to face me. I was not fighting with my sword, touched by the gods, but I would not need it. The Frisian fell to his knees, "Mercy. I will give you gold. Do not kill me!"

"Stand and be a man. You are a murderous assassin and you have done me and mine wrong. Fight me or I will kill you where you stand."

He dropped his head and then, like a snake, darted his blade towards me. I had thought he might try something like that and I spun around bringing my sword across his buttocks. It bit deeply and I tore it as I spun around. He screamed in agony. As I turned I saw Haaken and my Ulfheonar. I shouted, "Fetch the men, we leave in this drekar." Haaken waved and ran off.

"You have drawn blood. You have won."

"You are not your father's son. He had cunning and was without honour but at least he knew how to fight."

He swung his sword at me wildly. He tried to stab me in the knee. I stepped back and he fell in the sand. He picked a handful up and, as he stood, threw it at me. Had I had my own helmet then it would have done no harm. The open face of the one I wore meant it went into my eyes blinding me. He seized his chance and tried to end it there and then. When you have fought for as many years as I have then you use instincts and senses you do not know you possess. I could not see the blade but I knew where it was. My sword and seax came together to make a cross. His sword clanged into them. His face was so close to me that I could smell the drink he had consumed. I brought my knee up between his legs. Every ounce of strength I had was in that strike and he fell backwards into the surf for the tide had turned. The drekar was now floating.

I wiped my eyes with the back of my hand and cleared them. I walked slowly over to him. He was moaning and groaning. I brought my sword over and hacked off his right hand. He screamed. I kicked his sword away. "My son did not go to Valhalla because your assassins slew him without a sword. You have no sword nor do you have a hand."

Behind me, I heard Haaken shout, "Jarl! Finish it! They come!"

Ragnar Ruriksson tried to take out his seax with his left hand. I let him do it and then I hacked it off too. The blood was pouring from his two stumps. He was dying. I stepped over him and looked into his eyes. "You have no honour and you will wander the Otherworld for all eternity. I will never see you again nor do I want to for you are a nithing."

My men began to pour across the sand and clamber aboard the drekar. For me, time seemed to have stood still. I watched as he tried to speak. He could not. Swords clashed behind me. I was aware of arrows flying towards the enemy but I stared at this man who had taken so much from me and this did not seem enough. I waited until the light went from his eyes and the sea washed over his body. Then I turned and raised my sword. The men who were hurtling towards us stopped. I bellowed, "Thus all enemies of the Dragonheart die! Fear me!"

My men began to chant, "Dragonheart" over and over. Haaken and Snorri hurried me back to the sea and hands pulled me aboard. The wounded had been brought back and Alf was organising the rowers. The other drekar which bobbed about on the water had just deck watches aboard. They would not hinder our passage. Cnut Cnutson had survived and he went to the steering board. He had served as a ships' boy when he had been little. Haaken and Olaf chivvied and chased men to their oars. They were still full of the joy of battle. We did not bother with the sail. We had to row around to our bay and it was not far.

I looked down the drekar. We had lost men. I would discover who had gone to Valhalla later. Haaken looked up from his oar and said, "That was not a good death. He got what he deserved. I cannot understand why men would follow him."

Snorri cocked his head to one side, "There are still Frisians on the other drekar in the estuary. It would not surprise me to find that the real leader is there."

"Are you a galdramenn, Snorri? Can you see men's thoughts?"

"No Haaken One Eye but I had ears. When we crept around their sentries slitting throats and loosing arrows I heard men talk. The word 'prince' was used mockingly. I learned that was this Ragnar but they also spoke of the 'jarl on the drekar' and 'Jarl of the skulls'. We wondered why so few were in the camp and it was mainly those fortune hunters who came to seek glory. Alf said there are Frisian ships with their crews aboard in the Sabrina. Why do they wait there?"

It suddenly became clear to me that Ragnar Ruriksson had not been clever enough nor cunning enough to have been the man who made the plot to lure me away from my home. I remembered Harald Black Teeth's words. He had also spoken of a Jarl on the ships and a disagreement. I saw that this was not so. I looked aft, towards the distant Sabrina. "He knew I would come and these drekar were bait. This mysterious Jarl has been waiting for me to make my move."

"Are you certain, Dragonheart? It seems overly complicated."

"Then tell me, Haaken, why are there drekar with crews aboard? Why are they waiting? They had enough men to come to Cyninges-tūn and attack in force. No, there is cunning at work here. They choose a place to gather where I can attack easily. Why did they not gather close to Portesmūða? It is a larger harbour and close to the King. This is isolated and easy for us to approach. I wonder if Raibeart was recognised and they used him to trick me."

"They could have taken him."

"Aye Olaf but why take a minnow if you wish to catch a shark."

Cnut shouted, "I see *'Red Snake'*."

I looked ahead and saw my drekar around the headland we had just passed.

Snorri asked, "So what do we do?"

I lifted my head and turned so that I could gauge the wind. It was from the south and the east. "We use this wind that Njörðr has sent." I saw the sun rising in the east. "We let them wonder where we will be during the day."

Snorri pointed to the land. "They will see for I doubt not they will have men scouring the land for us."

"And we make them think that we are hurt and tempt them to come for us. Let us see if we can be as cunning as they are. First, we get the wounded aboard our drekar and their hurts tended to. Then we eat. When I had spoken with Erik Short Toe I will have a better idea of what I intend."

I was not being secretive. That was not my way but the idea which had formed was vague. I could sail but I was no sailor. I needed Erik's skills. We left the new Ulfheonar on the captured drekar. We discovered that her name was ' *Njörðr*'. The dragon prow had a man's face. Perhaps that was why the god had favoured us. He did not like his name being misused this way.

We rode at anchor and watched the morning arrive. We saw no sun and the wind brought damp clouds and squally showers. I sat on my chest with Erik. I now had Ragnar's Spirit strapped to my waist and that made me feel better. With my own armour and helmet, I would face anyone! "How many ships does he have in the river, Jarl?"

"Alf said six. Five Frisians and one Dane."

"Then that is good. Frisian ships are not as lithe as Norse or Dane. They are wider but they carry more men however they turn like a pregnant cow; slowly and awkwardly."

"Will they come here?" We had the ships' boys at the top of the masts of the two ships watching for them.

"With this wind the way it is? No. If they wish to catch us then they will make a line. We would have speed when we approached them but they would be able to cut us off. The only other way home for us is the long way along the coast of Wessex, up the east coast and around the islands at the top of the world. This time of year brings sudden storms. This Frisian Jarl sounds too wise to waste time sailing south."

Just then Karl Magnusson shouted, "Jarl, riders on the headland."

We looked over and saw four mailed men astride horses. Haaken said, "They know where we are then. So Jarl, will you now confide in us this plan of yours?"

I nodded and began. "There could be ten drekar waiting for us off the coast. The men we saw in the camp will man those drekar. We are a good crew but how could we fight such numbers? We could, perhaps, try to head for Hibernia and sneak past them however with the wind and their numbers it is likely that they would cut us off. We need to make them think that we go berserk."

Olaf Leather Neck laughed, "In a drekar?"

"When we were in camp I heard Harald Black Teeth. He spoke of Ulfheonar being almost berserkers and that I was distraught with grief. He said I had the death wish. Others might think so. We sail towards the centre of their line with the two drekar."

"Jarl, we do not have enough men to man both drekar!"

"I know Erik. Njörðr has sent us the wind which means we do not need to row. We make the captured ship a fire ship. We will sail at dusk. They will try to close with us before dark. If I was this leader I would not want us sneaking off in the night. We let the '*Njörðr*' go ahead. The crew light the ship and steer it towards the enemy. They will escape in the longboat and when they are close to us we throw them ropes and pull them aboard. The fire ship will make them move and we escape in the confusion."

Haaken nodded, "A good plan but it requires courage and judgement. Who will command these men who may not survive?"

"There is but one man for this task; me!"

They spent some time trying to dissuade me. They wasted their breath. I would not order any man to risk his life. My Ulfheonar had done enough already. When I told them whom I would take with me they argued again. "No, Haaken, I know whom I will choose. Guthrum is an experienced ship's boy and a good swimmer. Cnut Cnutson can steer. Alf Jansson and Karl Karlsson chose themselves for they captured the drekar. It will be enough."

I took off my armour. The only weapons I would need would be my sword and my dragon amulet. We transferred all the kindling and seal oil we could to the fireship and brought off the surplus crew. We were being observed from the headland but we were too far away for them to make sense of our actions. They were just watching to make sure that we did not escape. As we waited for the sun to become lower in the sky I said to my four-man crew, "This will make a great tale for Haaken to sing."

Alf said, with a smile on his face, "It would be good, Jarl, if we were there to hear it!"

I laughed, "I have no intention of dying, Alf. If Guthrum is as good a sailor as I think he is then we will soon be aboard the *'Red Snake'* and back in armour. I have to be aboard this drekar to make them believe that I have the death wish."

Alf shook his head, "You misunderstand me, Jarl. I am honoured, as we all are, that you chose us. If this is our last day in this world then we could not choose a better end."

Cnut stood at the steering board as we all hauled up the sail. It took longer than it should have. There were but four of us. When it was done we began to move. *'Red Snake'* would follow in our wake. I went to the prow. I had washed out the cochineal from my hair and beard and I was Dragonheart once more. I drew Ragnar's Spirit and stood at the prow of this ill-named drekar. As we rounded the headland I saw the sun beginning to set in the west and there, in a long line, were the enemy ships. The furthest ship was almost two miles away. I frowned. Three were missing. I turned and shouted, "Which ships are missing?"

After a while, Alf's voice came back. *'Eagles Heart'* is one. I know not the others."

Then Harald Black Teeth had deserted them. That gave me hope for it meant there were three ships less to deal with. At the same time, it meant danger for Jarl Gunnar Thorfinnson. The Weird Sisters had excelled themselves. The ships had not passed us which meant they had travelled north. I hoped my men were alert for three drekar, even with small crews, could cause much damage to my home.

I turned my attention back to the enemy. They had the Frisian ships in the middle. I saw a red skull painted on the sail of the centre one. Almost all of the shields along the side had a skull, either red or white, painted on them. Red paint made it appear as though blood was dripping from the skull's mouth. I took those to be this mysterious jarl.

"Steer for the skull!"

"Aye Jarl!

We were moving quickly now with the wind behind. "Alf, Knut, ready the fire but wait until I give the command!"

I wanted the enemy's attention on me. I braced myself on the prow and raised my sword. We were less than a mile away and approaching rapidly with a strong wind astern. I turned and said, "Light it now. Guthrum, get to the longboat."

I heard the chorus of assent from behind me. We were now less than half a mile away and I shouted, "I am Jarl Dragonheart from the Land of the Wolf. I come here to wreak vengeance upon you for the death of my son! Today you will all die!"

I know not if my voice carried but I heard the clamour of swords on shields from the Frisians.

Behind me, Alf said, "It is time Jarl."

Glancing at the fire which burned well close to the mast I said, "Not yet. We have time." I noticed that the outside drekar were rowing towards the centre. When we were less than half a mile away and the oars of the Frisians were sending their ships towards us I said, "Now is the time." Sheathing my sword I ran back to the steering board. Cnut was lashing it in position. As I passed Alf he kicked over the jar of seal oil while Karl hurled the pig fat. As I reached the steering board there was a whoosh as the fat and oil ignited sending flames leaping up into the mast and sail. The following wind took the fire. The front half of the drekar was covered in fire as we clambered down the ropes to the longboat.

We each took an oar as Guthrum steered us towards *'Red Snake'* now less than two hundred paces from us. I saw the panic amongst the Frisians. The skull ship turned to the east away from the fire ship. The next ship tried to follow. As the wind caught the enemy's sails it sent them into disarray.

As we approached *'Red Snake'* Guthrum shouted, "In oars!"

Cnut laughed, "Just like a sea captain!"

Guthrum was grinning. As *'Red Snake'* came close the wake threatened to capsize us. There was also a danger that they would fly past us. Ropes snaked down and Haaken shouted, "Grab them. We will haul you aboard!"

I took hold of the nearest one and immediately felt myself lifted into the air. I braced my legs as I was swung towards the side of *'Red Snake'*. It was fortunate that I did so else I would have been smashed against her side. I used my feet to clamber and climb up the strakes. Hands pulled me to safety. I heard Erik shout, "Let loose the sail!"

I glanced up and saw that they had been sailing under furled sails to allow them to pick us up. When I looked north I saw that there was a gap between the ships. The two to the west of us were racing across the choppy golden and red flecked sea towards us. The sun illuminated them. To the east, the captured drekar was burning fiercely but her forward momentum was slowing. The Frisians could avoid her. Two had fouled themselves against each other while the others were trying to turn to sail towards us.

We were now in the hands of Erik Short Toe. He would have to use all of his skills to avoid us being caught by the Danish and Frisian ships which sailed towards us. They intended to position themselves at our bow and our stern so that we could not escape. Erik shouted, "Take your oars but do not run them out yet!"

My crew knew what they had to do. I went to the prow. Donning my new helmet with the golden wolf I stood there for all to see. I would be the bait this time. To the east two of the ships, the skull ship and a Norse had managed to turn and their oars were pulling them towards us. We would be caught in a neat little triangle of drekar. Erik judged it to perfection. The sun was a thin line of red to the west when he shouted, "Out oars! Haaken row!" The light seemed to glint off the wolf.

He began a song we had not used for some time but it was one which enabled the men to row quickly for it had a rapid beat.

'Ulfheonar, warriors strong
Ulfheonar, warriors brave
Ulfheonar, fierce as the wolf
Ulfheonar, hides in plain sight
Ulfheonar, Dragon Heart's wolves
Ulfheonar, serving the sword
Ulfheonar, Dragon Heart's wolves
Ulfheonar, serving the sword'

As the oars bit into the sea Erik threw the drekar across the wind. We heeled but she was well balanced and righted herself. The two ships sailing from the west were travelling so quickly that they barely had the chance to react. The Dane put his steering board over to ram us.

'Ulfheonar, warriors strong
Ulfheonar, warriors brave
Ulfheonar, fierce as the wolf
Ulfheonar, hides in plain sight
Ulfheonar, Dragon Heart's wolves
Ulfheonar, serving the sword
Ulfheonar, Dragon Heart's wolves
Ulfheonar, serving the sword'

The surge from the oars almost took us beyond them into the dark night but the Weird Sisters had not finished with us. The Dane caught us a glancing blow to our stern. I felt the hull shiver. Every warrior was rowing on both boats and there was no opportunity to either hurl a spear or release and arrow. We burst between them. I saw one trying to turn but the Dane had suffered damage. I saw men bailing as the bow began to settle.

I hurried back to the stern.

"Are we hurt?"

"I know not yet."He waved over one of his sons, Arne Eriksson. This was his first voyage. "Get below decks and see if we have sprung."

"Aye captain."

I went with him to lift up the two short planks which gave us access to the hold. The small boy wriggled below the deck while we waited anxiously. "You can slow down now, Haaken. There is no point tiring yourselves out.

The Saxon King had a mighty home
Protected by rock, sea and foam
Safe he thought from all his foes
But the Dragonheart would bring new woes
Ulfheonar never forget
Ulfheonar never forgive
Ulfheonar fight to the death
The snake had fled and was hiding there
Safe he thought in the Saxon lair
With heart of dragon and veins of ice
Dragonheart knew nine would suffice
Ulfheonar never forget
Ulfheonar never forgive
Ulfheonar fight to the death

He changed to a more measured song which would not tire the men out. I looked astern. The darkness of the east was illuminated by a distant glow as the fireship settled beneath the waves. The shapes of three drekar were visible. They were following. They need not see us for they knew where we would go. We would be sailing north; we would be sailing home.

It was completely dark as Arne Eriksson wriggled up. "Well?"

"There is some water, Jarl, but it is seeping rather than flooding."

I saw Erik breathe a visible sigh of relief. "Thank the Allfather for that. We were lucky. Prepare to come about!" We would turn to sail due north so that we had the wind with us and the men could rest. "Come about! Oars in."

I took the opportunity, as the oars were pulled in, to discover who we had lost. It seemed a lifetime ago that we had fought in the camp and fled. The wounded lay on the decks still. I saw that they had been bandaged. Finni and Erik Eriksson both had wounds to the legs. They were sitting up but, if we were attacked, then they could not fight. Three of the new warriors from the town were also lying bandaged.

"How many did we lose, Snorri?"

"Five went to Valhalla, Jarl. They died well but the odds were too great."

"What happened?"

188

"We slew the sentries. That was not difficult for we had the night to help us. Einar began the fight as you asked him to. When the guards came from the hall then we slipped in and killed them. The new men held off the others. It worked out well at first because many were drunk and wanted an excuse to fight with anyone. Harald Black Teeth and his men kept out of it and it was they who slew our men when they realised what they were doing. Einar did well for he managed to make a shield wall and a fighting retreat. We hurried after you for we knew not how many men were with this Ragnar Ruriksson."

"I think he was just the figurehead, Snorri. They were trading on his father's name and reputation. There is another who is the power behind the throne. He is the Jarl who has the white and red skulls on his ships and his shields."

"Harald Black Teeth has a white skull but no blood. Perhaps he is kin to this jarl."

"Perhaps but if that is the case then there is no blood loyalty for he has fled."

We kept a close watch astern but an even closer one ahead for we would be passing our enemies on Man. The night wore on and Erik kept the steering board aimed due north. The wind helped and it was the shortest route. The wounded warriors had meant we had to rearrange the rowers. Cnut Cnutson was on a chest behind Olaf Leather Neck. Although the wind meant we did not have to row they stayed at their chests in case we had to. Olaf was chatting to Cnut and Haaken. I knew that it would be about his father. He had been the warrior who had stood next to me at Hrams-a when the lightning had struck my sword. How my life had changed since then.

In the dark of night, the wind began to veer and to freshen. It moved first south and then south-west. I guessed it would eventually come from the west. That was the way it normally worked. That meant the seas would be rolling in from the far seas to the west and they would be big. Our threttanessa was lithe but she was light. With no cargo in our holds and water seeping in from our collision I prayed for dawn and the sight of land. The wind became even stronger and we were struck by increasingly large waves. One wave, larger than the rest, rose like a sea monster and struck the drekar beam on. There was an alarming crack and Guthrum shouted, "The steering board! It has sheared!"

Erik Short Toe did not panic. "Get on the oars! Until we can rig something up you have to use the oars to steer!"

We were no longer making way. With no rudder, the normally responsive ship rolled sluggishly from side to side. She was like an overladen knarr. Guthrum and the ship's boys raced up the shrouds and began to furl the sail. We had to shorten it or risk breaching.

Erik shouted, "Jarl, find the spare oars we will have to use two of them as a sweep." I found the best two we had and took them to Erik. He cut some rope and began to bind them together. "Jarl, You will need to keep them on course. Keep the wind on our quarter. We will be more stable."

I stood between the rowers and held my hands out. That was the best way to gauge the wind. It was coming from directly behind. I waved to Haaken's side, "Up oars!"

As Snorri's side's oars bit into the water we began to straighten.

I pointed to Haaken's side, "Row!"

This was the test of a crew. They had to work in a way which was not normal. There was good humour and no panic. Haaken shouted, "With your hands like that, Jarl, you could be the White Christ they have in their churches. Perhaps that was what he was doing; steering a ship!"

It made the men laugh. Behind me, I heard Erik cursing as he tried to attach the sweep to the withy. It was not easy. I shouted, "Guthrum, help Erik Short Toe!"

He slid down the shroud and landed lightly on his feet. With two of them working together they managed to fashion a steering board. It was not as efficient as the one which had broken but it was easier to use than having the two sides compensate for the lack of one. Erik and Guthrum tried a few tentative moves and it appeared to work. "Thank you Jarl, We can manage now." The two of them steered together.

I turned, "Can we risk more sail?"

He shook his head, "This is delicate and if this breaks then we are in trouble. If we have to then we will try it but I would rather not take the chance. Karl, get to the masthead and watch aft."

"But it is still night, captain!"

"And soon it will be dawn. Look, to the east, the sky is lighter."

I donned my wolf cloak and began to prepare for war. The Norns had not broken our steering board just to see if Erik could mend it. We had escaped too easily. We would have to fight. I found my shield and donned my helmet. Haaken saw what I did and nodded. "It is *wyrd*!"

The sun had cleared the mountains to the east of us before Karl shouted, "Sails, to the east of us. Three drekar. They are the ones who followed us. I can see the skull on the sail."

Erik said, "So be it. We have to gamble now. Karl, lower the sail! We run before the wind. The bones are cast."

I went to the steer board side and peered east. I could see Wyddfa which meant we would have to alter course soon. Had we been in better condition then we could have risked the straits. I knew that we were too fragile for such a course. We would have to sail north and west and pass between Ynys Môn and Hibernia. The three ships would catch us.

Chapter 18

As the sail filled Erik put us over on to our new course as gently as he could. The normally speedy drekar now felt as though she was limping. Karl shouted, "Captain, two of the enemy are heading north. Just one follows us."

I went to the stern. "This Jarl knows these waters."

"Aye, more's the pity."

An idea formed, "Karl, the one which follows us, how many oars does she have?"

I waited while he counted. "Sixteen on each side."

I turned to Erik, "Then she is little bigger than we are. We fight her. We cannot fight three of them but we stand a chance with one."

"You are right."

I shouted, "Change into armour and get your weapons. One man in each pair."

We kept our way for we had half the men rowing but we slowed and that would encourage our enemy. I saw Ynys Môn just twenty miles off the opposite side to the steering board. Soon we would turn and we would have the advantage of the wind but, at that moment, we were barely making way and the Frisian was racing to close with us.

By the time all the men were armed and back at their oars, the drekar was just five lengths behind us. As our oars bit so we increased our lead. It was not by much but it bought us time. The little rock, covered in seabirds, which marked the end of Ynys Môn was the point at which we would turn. We could not throw the drekar over as we might have done had we been whole. It would be a gentle turn.

I had the chance to examine the Frisian. It had a skull for a prow. I had never seen one like that before. Perhaps all of them did. This one had shields with a yellow skull. I took heart from the fact that all the crew were rowing. None were sending arrows and stones our way. It was slightly wider than our drekar which would make it slower. It explained why we were able to hold our lead. Once we turned it would be different. Our turn would, perforce, be slower.

Erik shouted, "Stand by to turn!" As he put over the improvised steering board he shouted, "Haaken's side row, Snorri's side ship oars."

It was little enough but it turned us quicker than using just the two sweeps. Snorri and the warriors on his side donned helmets and fitted their shields to their arms. Snorri asked, "How do we do this, Jarl?"

192

"He has more men but they may not expect us to put up much of a fight. I intend to use the Ulfheonar to strike and strike hard. We disable their steering board. Then we head for Hibernia. Their leader is clever. He uses this drekar to keep watch on us but if it cannot follow then we can disappear."

"In oars!"

Haaken and the rest of the crew began to prepare. The Frisian was closing rapidly with us. He had been able to turn inside us. I do not think it was intentional for he must have realised that the other two would be coming from the east. He had to sail to the west of us if he was to be a sheepdog! Our slow turn had taken him by surprise. He began to turn to the west.

"Erik, I want you to turn and lay us alongside his steerboard side as soon as he passes us."

"It is a risk, Jarl."

"If this works it matters not that we break your sweep; we can make another."

"Aye Jarl."

"Ulfheonar be ready to board. The rest of you stop them from boarding us!"

The Frisian had his men rowing and they began to overtake us. Suddenly Erik and Guthrum put the steering board over and we lurched to the west. Although it took the Frisian by surprise there was a crack as the improvised rudder broke but it had done its work. We slammed through the oars of the Frisian and into his hull. Snorri and Beorn threw the grappling hooks and pulled. Olaf and Rolf Horse Killer leapt recklessly over the side while the sea still swirled below us. Haaken and I followed.

Some of the steer board side rowers had been injured by the collision. One man held a shattered piece of oar which was rammed into his leg. Olaf and Rolf swung their axes to clear a path to the helmsman. Haaken and I sprang through the gap. I hacked across the middle of the helmsman. He fell in a bloody heap. Snorri rammed his sword into the Captain of the drekar. He fell too. "Get the steering board destroyed!

"Aye Jarl."

Haaken and I turned to join Beorn and Leif as we fought our way to Olaf and Rolf. None could approach our two axemen. They swung in rhythm with each other. Heads were shattered; limbs lopped. The deck was so slippery with blood that it was hard to keep a firm footing. We were seriously outnumbered but our numbers filled the hull and we had enough blades to hold them off while Snorri and Beorn did their work. A spear found a gap and scored a hit against the side of Olaf Leather Neck.

His mail parted and I saw blood. Leif the Banner darted in and eviscerated the spearman. Snorri shouted, "It is done!"

"Back to the ship!" The steer board shroud was close to me and I hacked through it. The sail began to flap. Cnut Cnutson had boarded with us and he suddenly took off down the centre of the ship. It took everyone by surprise. He hacked his way down the ship and stood at the prow defying the whole of the crew. Haaken and I took two more warriors who tried to stop us leaving. It was brave but foolish. I shouted, "That is enough! Back!"

Haaken and I stood on the gunwale as our men jumped across. Arrows fell from our ship into the Frisians. Cnut seemed to bear a charmed life. He had taken everyone by surprise. He slashed through the stays. Until they were repaired the ship was going nowhere. Cnut then stood with his back to the prow as the crew advanced on him.

Haaken and I jumped aboard our ship. The ropes were cut and the wind forced us along the side of the drekar. Cnut slew two warriors as Haaken shouted, "Jump!" Cnut ran and leapt into the air. His father must have been watching over him. As *'Red Snake'* came close Cnut crashed across the gunwale of our drekar. Einar Hammer Arm and Olvir Grey Eye pulled him to safety. His leg and his arm had been slashed but he had survived.

Haaken said, "I think Cnut the Eagle that you are now one of the Ulfheonar!"

"Let us get out of this predicament before we begin to congratulate ourselves! Take to your oars and I will direct you again until the sweep is repaired."

The men complied. They did not bother to take off their helmets. We were three boat lengths from the stricken Frisian and we needed to make ourselves invisible. Guthrum and Erik had learned from their first effort and by the time the Frisian was a mile away, they could steer again.

Erik looked worried, "Jarl, I would make for Dyflin. The wind may be against us but I would not risk Man. The wind would take us thence."

I nodded, "Make for Dyflin."

We were in a sorry state. When Arne Eriksson wriggled back from beneath the deck his face told the story. "We are taking on water."

Erik Short Toe nodded, "When we struck the Frisian it was too much for her. Son, have the ships' boys go below with you. Guthrum you stay deck side. Use the empty beer pail to bail. Jarl, I need you here with me!"

I joined him and soon realised why he needed help. A steering board moved the ship easily. This improvised version was something you fought. Soon we were both bathed in sweat as we tried to keep the drekar on course. The water kept coming from below. It was a race against both time and the sea. The sea was winning.

The thin line ahead told us that the coast was getting closer but as we began to get our hopes up they were dashed by Haaken, "Jarl, our two friends have caught us up. They are coming at us from two different directions. They intend to outflank us."

I looked at Erik, "There is no point in stopping rowing. We get as close to the shore as we can."

"You are right Jarl but the excess water is making us slower. They will catch up with us before we reach the coast."

"We do not give up! That is not our way!" I gripped my dragon, "May the spirits of my ancestor and the Allfather come to our aid!"

Haaken began the chant. My men were exhausted but a chant helped them and revived their spirits.

'Ulfheonar, warriors strong
Ulfheonar, warriors brave
Ulfheonar, fierce as the wolf
Ulfheonar, hides in plain sight
Ulfheonar, Dragon Heart's wolves
Ulfheonar, serving the sword
Ulfheonar, Dragon Heart's wolves
Ulfheonar, serving the sword'

I let Erik watch the shore. I held on to the oar with him but I watched astern. The larger drekar was the one captained by the mysterious Jarl. It was to the east of us, cutting off an escape to our home. The other was another with sixteen oars on each side. It was smaller and faster. It was beating up to stop us from reaching the shore. "Erik they will catch us long before we reach the shore. The one which will catch us is easier to defeat. When they come alongside I will board him. You and your ships' boys join us. Better we die together than get picked off."

"Aye Jarl, but we will bail until we touch. I will not abandon this drekar so easily. She is brave and has spirit! She deserves to live."

"Stop rowing and arm yourselves. Arm the wounded. We die with our swords in our hands!"

The cheer from my depleted crew gave me hope. The sight of the nearest Frisian, just four boat lengths away filled me with despair. The larger one was further back.

"Get your boys on deck and arm them, Erik Short Toe. This is a good day to die!"

I donned my helmet and hefted my shield. We would be fighting overwhelming odds and I needed all the help I could get. As the bow of the drekar came abeam of us Erik and I pushed the makeshift steering board hard over. It was a violent move and it shattered the sweep but it took us across the bows of the drekar. The skull prow rose over our gunwale and seemed to bite into the mast. We had no need to throw ropes and my men hurled themselves over the prow. It gave us a chance, albeit slight, for the Frisians were gathered on the steering board side.

Olaf Leather Neck inevitably led the way. His wound did not slow him down. He swung his axe before him. It was lightly armed men who met him. Their spears seemed not to bother him. His axe smashed heads and arms. Those that hid and survived his onslaught were felled by Rolf Horse Killer.

Haaken and I led the attack down the other side. I held my seax behind my shield and wielded Ragnar's Spirit. We fought together as we had done since we were boys. I blocked a skeggox and slashed my sword under armed to rip open the Frisian's belly. Haaken smashed his shield into the face of one warrior as he casually took the head of a second. It seemed we were doing the impossible and beating the Frisians. However, the sheer weight of numbers slowed us down. Rolf and Olaf were finally stopped by the mast. Wounded Finni and Erik Eriksson joined them. They had fought together for the longest time.

Snorri, Beorn, Leif and Rollo Thin Hair stood behind Haaken and me. The press of our enemies was so tight that we could barely swing our arms. I head-butted the nearest Frisian so hard that he tumbled over the gunwale. That gave me the chance to slide my sword into the side of another. A sword clanged against my helmet. Arrows came from behind us. A warrior who was about to stab Haaken fell backwards with an arrow in his eye.

It seemed to energise Haaken. He shouted, "Come on, warriors of Cyninges-tūn! Push these scum over the side. They are not warriors they are bandits!"

Leif the Banner, Snorri and Beorn pushed against us. I ripped my seax sideways and opened the entrails of a warrior. The deck was slippery now with blood and gore but we were winning. We pushed them back. Haaken and I had enough room now to swing our swords. With Snorri next to us the three of us scythed our swords towards the fearful Frisians. I began to think we stood a chance when I heard a cry from behind. It was Sven Svensson. "Jarl the other ship is here. We are surrounded!"

"Then let us make a shield wall and make them pay dearly for our lives."

My men all locked shields. Rollo Thin Hair hacked a Frisian who was coming at my left side and joined his shield to that of me and Rolf Horse Killer. I jabbed my sword over the top of the shield. The Frisian who stood there recoiled. Had there been just this one drekar then we would have won but the second had over sixty men on board. As soon as they clambered over the deck of *'Red Snake'* then the slaughter would start. I felt a movement behind me. I risked looking to see if it was danger. It was the ship's boys led by Guthrum. They had cut the stays of the enemy ship and swung across.

Guthrum had been cut across his cheek and his eye but he grinned, "I will tell my grandchildren of the day I fought with the Dragonheart!" He pulled back and sent an arrow to smash through the face of the Frisian chief who was rallying his men.

Then the dying began. Bjorn Eiriksson and Sven Svensson fell one after the other. It took six blows to kill Sven and he took three more men before he died. When Beorn took the last spear in his stomach he grabbed two men and took them over the side with him. They died well. Snorri suddenly dropped to one knee as his other was hacked by a Frisian sword. I chopped across the side of the warrior's head. I smashed his skull open and his brains spurted out.

I helped Snorri to his feet. "Come, my friend, rest on me."

"I am sorry, Jarl. I must be getting old!"

"Never! We are just getting our second wind!"

Haaken began to sing.

> *"Around the mast, the oathsworn stood*
> *Deep in gore, deep in blood.*
> *Brothers in arms they fought as one*
> *They fought when hope had all but gone.*
> *Ulfheonar never forget*
> *Ulfheonar never forgive*
> *Ulfheonar fight to the death*
> *Remember this fight at the end of days*
> *Warriors dying but hopes still raised*
> *Oathsworn all and the Dragonheart*
> *They died together were never apart*
> *Ulfheonar never forget*
> *Ulfheonar never forgive*
> *Ulfheonar fight to the death"*

It was a strange experience as Haaken's voice rang out. He always had a fine voice and to have created his own death song in the midst of the battle was truly wondrous. All those who stood and breathed chanted the chorus and perhaps the gods heard for Arne Eriksson, who was clinging to the shrouds suddenly shouted, "*'Heart of the Dragon'*, *'Crow'* and *'Odin's Gift'*! They have come!"

When all hope had gone the gods sent us help. We redoubled our efforts and the Frisians either threw down their weapons or threw themselves over the side. We had survived.

I quickly tied a cloth around Snorri's leg and then touched the dragon amulet and thanked the spirits for our salvation.

Epilogue

Three weeks later the last of the wounded left Kara's hall. We had lost twelve warriors but the eight who had been wounded all survived. Men did not mourn those who had died because the fight was worthy of retelling. The mysterious Jarl had disappeared when our ships had approached. *'Red Snake'* was too badly damaged to be left and so she was tied between *'Crow'* and *'Heart of the Dragon'* and brought home with four sets of ships' boys bailing. *'Odin's Breath'* followed the Frisian until it disappeared beyond the wild islands of the north. I would meet the Frisian again; of that, I had no doubt. The survivors whom we enslaved were just poor warriors. They only knew his nickname, 'The Skull'. We did have a description. He had no hair at all and red eyes. As Haaken said, 'If we can't find him then we are poor hunters!"

The dead were buried with honour at Cyninges-tūn. It was a place of reverence and contemplation. Warriors went there to remember what it was to be a warrior. I was sad that Karl Karlsson had died. A fine ships' boy, we had had hopes for him. Erik Short Toe had lost an eye while his son, two fingers. Guthrum had a scar to the end of his days but none would change their wounds. They were all badges of honour.

I sent Beorn to Jorvik. He discovered that Hermund the Bent had fled there and was hiring men to raid Jarl Gunnar Thorfinnsson. I sent Raibeart in *'Weregeld'* to warn him.

I sat in Kara's hall with my whole family around me. Elfrida had come with Ragnar. We had spoken of many things but not the most important. Kara was never afraid of broaching difficult matters and she asked outright, "Was it worth it, father?"

"What?"

"The treasure you took; was it worth it?"

She was not being critical but she had to ask the question. Since my return, I had wrestled with it. I had been at Erika's grave and begged forgiveness. I had travelled to Olaf's peak and sought the spirits. None had given me solace. Kara was right to ask me. Every face turned towards me.

"Was the treasure worth the death of my son and grandson? Was it worth the death of warriors like Sven Svensson and Bjorn Eiriksson and young boys like Karl Karlsson? The answer is no. And that is obvious to all in this room but if you ask me would I do it again then the answer would be yes, as you know my daughter for it was meant to be. It was *wyrd*. The Weird Sisters willed it so. A man cannot escape what must be but I tell you this I now realise the true measure of a Viking's treasure. I understand what it is." I saw Ragnar and Gruffyd lean forward eagerly. "It is his blood, his family and it is his oathsworn. That is the true Viking treasure. It is not my sword nor my jewels. It is not gold. It is something which cannot be weighed and it is in here," I patted my chest, "in the Dragonheart."

The End

Glossary

Afon Hafron- River Severn in Welsh

Alpín mac Echdach – the father of Kenneth MacAlpin, reputedly the first king of the Scots

Alt Clut- Dumbarton Castle on the Clyde

Balley Chashtal -Castleton (Isle of Man)

Bardanes Tourkos- Rebel Byzantine General

Bebbanburgh- Bamburgh Castle, Northumbria Also know as Din Guardi in the ancient tongue

Beck- a stream

Beinn na bhFadhla- Benbecula in the Outer Hebrides

Belesduna - Basildon

Blót – a blood sacrifice made by a jarl

Blue Sea- The Mediterranean

Bondi- Viking farmers who fight

Bourde- Bordeaux

Bjarnarøy –Great Bernera (Bear Island)

Byrnie- a mail or leather shirt reaching down to the knees

Caerlleon- Welsh for Chester

Caestir - Chester (old English)

Casnewydd –Newport, Wales

Cephas- Greek for Simon Peter (St. Peter)

Chape- the tip of a scabbard

Charlemagne- Holy Roman Emperor at the end of the 8th and beginning of the 9th centuries

Celchyth - Chelsea

Cherestanc- Garstang (Lancashire)

Corn Walum or Om Walum- Cornwall

Cymri- Welsh

Cymru- Wales

Cyninges-tūn – Coniston. It means the estate of the king (Cumbria)

Dùn Èideann –Edinburgh (Gaelic)

Din Guardi- Bamburgh castle

Drekar- a Dragon ship (a Viking warship)

Duboglassio –Douglas, Isle of Man

Dun Holme- Durham

Dyrøy –Jura (Inner Hebrides)

Dyflin- Old Norse for Dublin

Ēa Lōn - River Lune

Ein-mánuðr - middle of March to the middle of April
Eoforwic- Saxon for York
Faro Bregancio- Corunna (Spain)
Ferneberga -Farnborough (Hampshire)
Fey- having second sight
Firkin- a barrel containing eight gallons (usually beer)
Fret-a sea mist
Frankia- France and part of Germany
Fyrd-the Saxon levy
Garth- Dragon Heart
Gaill- Irish for foreigners
Galdramenn- wizard
Gesith- A Saxon nobleman. After 850 AD they were known as thegns
Glaesum –amber
Gleawecastre- Gloucester
Gói- the end of February to the middle of March
Grendel- the monster slain by Beowulf
Grenewic- Greenwich
Gulle - Goole (Humberside)
Hagustaldes ham -Hexham
Hamwic -Southampton
Haughs- small hills in Norse (As in Tarn Hows)
Heels- when a ship leans to one side under the pressure of the wind
Hel - Queen of Niflheim, the Norse underworld.
Here Wic- Harwich
Hersir- a Viking landowner and minor noble. Ranks below a jarl
Hetaereiarch – Byzantine general
Hí- Iona (Gaelic)
Hjáp - Shap- Cumbria (Norse for stone circle)
Hoggs or Hogging- when the pressure of the wind causes the stern or the bow to droop
Hrams-a – Ramsey, Isle of Man
Hwitebi - Whitby, North Yorkshire
Hywel ap Rhodri Molwynog- King of Gwynedd 814-825
Icaunis- a British river god
Issicauna -River Seine
Itouna- River Eden Cumbria
Jarl- Norse earl or lord
Joro-goddess of the earth
kjerringa - Old Woman- the solid block in which the mast rested
Knarr- a merchant ship or a coastal vessel

Kyrtle-woven top
Lambehitha- Lambeth
Leathes Water- Thirlmere
Ljoðhús- Lewis
Legacaestir- Anglo Saxon for Chester
Lochlannach – Irish for Northerners (Vikings)
Lothuwistoft- Lowestoft
Louis the Pious- King of the Franks and son of Charlemagne
Lundenburgh- the fort in the heart of London (the former Roman fort)
Lundenwic - London
Maeresea- River Mersey
Mammceaster- Manchester
Manau/Mann – The Isle of Man(n) (Saxon)
Marcia Hispanic- Spanish Marches (the land around Barcelona)
Mast fish- two large racks on a ship designed to store the mast when not required
Melita- Malta
Midden- a place where they dumped human waste
Miklagård - Constantinople
Nikephoros- Emperor of Byzantium 802-811
Njoror- God of the sea
Nithing- A man without honour (Saxon)
Odin - The "All Father" God of war, also associated with wisdom, poetry, and magic (The Ruler of the gods).
Olissipo- Lisbon
Orkneyjar-Orkney
Penrhudd – Penrith Cumbria
Portesmūða -Portsmouth
Pillars of Hercules- Straits of Gibraltar
Ran- Goddess of the sea
Roof rock- slate
Rinaz –The Rhine
Sabrina- Latin and Celtic for the River Severn. Also the name of a female Celtic deity
Saami- the people who live in what is now Northern Norway/Sweden
Samhain- a Celtic festival of the dead between 31st October and1st November (Halloween)
St. Cybi- Holyhead
Scree- loose rocks in a glacial valley
Seax – short sword

Sheerstrake- the uppermost strake in the hull
Sheet- a rope fastened to the lower corner of a sail
Shroud- a rope from the masthead to the hull amidships
Skeggox – an axe with a shorter beard on one side of the blade
South Folk- Suffolk
Stad- Norse settlement
Stays- ropes running from the mast-head to the bow
Strake- the wood on the side of a drekar
Suthriganaworc - Southwark (London)
Syllingar Insula, Syllingar- Scilly Isles
Tarn- small lake (Norse)
Temese- River Thames (also called the Tamese)
The Norns- The three sisters who weave webs of intrigue for men
Tilaburg - Tilbury
Thing-Norse for a parliament or a debate (Tynwald)
Thor's day- Thursday
Threttanessa- a drekar with 13 oars on each side.
Thrall- slave
Tinea- Tyne
Trenail- a round wooden peg used to secure strakes
Tynwald- the Parliament on the Isle of Man
Úlfarrberg- Helvellyn
Úlfarrland- Cumbria
Úlfarr- Wolf Warrior
Úlfarrston- Ulverston
Ullr-Norse God of Hunting
Ulfheonar-an elite Norse warrior who wore a wolf skin over his
armour
Vectis- The Isle of Wight
Volva- a witch or healing woman in Norse culture
Waeclinga Straet- Watling Street (A5) Windlesore-Windsor
Waite- a Viking word for farm
Werham -Wareham (Dorset)
Wintan-ceastre -Winchester
Withy- the mechanism connecting the steering board to the ship
Woden's day- Wednesday
Wulfhere-Old English for Wolf Army
Wyddfa-Snowdon
Wyrd- Fate
Yard- a timber from which the sail is suspended
Ynys Enlli- Bardsey Island
Ynys Môn-Anglesey

Historical note

The Viking raids began, according to records left by the monks, in the 790s when Lindisfarne was pillaged. However, there were many small settlements along the east coast and most were undefended. I have chosen a fictitious village on the Tees as the home of Garth who is enslaved and then, when he gains his freedom, becomes Dragon Heart. As buildings were all made of wood then any evidence of their existence would have rotted long ago, save for a few post holes. The Norse began to raid well before 790. There was a rise in the populations of Norway and Denmark and Britain was not well prepared for defence against such random attacks.

My raiders represent the Norse warriors who wanted the plunder of the soft Saxon kingdom. There is a myth that the Vikings raided in large numbers but this is not so. It was only in the tenth and eleventh centuries that the numbers grew. They also did not have allegiances to kings. The Norse settlements were often isolated family groups. The term Viking was not used in what we now term the Viking Age beyond the lands of Norway and Denmark. Warriors went a-Viking which meant that they sailed for adventure or pirating. Their lives were hard. Slavery was commonplace. The Norse for slave is thrall and I have used both terms.

The ship, '*The Heart of the Dragon'* is based on the Gokstad ship which was found in 1880 in Norway. It is 23.24 metres long and 5.25 metres wide at its widest point. It was made entirely of oak except for the pine decking. There are 16 strakes on each side and from the base to the gunwale is 2.02 metres giving it a high freeboard. The keel is cut from a piece of oak 17.6 metres long. There are 19 ribs. The pine mast was 13 metres high. The ship could carry 70 men although there were just sixteen oars on each side. This meant that half the crew could rest while the other half rowed. Sea battles could be brutal. The drekar was the most efficient warship of its day. The world would have to wait until the frigates of the eighteenth century to see such a dominant ship again. When the Saxons before Alfred the Great tried to meet Vikings at sea it ended in disaster. It was Alfred who created a warship which stood a chance against the Vikings but they never really competed. The same ships as Dragonheart used carried King William to England in 1066.

I used the following books for research

British Museum - 'Vikings- Life and Legends'
'Saxon, Norman and Viking' by Terence Wise (Osprey)
Ian Heath - 'The Vikings'. (Osprey)

Ian Heath- 'Byzantine Armies 668-1118 (Osprey)
David Nicholle- 'Romano-Byzantine Armies 4th-9th Century (Osprey)
Stephen Turnbull- 'The Walls of Constantinople AD 324-1453' (Osprey)
Keith Durham- 'Viking Longship' (Osprey)
Anglo-Danish Project- 'The Vikings in England'
Anglo Saxon Thegn AD 449-1066- Mark Harrison (Osprey)
Viking Hersir- 793-1066 AD - Mark Harrison (Osprey)
Hadrian's Wall- David Breeze (English Heritage)

Griff Hosker May 2016

Other books by Griff Hosker

If you enjoyed reading this book, then why not read another one by the author?

Ancient History

The Sword of Cartimandua Series
(Germania and Britannia 50 A.D. – 128 A.D.)
Ulpius Felix- Roman Warrior (prequel)
The Sword of Cartimandua
The Horse Warriors
Invasion Caledonia
Roman Retreat
Revolt of the Red Witch
Druid's Gold
Trajan's Hunters
The Last Frontier
Hero of Rome
Roman Hawk
Roman Treachery
Roman Wall
Roman Courage

The Wolf Warrior series
(Britain in the late 6th Century)
Saxon Dawn
Saxon Revenge
Saxon England
Saxon Blood
Saxon Slayer
Saxon Slaughter
Saxon Bane
Saxon Fall: Rise of the Warlord
Saxon Throne
Saxon Sword

Medieval History

The Dragon Heart Series
Viking Slave
Viking Warrior
Viking Jarl
Viking Kingdom
Viking Wolf
Viking War
Viking Sword
Viking Wrath
Viking Raid
Viking Legend
Viking Vengeance
Viking Dragon
Viking Treasure
Viking Enemy
Viking Witch
Viking Blood
Viking Weregeld
Viking Storm
Viking Warband
Viking Shadow
Viking Legacy
Viking Clan
Viking Bravery

The Norman Genesis Series
Hrolf the Viking
Horseman
The Battle for a Home
Revenge of the Franks
The Land of the Northmen
Ragnvald Hrolfsson
Brothers in Blood
Lord of Rouen
Drekar in the Seine

Viking Treasure

Duke of Normandy
The Duke and the King

Danelaw
(England and Denmark in the 11th Century)
Dragon Sword
Oathsword

New World Series
Blood on the Blade
Across the Seas
The Savage Wilderness
The Bear and the Wolf
Erik The Navigator

The Vengeance Trail

The Reconquista Chronicles
Castilian Knight
El Campeador
The Lord of Valencia

The Aelfraed Series
(Britain and Byzantium 1050 A.D. - 1085 A.D.)
Housecarl
Outlaw
Varangian

**The Anarchy Series England
1120-1180**
English Knight
Knight of the Empress
Northern Knight
Baron of the North
Earl
King Henry's Champion
The King is Dead
Warlord of the North

Viking Treasure

Enemy at the Gate
The Fallen Crown
Warlord's War
Kingmaker
Henry II
Crusader
The Welsh Marches
Irish War
Poisonous Plots
The Princes' Revolt
Earl Marshal
The Perfect Knight

Border Knight
1182-1300
Sword for Hire
Return of the Knight
Baron's War
Magna Carta
Welsh Wars
Henry III
The Bloody Border
Baron's Crusade
Sentinel of the North
War in the West
Debt of Honour

Sir John Hawkwood Series
France and Italy 1339- 1387
Crécy: The Age of the Archer
Man At Arms
The White Company

Lord Edward's Archer
Lord Edward's Archer
King in Waiting
An Archer's Crusade
Targets of Treachery

Viking Treasure

Struggle for a Crown
1360- 1485
Blood on the Crown
To Murder A King
The Throne
King Henry IV
The Road to Agincourt
St Crispin's Day
The Battle For France
The Last Knight

Tales from the Sword I
(Short stories from the Medieval period)

Tudor Warrior series
England and Scotland in the late 145th and early 15th
century
Tudor Warrior

Conquistador
England and America in the 16th Century
Conquistador

Modern History

The Napoleonic Horseman Series
Chasseur à Cheval
Napoleon's Guard
British Light Dragoon
Soldier Spy
1808: The Road to Coruña
Talavera
The Lines of Torres Vedras
Bloody Badajoz
The Road to France
Waterloo

Viking Treasure

The Lucky Jack American Civil War series
Rebel Raiders
Confederate Rangers
The Road to Gettysburg

The British Ace Series
1914
1915 Fokker Scourge
1916 Angels over the Somme
1917 Eagles Fall
1918 We will remember them
From Arctic Snow to Desert Sand
Wings over Persia

Combined Operations series
1940-1945
Commando
Raider
Behind Enemy Lines
Dieppe
Toehold in Europe
Sword Beach
Breakout
The Battle for Antwerp
King Tiger
Beyond the Rhine
Korea
Korean Winter

Tales from the Sword II
(Short stories from the Modern period)

Other Books
Great Granny's Ghost (Aimed at 9-14-year-old young people)

For more information on all of the books then please visit the
author's website at www.griffhosker.com where there is a link to

contact him or visit his Facebook page: GriffHosker at Sword
Books

Made in the USA
Coppell, TX
28 December 2021

70241043R00122